Sword of Inquest

Sword of Inquest – Book One, La Patron's Sword Series
Sydney Addae

ISBN: 9781937334598
First Edition Electronic September 2014

Published by Sitting Bull Publications, LLC.

Sword of Inquest – Book one of La Patron's Sword Series

Altered both mentally and physically, Asia Montgomery finally has a lead to unlock the mystery of her past. Gunnolf, her former mentor has reached out to her, some say from the grave. Desperate to learn real nuggets of her personal history before the Liege changed her, she embarks on a journey that takes her into the bowels of Lancaster Castle, which belongs to one of the Liege Lords.

Hawke has been an altered prisoner of Lord Boris Lancaster so long his wolf has all but given up hope of ever being free. When Asia steps into the lab looking like Tate, his wolf springs to the surface to investigate. Confused and happy he makes a plea for assistance for the first time in decades.

With an eight-million-dollar bounty on her head, Asia is hesitant to trust anyone in the castle, no matter what her wolf wants. The Liege has spent millions of dollars Hawke and Asia and will stop at nothing to regain their property. Can Asia trust long enough to assist another victim of the Liege? Will Hawke accept Asia for the person she is at her core? Time and again, Asia and Hawke must bend for each other or break the bond holding them together in Sword of Inquest as they rush to fulfill La Patron's command.

This book may be read alone, however, it is a continuation of the La Patron, Alphas Alpha series. To understand the depth of the relationships between Jasmine, Silas, Asia, Angus and Hawke, I suggest you read the following books. BirthRight, book one is a free read and sets the tone for the series.

Book one is BirthRight,
Book two is BirthControl
Book three is BirthMark
Book four is BirthStone
Book five is BirthDate
Book six is BirthSign

I want to thank everyone who enjoys the La Patron Series you are the best. I also want to thank those of you beginning the Sword series with me, hold onto to your hats it will be an awesome ride taking us back to the den.

A special shout out to Sally R., Karen M., and Kelly, I could not have presented this story without your help.

Thanks!

Prologue

Isa...Isa? Are you there? Are you hurt? Did they hurt you?" The honest concern in the stranger's voice entered her private area inside where she had locked down her emotions a decade ago.

"*No...yes, but that's okay. Who are you?*" she held her breath and waited for his response.

A long whistling sound came through her link; she assumed it was a sigh. "*I was afraid of this...not only did they betray me, but they tampered with you. I am Gunnolf... your teacher. I have been imprisoned for over fifty years waiting for word of you and the others.*"

Others? She frowned as a mist rose in her mind and cleared with an image of a tall male with long black hair, stood tall giving a young girl instruction.

"*Do it again, this time watch your hands...they must remain in position to protect your face.*"

The child, who couldn't be more than ten years old, executed a perfect drop kick against a stuffed bag. "*Gunnolf... you taught me?*

When I was younger? You know me? My family? Where I am from?"

"*I swear to the Goddess those bastards will pay for what they have done to you...yes. You are Isa. Your parents met the Goddess when you were a young child; you were placed in an orphanage. That is where I found you.*"

Her heart beat so hard she thought it would leave her chest. Tidbits of light penetrated the darkness and she saw herself as a child. Tears ran down her face, she didn't bother to wipe them, she had been weeping on the inside for decades.

"Asia, are you okay?" Angus asked.

"No. Not really." She faced him, her heart beat with fear and excitement which was more than she had felt in a long time. Was it possible? Could Gunnolf truly fill the gaping holes in her memory? He frowned. "Is it the bracelet?" ... "Give me your hand." She extended it to him hoping he would not take the bracelet; it could help her get in and out of places.

He placed his palm over her wrist. The bracelet warmed and then normalized. "I have given you full control of your bracelet. No one can use it but you. No one can see it but you. Also, I gave you one of the most powerful ones; it should last for years without maintenance. Perhaps this is the next assignment the Goddess meant for you."

*****

"I still haven't heard from Asia," Jasmine said. *"I know she feels she needs to trace her past, but I'm still worried. She has no back-up and no pack over there to help. We should send someone."*

"No." He released a breath.

She placed her hand on his arm and squeezed. Would he remember their conversation from yesterday? She would see if he meant what he said about listening to her feelings. "*I'm really worried about her.*"

"*According to Angus she is determined to release Gunnolf. That's a good thing; the full-blood is older than me and very strong.*" He frowned at her raised brow. "*He was. I'm not sure I understand how they've kept him all this time. The point is, she is in the backyard of one of the Liege Lords. The moment unknown full-bloods start showing up, it'll put her in more danger.*" He touched her lip. "*You and I can help her from here, better than sending others to get in her way. Besides, Gunnolf trained hundreds of orphaned full-bloods. Once he is released, he could probably call an army together.*"

Disappointment in his response laced her chest. He still didn't get it; apologies were fine, but didn't change the outcome. He needed to change and take her "suggestions" seriously. "*I don't know Silas; he has been a prisoner a long time. They could have a chip in his head and know he's calling her. This could be a trap.*"

"When she contacts you, tell her what you feel and offer to send someone, if she accepts, I'll send Brix and Leon."

That made her feel slightly better, although she'd rather Asia come home where she'd be safe. Silas grabbed her around the shoulder and pulled her back against him.

"You can't coddle them, Sweet Bitch. Asia, Rese, Rone, Cam... they have their own destinies to fulfill. They'll probably get hurt, but they'll be living their lives and carving their histories. Let her go... be there for her when she needs you, that's the best you can do."

Chapter 1

It was noon with overcast skies and a bit of chill in the September air. A custom-made day designed to send a man looking for companionship. This time he would choose her. She had worked in this old, two-storied, converted mansion a week, waiting and changing her appearance to catch his eye. From all she heard, today she hit all of his preferences on the head.

Dressed in a charcoal gray tight skirt, matching jacket and a wide black belt, she shook her head so that the soft curls would settle around her shoulders as she strutted across the tiled floor in Madame's Boudoir. It had been a long time since part of her assignment included seduction and she was out of practice. Give her a gun or blade instead of makeup and fancy clothes and she'd make a clean kill without blinking. In this place she had to play nice, civilized.

She added an extra swing to her hips, prepared to catch her prey. In the dim light of the small parlor her red lipstick added a layer of drama while she paraded around the room with a can't-touch-this-attitude. Bored and tired of waiting she searched the other rooms for him.

Greggor preferred tall females, muscular, flat chested, long black hair and any color but brown eyes. She'd used her chameleon bracelet to create the perfect tease. Ignoring every other request, her heart beat raced in anticipation. Earlier that week she made her preferences clear to the Madam of the house, earning praise and gratitude for taking on that particular client.

The air in the room stilled. She sensed him before she saw him. Without turning, their eyes met in the mirror she faced. His gaze roamed down her back and remained on her long legs and the curve of her barely covered hips. She turned and walked toward the opposite side of the room. He stepped forward halting her, threw more bills than necessary on the table and motioned for her to follow him up the stairs.

A grin of satisfaction crossed her lips.

Jacket and belt removed, he slapped hard, cold metal around her wrists, holding her arms securely in place against the rough fabric of the bench. While his back was turned, she gave her arms a quick tug, and relaxed, satisfied that she could break free if necessary. He glanced over his shoulder with a wicked grin and then showed her the blade. Her gaze flicked across his slender arms and then remained on the glint of the steel as he moved closer.

She looked up. Their gazes clashed.

He held the blade over her chest and then sliced through the lightweight material of her blouse to the hem of her skirt with a steady downward arc, never touching her flesh. Remnants of her outfit pooled on the floor as he snapped his blade shut, looked at her and grinned. The gap between his two front teeth was more pronounced because of their unevenness.

"You want to play with Greggor, my dark pretty one. We shall play." He spoke in broken, choppy English, but she understood his hand gestures. Some things were universal. He dropped to one knee and secured her ankles with silky materials, stretching them far apart.

The heat in the small room escalated, sweat beaded across her brow and ran down her face and then chest. Two hulking men remained by the door blocking any air that might seep through the cracks as well as the one exit. Clothed in a skimpy bra and panties she ignored the heat and remembered her purpose for being in this room.

"Oooh, Greggor likes to play rough," she said in a husky tone playing her role as instructed.

He looked up at her, his dark brown eyes filled with cruel intent.

"I paid many grivna for you tonight and you will obey me."

She stared down at the whiplash thin man and smiled. "Yes, Master. I will please you."

He stood, pulled his shirt over his head and tossed the shirt to one of the men. He caught it mid-air. She grinned, as she had been instructed, at his mastery over the much larger males.

"You are strong. I like that about you," she purred, pouring it on thick for the egomaniac. He pushed out his chest, placed a finger in his waistband and smiled. "Yes, yes I am." He pulled the belt from his pants.

Her eyes rounded.

"Bend over," he demanded slapping the belt across his palm.

She frowned, trying to inject some fear into her response and played the role the house Madam instructed her to play. “Please don’t hurt me.”

The sting of the leather across her ass pissed her off more than caused any pain. “Ouch, that hurts,” she said as the leather strap landed again and again across her ass and thighs.

“You ignore me, turn to others. I hate you,” he said swinging the strap harder.

She turned aside, her long black hair covered her eye roll. Everybody had issues, even the manager of the castle. But she needed to play the game to complete the mission. Greggor needed to get on with it, preferably in silence.

“I said I hate you,” he said again prompting her.

Damn, she missed her cue. “But I love you. I love you, Greggor.”

She said infusing a hint of regret, and hurt.

“You do?”

“Yes, I love you and want only you. The others mean nothing, they are just a job. But you, are my everything.” She met his gaze, surprised when his eyes softened. The man was really into this shit.

He dropped the belt, untied her ankles and unlocked her cuffs. The next moment underscored the past four days of seeking information, watching him and seeking to be in this room. He wrapped his arms around her and squeezed.

Asia stroked his head, and activated her chameleon bracelet. Tingling sensations raced through her and with each touch she stole information on a new employee. Information she needed to break into Lord Boris’ castle and rescue Gunnolf.

Chapter 2

Greggor's thoughts had been accurate. Asia had waited to catch the newest employee of Lancaster Castle, Tate Whiner, on his way home from the market. Each day she kept a 24-hour vigil on his flat only to discover he had been out of town until last night. Tired from a lack of sleep she almost missed when he left for work. She ran down an opposite street and caught him two blocks before he entered the road leading to the castle. Asia bumped into him, knocking him down and offering heartfelt apologies, exchanged bodies.

Rushed, she left him leaning against a wall. Not the smoothest transition she had ever done. After she took over his body she learned he would move into the dorm that day and not leave again for a month. Unless she came up with a plan, the bowels of Lord Boris' castle would be home for a while. That was unacceptable to her.

"Tate, you're late, it's crazy in here today. I need help feeding the inmates in section B, we're shorthanded again," Chuck said pointing to a full cart with half cooked steaks and raw vegetables.

Asia strode across the room fully aware she appeared as an average height, unassuming white male. Unremarkable and easy to forget. "Okay, want me to take these?" Standing behind the cart, she counted the platters and placed the water jugs on top.

"Just a sec, almost done." Chuck squeezed three more large plates onto the cart and another basket of hard rolls. The hard bread would be difficult to eat, but being the new guy, she followed instructions rather than offered suggestions.

"Go ahead take it and come back for the food for your sector. I should have it ready by then. Later I need you to take his Majesty his

meal. If we are lucky, he'll take it easy on you because you are new."

Tate nodded, having no idea what Chuck meant and didn't care. The past few days she'd spent every free moment seeking clues about Gunnolf 's location and came up empty. As the lowest on the employee seniority pole she had no access above ground and had searched everywhere on this level. Other than asking questions, or leaving a body trail, she didn't know which direction to take next.

Asia placed her palm on the security scan for sector B, the door slid open. No one looked at her as she rolled the food cart to the end of the row. One by one, she slid open the small door at the front of the cage. If a plate was on the drawer she placed steak, vegetables and a roll on it. No plate, no food. Each cage had a funnel for water. Using the jugs, she refilled everyone's supply in silence without meeting their gazes.

"You're different," an older female said, staring at her.

"He's new. They're all the same," another woman said in a dismissive tone.

Asia didn't hang around for the discussion. By the time she returned, Chuck had finished her cart and had taken a cart to his sector. She exchanged carts and headed to her area while scanning for Gunnolf.

Ready to finish her chores so she could decide her next move, she pushed the food cart into her sector. After a few days she'd become accustomed to the derision in the gazes of the test wolves. The desire to rip her apart lay just beneath the surface of their skin. These guys hated their captivity and each day it became harder to face them. Either she found Gunnolf here, or she'd leave this place.

Angus, La Patron's litter-mate, or as Jasmine would say, his brother, had given her a chameleon bracelet which allowed her to hide and change her appearance at will. It saved her life more than once since the rest of her team returned to the states. She glanced at her wrist, unable to see the bracelet, but felt its weight. Good, she may need to morph into one of her co-workers to search the upstairs.

Asia had remained in this country for one reason. To set Gunnolf free in the hopes his knowledge would in turn set her free. As the lead experiment specimen for decades, her memories were dotty and missing. He had answers to her questions about her past, her family and most importantly how she'd entered servitude to the Liege. Asia had to find him.

She placed her palm on the keypad and the door opened. Inside every cage were men, women, and teens. All full-bloods. Snarls and snapping sounds rose in her breast from her wolf at the captivity of the animals.

"You're late," an older man snapped when she entered the room. The guy had never spoken to her before and his attitude did nothing to gain a response from her. She repeated the dinner ritual, serving each person and then refilled their water.

"What happened to the other one? The one before you?" the old man asked again.

Asia looked at him and shrugged.

Evening meal complete, she returned to sector B, grabbed the hose and washed everything down, including the people, their waste and their plates. How anyone could be treated in this manner? None of it made sense to her. The lab in Pennsylvania had rooms with separate bathing areas and as much as she'd hated it then, she realized it was a penthouse compared to this caged existence.

To ease her conscience, she spent a little more time on the baths of anyone who tried to clean themselves. When she turned off the water a few of them thanked her. Surprised, she nodded and then headed to her sector to repeat the process.

"Great, thanks man, you took care of cleaning sector B," Chuck said. "I'll take sector D. After you finish clean-up in your sector, the tray for Hawke is ready. Press in your code in the lift and it'll take you below. He's the only door down there, just walk straight ahead out the lift. Promise you won't miss it. Try not to take too long, he gets' uber cranky when his food is too late."

Nodding, she headed to her sector. "Where are you from?" the older man asked when she entered her area.

Test wolves weren't supposed to talk to her. They never talked. She stared at him and turned on the water.

"Could you clean my mate first?" he pointed to the female in the cage next to him. "She had a rough day today."

Asia washed the woman down, spending a fair amount of time on her until the older female waved she'd had enough. It took longer than the other sector because there were more people. When finished, she grabbed the tray and headed down to the lab. Strange, she hadn't heard a word from him since she entered the castle four days ago. Before that he called out to her every day. What happened to him? Where could he be? She had no idea but each hour she grew confident it was not on this level with all the others.

Prickles of unease ran through her.

She scanned the area for Gunnolf. No luck. As she strode down the hall her wolf became agitated. Agitated may not be the right word, excited was more precise.

She placed her palm on the security pad, after a few beeps the door slid open and she stepped into the darkened lab. Dread swept up her back. Flashbacks of her captivity swamped her. The taste of antiseptic hit the back of her tongue. Chloroform and other noxious odors filled her nostrils. The clicking of equipment replayed in her ear. She slammed the door on those debilitating memories and refocused.

"If you insist on standing in the doorway, do so from the other side." The rude comment snapped her out of it.

"Dinner."

"I can see that. Place it on the lift and leave." He turned his back on her and sat at the keyboard.

Asia looked around the large sterile room while walking to the lift, and then placed the tray on the built-in ledge.

Shit. This lab made the one they destroyed in Pennsylvania look like pre-kindergarten. What kind of experiments did they run here?

The metal on the table restraints looked familiar. A bone-deep chill raced through her at the enormity of this place. No wonder they sacrificed the other lab, it couldn't compare to this one. She hadn't seen this many computers and robotic equipment in any of the other labs.

"Get out." He didn't raise his voice; he didn't need to, his words held a cutting edge that made her hackles rise.

"Yes, your majesty."

"I heard that."

She smiled and walked toward the door.

"Wait." She stopped and looked over her shoulder.

"Your name?"

His scent hit her and her wolf went ballistic. Shock immobilized her. The hunk of man was a full-blood wolf. Full-bloods did not make good lab specimens because their wolves would not obey humans and yet she stared at proof this could happen. Scars crisscrossed his arms, his back and from what she could see, the top of his chest. Someone had performed numerous surgeries on this wolf. Overhead light beams danced across his shoulder, highlighting his shaggy jet-black hair. She frowned, the color struck a chord, where had she seen it before? How much wolf remained in the man, or had the Liege found a way to neutralize the beast altogether. La Patron would want to know the answer to that question.

"Your name?"

Asia cleared her throat. "Tate."

Did he run this lab? She knew better than most the kind of experiments the Liege performed. The notion that a full-blood ran tests on other wolves for the Liege blind-sided her. It just didn't happen. As a full-blood, she'd done dirty deeds on behalf of the Liege for decades but it took constant reprogramming and she had scars to prove it. Her wolf always looked for opportunities to break the hold they had on her. One thing for sure, they never left her alone in a room full of equipment. Never.

A low throb beat at the base of her neck. Her beast whined pushing her to shift.

"Which sector are you working?"

"Sector C and B today."

He nodded and turned. "Next time bring my food on time, Tate."

She threw him the finger as she left.

"I saw that," he said as the door closed behind her.

Chapter 3

Asia lay on the pallet in the main area between both of her sectors. Although assigned a bunk and locker in the dorms, she'd never used them. Short staffed, she and the others remained below working rotating shifts. She had used every free minute to seek her mentor. Not finding him with the other test wolves wore on her nerves.

The day Gunnolf reached out to her seemed like a dream, perhaps it had been. She'd been ready to board the plane to take her to London along with Tyrese, Angus, Leon, Brix and Danielle, Tyrese's mate when Gunnolf called her name.

"*Isa... Isa, child is that you? What has taken you so long to return? Are you well?*" From that point on, she'd changed plans and remained in Krajdn, seeking information to rescue him. At first, she had been full of hope and excitement. Gunnolf knew her as a child, knew her parents, her history. He'd shared bits and pieces with her but not near enough. Starved for knowledge she set out to rescue him.

Jasmine offered to send help, but Asia had refused. This was a personal mission and if it made a wrong turn she alone would suffer. After a long heated discussion, her Mistress agreed to allow her to remain alone if she promised to use the chameleon bracelet as a main weapon. With a bounty of five million on her head, Lord Boris wanted her dead for killing another Liege Lord; Asia had been quick to agree. The Liege could not know she was in the country let alone in one of their holdings.

She had spent days seeking answers about the castle and the inhabitants from the local towns people. Sketchy and conflicting information slowed her progress but everyone agreed Lord Boris Lancaster was not in residence. In fact he seldom visited the place and left his nephew in charge. All the other ramblings of ghosts, mass killings, and Frankenstein experiments she filed in the local folklore column. Angus said her former mentor had been a great man, but no one heard from him in decades.

Stranger still, she hadn't heard a word from Gunnolf since she entered the castle four days ago. Before that he called out to her every day. What happened to him? Where could he be?

Frustrated, each hour she grew confident he was not with the other test wolves. Based on what she had learned so far, if Gunnolf were alive, he would be on this level.

"Mistress?" She called Jasmine through their link. After her accident and brush with death in an old lab in Pennsylvania, all of Asia's links quit working, except Jasmine's and within the past two weeks, Gunnolf.

Thoughts of the explosion that shut down the computer chip in her brain, compliments of the Liege, sent chills rippling across her body. The price paid to be free of those men had indeed been high.

"Asia, I'm glad to hear you. Are you okay?"

The warm concern from her Mistress' voice eased the tension knotting in her shoulders. She tipped her head from side to side to release more pressure. Unaccustomed to pack, Asia was learning to accept the care of others in slow degrees. In her flawed memory of her upbringing she had been devoid of emotional bonding. Jasmine decided to change all of that. With every connection, and every discussion the woman reminded Asia, either in word or actions, that she had a family who stood behind her. Although thousands of miles and an ocean separated them, Asia wasn't alone.

"I'm okay. Still in the castle."

"Did *you find out any more information?*"

"No, *I still have not located Gunnolf.*"

"You've been there almost a week. Is there a problem?"

"Yes. I don't think he's here." She told Jasmine everything that had happened to that point. Seeking out Lord Boris nephew, chasing him until he caught her, taking information, exchanging places with the new hire Tate and her subsequent search of the castle.

"Sound like you've done all you can. You haven't heard from him since you entered the castle?"

"No, Ma'am. That link is dead. I don't know what happened." She had a few ideas, but nothing concrete.

"What now?"

"I'm ready to come home, but..."

"But?"

And then she told Jasmine about the test wolves, and their living conditions.

"You can't get involved. Silas forbids it. It was one thing to remove Gunnolf, he's an old and revered friend. But you're a guest on another Alpha's turf. He's turned a blind eye as a courtesy to Silas, but he has no allegiance to us. He'd probably side with the Liege if things went wrong."

The truth left a bitter taste on her tongue. "*The Liege corrupted a full-blood, he runs their lab. If they can do that... we are all at risk.*" She tried to sound unaffected by the man in the lab but she could not. Despite the little she knew of him, something about him called to her.

"*What?*" Jasmine shouted. "*A full-blood? Hold on a sec, I need to tell Silas.*"

Asia filtered through the sounds in the lower area. Chuck snored.

Henry worked the other side with his friend, Armand.

"*Are you sure he ran the lab?*"

"*Yes, he's a bit of an ass, everyone caters to him. But I am certain of the wolf.*" She yawned and pulled the cover to her chin. "*I'll let you know when I figure a way to get out of here and come home.*"

"*Okay, I'm sorry things didn't work out the way you planned.*"

Chapter 4

"Tate, you're on to take these beauties to his majesty. Since he didn't kill you the other night for the late meal, you get to spend more time in the lab. Exciting, right?" Chuck laughed and pointed at the cages. "Plus, it's mating day, chances are he's hot and ready to get the party started." Chuck slapped the top of two cages earning snarls from the bitches behind the bars. Asia gritted her teeth at the crude remarks and pushed the cart.

"Oh yeah, here take this." Chuck threw a dog whistle on a long chain to her. "Sometimes he needs a little help to shift, use this. I don't know why but it helps."

Lips pressed together, she exhaled and pushed the cart forward. "A dog whistle, what the hell?" she murmured once she cleared the lower lift. "That's insulting as fuck."

She placed her hand on the scanner, the door opened and she pushed the cart inside the lab. The wolf stood on all fours a distance from the door; she exhaled and tossed the chain aside. "Good you've already shifted, no need to help you then." The cart seemed heavier, and she gave it a hard shove sending it further into the room and then lowered it on a lift. He trotted in her direction and she looked at him. "Shit." Certain she was seeing things she shook her head. "Oh shit, you're a black wolf," she said looking at the magnificent beast. "How is that possible?" The lift moved down, and she continued to stare. Her wolf howled and pushed to be free.

The black wolf whined as he watched her move downward. Once the lift reached the bottom, she opened the cages. Snarling and snapping, the bitches leapt out the cages and ran to the other side of the lab. Safe behind the cages, she hit the button, and the lift moved upward.

The black wolf howled.

Asia really looked at him. The only other wolves she had seen close to his size were La Patron and his brother Angus. He ignored the bitches and stared at her. His sad sherry colored eyes tugged on her heart, which made no sense.

"Easy big guy, I'll be back," she said knowing cameras were everywhere. She hated her black wolf outburst and hoped she didn't get in trouble. Following Tate's script she continued. "It's that time of the month, have fun with the ladies. Fingers crossed, we need pups." She raised her hand displaying crossed fingers.

Another breeding project, she should have guessed. But why allow the full-blood access to computers? Too many questions and as Mistress said, answering them about a black wolf was not the mission.

"*Please, help me.*"

Those three words sent shock waves through her system. The black wolf spoke to her on a link burning in her mind. What? How? She didn't understand. No one had been able to access her links after her re-birth. Was this another trick? New technology?

Time to leave.

The black wolf howled again and jumped at the landing where she stood. His howls turned to snarls as he continued leaping toward the railing.

"*Please, I'm a prisoner. What's left of me can only speak as a wolf. Please, help...*" The plea burned in her mind, but she didn't trust him. First Gunnolf accessed her through a link, now the wolf tapped into her mind. She needed to find out if Gunnolf lived and get out of this damned castle.

Frustrated and confused, Asia placed her palm on the security pad. The door opened. She waited for the scan to complete and then stepped into the hall. The howl of the black wolf sliced through her, causing her to stumble. Sadness, heartache and pain were braided into the sound. In a few seconds, the wolf accomplished something no one had done in decades.

He made her feel.

Chapter 5

Asia noted the cameras lining the hall and headed to an area of the building where staff gathered. She nodded to the two other lab techs, grabbed her clip board and veered to the right.

"How was his majesty today?" Chuck asked.

"No different," she said sensing their low opinion of the full-blood.

"Did he thank you for the gift?"

"Did you tell him not to kill the bitches this time?" Henry asked. "I'm running low on stock. As hard as he fucks them, you'd think

they'd be spitting out pups ten at a time."

Asia's forced a smile, certain the lackey whose form she occupied would. Their words concerned her, and pissed off her wolf.

"*I'm a prisoner here...*" His pitiful words bled through her thoughts. Despite her wolf 's displeasure, she disregarded the wolf and continued down the hall away from that lab. The moment she turned the corner a barrage of scents and sounds hit her.

Henry met her gaze and shrugged. "For some reason they've been noisy today. Could be a reaction from his Majesty making all that noise. What's wrong with him today? Bastard's nose is usually too stuck up his ass to say thank you when we send bitches for him to

mate. Today he's making all kinds of noise."

"What's he doing? Is he mating with them yet?" She asked, allowing Tate's personality to surface.

"Not yet, I might need to give him a sedative but then he'd try to kill me if he ever saw me again. But how else can I get the bitches out of there?"

"Sedate all of them, then get your bitches." At least this one would be out of the way while she checked the castle one last time for Gunnolf.

"Hmm, I might have to do that. Let's hope he'll settle his big arse down and do the job. So far just two of his pups survived. If we don't want to be looking for other jobs we need to up those odds."

Asia nodded, although the thought ran through Tate's mind that their bosses would kill them before firing them. As she walked to the area Tate worked, she rifled through his memories again to search for clues. Since he'd never been upstairs, he had no idea what it looked like or who ran this business. Once, sometimes twice a day he reported to a supervisor who never came below but saw and knew everything that happened. Poor guy never expected to leave or have a family. For a new worker he had a pretty dismal view of the place.

"Where are you from?" the old man asked again. His mate glanced at her and then turned aside.

She ignored his question. The door slid closed, and she headed toward the desk and stopped. Tate would do a visual check on each wolf. With long steps she moved down the aisle uncertain what changes she needed to see. These wolves had undergone multiple surgeries and treatments, but since Tate didn't know the kinds of experiments, neither did she. They were a pitiful bunch. Cuts and bruises marred their faces which surprised her. Those should've healed clear.

A lone cage sat a few feet from the others. A few feet away she paused, sensing tighter security at what she assumed were someone's remains, until he released a tired sigh. The old man lacked both legs and an arm. The one arm left had been cut off at the elbow. Could he see? When he lifted his head, she noted the empty sockets and her heart dropped. A wolf would rather be dead than caged, this type of mutilation smacked of a sick mind. The need to leave this place burned in her gut. Sorrow and heartache rose in her chest for the old guy but she didn't speak or move closer, instead she returned to the desk. The moment she did, the monitor blinked.

"Report."

Asia gave a concise report based on her observations of the caged wolves. "Very good." A pause and then. "Hawke is ignoring the bitches and trying to jump over the railing. Did anything happen when you were in the room?"

"No. He had shifted already, in preparation I suppose. Guess he knew we'd bring the bitches this time today. Seems he whined a bit, which may be unusual but other than that, he seemed fine."

"Okay. Finish your report and help the others. There won't be a

shift change today, we are short staffed."

A shiver ran through Tate followed by the sure knowledge his replacements had been permanently terminated.

"Mistress?"

"Asia?"

"I am in the main area and haven't found Gunnolf, or heard from him. The lab tech I am wearing fears there's no way to leave alive. Everything is automated."

"That's not acceptable."

She exhaled, looked at the caged wolves and brightened. *"Can*

Jacques teach me a virus to shut the place down for a short window?"

"One sec."

Asia filled in the computerized forms on each wolf in case someone paid attention.

"Jacques says he needs information on the computer, can you send him anything?"

"No. I don't have access other than the lowest level."

"Jacques says that is enough. Type this."

After clearing the screen, she typed the strings into a file he specified expecting a flashing sign or neon lights. Nothing happen. The cursor stopped blinking, and the screen returned to normal. She looked at the wolves again. The old male gazed at her but didn't speak. Unable to face them, she left the room.

"Over here," Chuck waved at her. She jogged closer to help him with the cage. "Word came down to sedate Hawke and the bitches. Then take them out and let him sleep it off. I'd say cut off the bastard's

balls if I didn't think they'd cut mine off first."

Not interested in conversation, she nodded and helped push the platform holding the cages. Asia mimicked human behavior and resisted moving down the hall at a faster pace. The vision of the mutilated man nauseated her and she could not rid her mind of the image. Why would anyone do that to someone? What happened to his limbs? His eyes? How did he still survive?

"Heard they tanked Chives and Henly," Chuck said in a lowered voice, but not low enough that the cameras wouldn't pick up the conversation. "Now we're down to the four of us, they expect us to live down here with these animals full time. Fuck that. I didn't sign on for that bullshit."

"Be quiet before you're tanked like the others," she said amazed at his stupidity.

He snorted. "There's only one guard on duty above ground and the super. Chances are the super and the guard are somewhere shagging each other and not paying us a bit of attention, eh the bastards."

Maybe he wasn't stupid. "How do you know about them?"

Chuck preened. "You're new, the super used to work down here with us. Last super disappeared, they moved him upstairs. Everybody knows Hawke runs the place, the super is just to make sure the equipment doesn't fail."

Asia nodded, calculating the odds. The other three on this floor were no problem to dispose of; the real challenge was the super and the security guard. First, she needed to get through security to reach them. Moments later they stopped in front of the lab door.

Her wolf whined and pushed to break free, surprising her. Henry met them holding a tranq gun. He looked at the cages and then punched in the security code. A beep sounded, and the door opened, he walked inside. A howl and then snarling anger filled the air.

"*No!*" That one word filled with hurt, anger and despair shot through their link. She closed him out. He was not her mission. Gunnolf and freedom were her only concerns. A thumping sound came from the room. Chuck pushed the cart and then looked at her. She snapped out of it and helped push the cart into the room.

"I'll stand here with the tranq's," Henry said. "Put the bitches in the cages, leave him on the floor. He'll be mad as fire when he wakes but I'll show him the damn tape if I have to. Son of a bitch gave us no choice."

Chuck snorted. "That's not going to matter to Hawke. Bastard thinks he's perfect."

Asia helped pick up the sedated bitches and placed them inside the cages. When her wolf whined over Hawke's fate, Asia ignored her completely.

Henry wiped the sweat from his forehead and stretched. "I'm going to the back, get rest while you can. It's going to be a long night."

Chuck nodded, walked off in the opposite direction, opened his area and stepped inside the hall.

"Let's grab a bite before I go upstairs to take this stuff back." Henry waved her forward.

Asia nodded. The moment they walked into the break room, Henry grabbed her close. His hands roamed everywhere, kissing and touching. She pushed him off her.

"Wait, wait... I thought you and Armand were a couple." Henry smiled. "We are." He reached for her again.

She held him at arm's length. "I don't want any trouble. Leave me out of this."

"It's okay, he knows, he's cool. I'll see him later. Come on; let me initiate you into the brotherhood." Henry pulled her close again. Sensing the cameras, Asia played it out a bit even though she wanted to punch him for being an asshole, instead she used the chameleon. The familiar tingling raced through her body making the exchange while wrapped in his arms. Once done, she sat on the ground holding Tate's new body for a few moments. Kissed his cheek and stood.

"Welcome to the lower level, go ahead and sleep now." She stepped out the door and spoke into the wrist communicator. "I need access to level B to return tranq gun and tranquilizers."

There was a delay and then a small voice spoke. "Proceed." Excited for the next stage in her mission, Asia headed for the lift, placed her palm on the key-pad, and entered the door. Seconds later the door opened, and she met the lone security guard. A quick scan showed he was the only person on the floor. She had no idea where the super was.

"You got him?" The guard asked turning to walk down the hall.

Asia followed. "Yeah. Took two shots in him and one each for the other two."

"Whew, he's going to be pissed," the guard said opening a cabinet filled with weapons.

"Yeah. But I followed instructions, he wrote the damn protocols."

"Funny, but he didn't mean for them to be used on himself. Bastard never imagined himself out of control in the first place. Not to mention passing up two bitches in heat, he's going to be real angry," the guard chuckled putting the weapon away.

"No question," she said wondering how a full-blood had risen in the ranks of the Liege and commanded this kind of fear and respect. They headed back toward the lift. She noticed the guard appeared distracted.

"What's wrong?"

The guard frowned. "Nothing, he's been acting weird all day, locked himself in the computer room, watching cameras." He waved toward the camera in the hall. "Dance with me Henry, that'll get a rise out of him." He grabbed her and started dancing.

Asia laughed and grabbed a portion of his memories. His name, Jerry. His lover, Ponce. They'd started the same time, and he helped his lover get his current position by telling lies on the old supervisor. She bypassed all of that information for something she could use to find Gunnolf and leave the building.

After waving goodbye to Jerry, she headed into the lift, typed in a code and stepped out when it stopped. Immediately she typed in another code to hold it. She sensed Ponce in the room to her left. Something had spooked the young man. Chances were he realized she was on the floor. Using the code from Jerry's memory, she entered the communications room and tackled Ponce to the ground before accessing the database. Within minutes, she knew everything she needed to know.

Gunnolf was dead.

Hawke killed him. Liege Lord Boris Lancaster owned this place but hadn't visited in years. Her hopes of discovering more about herself ended. The information she'd received from Gunnolf was now suspect. How would she ever know if the things he shared were real, another memory stolen from someone else or manufactured to suit the Liege's purposes?

Anger, boiled and rippled through her. A masterful hand had played her like a well-tuned violin. *Son of a bitch.* She grabbed and threw the half empty bottled water across the room.

Ponce knew computers, and this system was high tech. With a series of keystrokes, passwords and security over-rides, she shut down and disabled every camera in the building erasing everything in the past twenty four hours.

Ready to leave, she unlocked and opened every door and exit. She swallowed her anger over the treatment of her fellow wolves; she turned on the loud speaker and howled long and loud. After a scream or two, she heard the mass exodus of her brethren.

Mission complete, she was going home.

Chapter 6

Asia turned to leave and stopped. Jerry, the security guard stared wide eyed, and he had company. Two vacant eyed hybrids stood behind nearby. Chuck had been wrong. There were others above ground, simply not others he would recognize.

"*Okay, Jacques is ready,*" Jasmine said.

Asia rested on the balls of her feet as Jerry typed on the keypad looking inside the room with a deep frown.

"*Incoming.*"

"*Incoming? Wait. Jacques said whatever you do don't shut the system down, it will trip alarms and alert the Liege. Don't use a hammer, is what he said.*"

Asia shook her head at the late advice. Heart racing, adrenaline pumped through her providing an outlet for her anger in preparation

to fight. "*Too late, already done, company's here.*"

The door slid open. "Ponce, what are you doing?" Jerry hissed pulling her close, looking around until and stopped on the floor where Henry lay dead on the ground.

"Shit, I didn't mean for you to kill anybody, we were just kidding around," he said and fired the weapon in his hand at the hybrid. Surprised, Asia stepped aside, and avoided being slammed into the controls when the other hybrid charged. Jerry emptied his pistol slowing down the hybrid, but she knew that wouldn't stop the breed. Nothing would until they completed the mission with their deaths.

Asia jumped up, flipped and landed behind the second hybrid. She punched the thing in the eye, withdrew her fist, and punched again. This time she ripped out the chip behind his eye. He screamed and held his face. Grabbing his head between her palms, she twisted, snapped its neck and silenced him at the same time.

"What... how'd you do that?" Jerry asked staring as flesh re-knitted over the metal on her arm. Since there was no reasonable answer, she gazed down at the other hybrid lying on the floor with a hole in his chest and neck. Jerry had destroyed his opponent with a laser. Asia hoped he wouldn't do the same to his lover.

"I think I read about it somewhere, come on let's go." She stepped over the hybrid and headed toward the door.

"Go? Go where," Jerry yelled and then raised a closed fist before lowering it. "There are chips in our brains, those bastards can find us anywhere in the world. Do you have any idea what you've done? Do you know what they do to people who fuck up?" He pointed to the dead tech.

Asia looked out the door.

Jerry grabbed her shoulders and shook her. Asia read his pain at what he needed to do. He loved Ponce and planned to kill them both to save them from the Liege. Instead of speaking she laid her palm across his cheek and morphed. Side by side, she placed the lovers before scanning through Jerry's memories. His knowledge of the castle seemed like a birthday present and Christmas rolled into one. A hidden door on an upper level met her immediate needs and she moved at an even pace, entered a code and headed down the stairs. Jerry and Ponce often left the building for picnics and outings through this exit. With each step to leave this accursed place, her wolf whined. Night had fallen by the time the copse of trees on the other side of the castle came into view.

Asia looked up at the dark, imposing building and spit on the ground. Gunnolf died years ago and somehow his memories lured unsuspecting protégés into a web of servitude. If she had explosives, she would blow the place apart.

Tired and hungry, she morphed into the guard who helped rescue Tyrese from Lyrill just in case the European pack was still in the area. Jasmine would have flight arrangements made, ready to take her home and it would be too difficult explaining a new person in the country.

Mission over, she headed toward the small house on the opposite side of the lake where she'd stayed before the job in the castle. Tonight she would rest, explain the situation to Jasmine and wait for an extraction. Now that she'd calmed down, she realized she'd violated a direct order from La Patron by releasing the test wolves. No telling how he would respond.

Greggor would be angry over the security breach and start the hunt soon. By disabling the cameras she'd covered her tracks temporarily, but leaving the continent was the safest bet. Eager to leave, she took off at a fast run until sensing full-bloods followed.

She didn't sense aggression and stopped to wait. A few seconds later a pitiful, rag tag bunch of people surrounded her. Recognizing them from the lab she wondered why they had not returned home or left the area. They stared as if she had answers. But why follow her? A stranger.

"Why are you following me?"

"We don't know where to go." The plain comment took her by surprise.

"It has been many years since I have seen the moon or felt dirt beneath my feet. Where do we go now that we left that place?" An older man she recognized from inside, his skin held a blue tinge that mystified her. Was she responsible for them? For this?

Asia looked at the wolves and sighed. Tonight had been a series of her messing up one after the other. What had she done? She didn't like being responsible for people.

No, she *was* responsible and somehow they knew.

To free the test wolves without thinking of the next step or what the cost would be had been a big mistake. Now they needed direction, and she had nothing. No place to take them, no pack for them to join, not even food to feed them or medicine to help them heal. In her anger, she hadn't thought this far ahead. It never occurred to her they would need more direction. The urge to run and disappear rode her hard.

Eager to leave the area, she waved for them to follow her. Together they moved through the woods at a decent pace until she scented Tobias, the beta from the European pack. Earlier that month, he and his pack mates helped Tyrese, La Patron's son and others fly out of the country. Jasmine had them wait for her to complete her mission and help her leave as well.

"Tobias," she extended her hand in greeting to the tall, red headed, full-blood. He shook her hand but his attention settled on the ragged wolves with her.

"La Patron asked my Alpha to have us look for you and offer help if needed. We've been waiting in the area all week."

Glad for the help she explained the dilemma without going into too much detail. She sensed he read between the lines.

"Soon I'll be returning home. Can you take them with you, reacquaint them to pack life?" Since he didn't know Silas had been in recent contact with Alpha Frederick she didn't offer that information.

"I need approval from my Alpha. But it should be okay. When do you leave?"

"I am waiting for arrangements, Gunnolf is dead –"

"Gunnolfs' been dead a long, time. Hawke tried to save him, but they used him instead. Heard they have a way of using the dead," one of the wolves said in an eerie voice sending chills up Asia's spine.

She looked at the older woman. "When did Gunnolf die? I swear he spoke to me."

The woman cackled showing browned teeth and missing canines. "Gunnolf speaks to everybody. All of us were in the orphanage at one time. A great man he was, great man. Pity they use him the way they do."

"How do they use him if he's dead?" Asia didn't understand, none of this made sense.

"Somehow they got hold of his memories and used those to lure us into the web. I heard his voice over twenty years ago, but he wasn't there." She eyed Asia and nodded with the self-assurance of someone who visited another spiritual plane often. "I still listen to his voice. I've been meaning to return to the village. Rumor says he warded the place and stashed his things there. Course that could be just the voices."

Asia nodded, ready to end the conversation. Too much time had passed, and she needed to rest after expending so much energy with the bracelet. That was a small price to pay. "You should get them out of here before it's too late." She stressed the last words so Tobias understood the danger.

He nodded. "You?"

"Just waiting for instructions, go ahead." She had to confess her actions and hope Jasmine forgave her.

The wolves followed him through the trees, she ran in the opposite direction wondering why she hadn't left with Tobias. Her wolf whined and howled. The small house came into view, and she breathed in relief no one had been inside to touch her things. The backpack lay in the cupboard; she grabbed the straps and left the hut for the forest. It didn't take long to find her tree.

It stood tall and majestic above the others. Asia slid the bag on her back and climbed upward. Halfway up the tree, the roar of engines in the distance filled the air. Tobias and the wolves were on their way.

Once she found the three branches close enough to lie across, she hung the backpack on a nearby limb and pulled out her jerky, dried fruit and nuts. She ate until her stomach agreed she could stop and drank from the canteen. The cool water eased her throat and rested well in her belly. In the morning she'd need to refill it in the nearby stream and go into town for more food. Beyond tired, she placed everything back into her bag and zipped it tight to keep out bugs.

Next she pulled her heavy knit cap and a lightweight jacket, and slid them on. Dressed for sleep, she did a preliminary scan of the area.

The sounds of the forest soothed her. Unaccustomed to handling an entire mission, from beginning, to implementation, to completion, she hated all the mistakes, but she'd learn. Yawning, she lay on her side and closed her eyes.

"*Where are you?*"

Her eyes flew open. "What the hell?" She whispered, scanning the forest for the black wolf. How'd he get in her head again?

"*You are the first person I have been able to speak with in decades; please I need your help.*"

Asia scoffed and rolled over despite her wolf 's objections. The last time a voice spoke in her head it wound up as a trick. She refused to waste time or fall for any more tricks.

"*They've used me to do... things; even now the computer in my brain is seeking to shut down this link.*"

Memories when a computer chip and scanner were locked in her brain sent chills through her. The Liege had monitored every step she made, heard and saw every person she talked to, and even used her as a weapon and instrument to gather intelligence. Life had been hell. La Patron had locked her in a cell with a blindfold to prevent the Liege from seeing the inside of his facility and to protect his secrets. No one understood how the computer chip took over your life better than she did.

But it could all be a part of some big lie to re-capture her for what she did to the castle. Asia could not afford to answer him. Links were intimate and a powerful intrusion in a person's life. Once she responded it would solidify the connection and he could find her anywhere. She refused that risk and remained silent.

Hawke lay on his side on the cold concrete floor of the lab. No one had brought dinner, and he had no desire to seek out a meal. A miracle happened today. His wolf rose to the surface with renewed vigor and determination, taking control from the computer chip in his brain that ran his life. He'd always suspected it could happen under the right circumstances, he just never realized what those circumstances would be.

That still puzzled him.

Tate sparked his interest when they first met. There was something different about the guy but Hawke hadn't been able to put his finger on what. Once he shifted to fuck the bitches, his wolf emerged stronger when Tate entered the room. For some reason his wolf linked with the easygoing young man. A true link. One his computerized mind could not shut down or penetrate. So it must be real. After all these years he had someone to talk to. Someone his wolf trusted.

"*I am a prisoner. My body has not been under my control for decades, yet my wolf has connected with you. Can you help us leave this place?*" There was no answer. Not even a courtesy fuck off.

Footsteps neared the doorway and Hawke stood on all fours, expecting dinner. He wasn't starved but he could eat. Two hybrids stepped inside first. Hope, fragile and in its infancy stage crumbled beneath the boots of the man who walked inside next.

Chapter 7

Greggor strode into the lab, looked around, and then down at the large black wolf standing on the lower level of the lab and released a nervous sigh. If anything happened to the beast, his uncle would kill him. He had one job, to make sure Hawke worked in a safe environment.

"I heard you were having a bad day," he said moving to the edge of the gate. "Figured it was time for me to check in on you." He eyed Hawke wondering why he hadn't shifted.

The next moment his breath caught, as magnificent as he thought Hawke's wolf was, it didn't compare to the man. Tall, dark and handsome didn't begin to describe the square cut of his jaw, sharp nose and full lips. Greggor had spent hours reviewing videos of Hawke working out in the gym, driving on the small range and on the computer. He could not get enough of the man and kept his physical distance preferring to overstuff himself on camera footage without an audience.

Hawke's mental aptitude scores had been off the charts, that's one of the reasons his Uncle Boris wanted Hawke, but Greggor appreciated the gorgeous hunk wrapped around the genius.

Hawke's head was down for a few seconds, he shuddered. Greggor's gaze widened in fascination as Hawke's muscles rippled across his chest and biceps bulged as he placed his palms on both sides of his head. When Hawke walked in the opposite direction, Greggor's gaze locked on his tight ass, thick muscular thighs and wide back. The man was walking perfection and oblivious to his own natural beauty. The inherent downfall of the computer lodged in Hawke's mind neutered vanity and emotional attachments. There were days Greggor hated the damn chip. Just once he'd like to know if Hawke ever saw him, really saw him.

"Hawke?"

"Yes?"

"What happened? We had a security breach."

Hawke stopped and looked at him. Greggor sensed he completed a self-scan first before moving to the keyboard to check his system. "My files have not been tampered with. There has been no security breach."

Greggor swallowed his irritation. "Because your system's not affected does not mean we didn't have a breach. Did anything unusual happen yesterday? Anything?" The moment the computer alarm rang, he'd activated a few hybrids to help Jerry, the security guard. Now, Jerry was missing, the hybrids destroyed, his lab techs were dead and his test subjects escaped. He would have shot himself if Hawke had disappeared as well.

He had a small respite, his Uncle Boris' current project in the states took priority and the man couldn't leave, which gave Greggor time to learn where the holes were in security before recapturing the wolves.

Hawke gave him a vacant eyed stare for a few seconds and shook his head. "Nothing that I recall."

Over the years Hawke's thoroughness reached legendary status. If he said nothing happened, then he believed it. Pleased, Greggor nodded.

"You should view the footage for that time to see if you concur with me, although I am correct."

Greggor nodded at the conceit embedded in the response. Often, he wondered how much was Hawke and how much was the computer. "I don't need to check, I trust you. Can you look at the main system; do an analysis on why and how the compromise happened? I

need to plug that hole before I bring the test subjects back."

"Good point. I'll check it now."

"Can you access the main system from here?" He hadn't been aware Hawke could do that, but then again, there wasn't much the man couldn't do. The installed computer chip served as a means to control Hawke but had little effect on the wolf. Typically, whenever Hawke shifted to wolf to mate or run in the below ground arena, he always returned to human form when he woke.

"I can but I run the risk of opening my system to whatever is on the main system and Master Boris forbids that. I cannot override his orders." Hawke said his deep voice lacked inflection and personality.

"Put some clothes on and I'll take you up to the room."

Hawke nodded, strode to a room with a large glass pane, and entered a code in the keypad. The door slid open, and he walked into the room. Greggor watched him slip on a pair of pants and a tee shirt that hugged his chest. Pity he couldn't stay naked but the cameras were back online and his uncle or any of his friends might visit this facility at any time. He would be the only person pleased at seeing a naked Hawke at the controls.

Once dressed, Hawke entered the lift and rose to meet Greggor. The entire time the computer in the lift checked and rechecked Hawke's chip, making sure he was stable. Greggor stepped back, looked up at his crush and swallowed hard. Masculinity personified defined Hawke who stood over six and a half feet tall, and starred as the long-time object of his night-time dreams.

Hawke passed him without any acknowledgement and placed his hand on the keypad. Anyone else in the castle could place their palm on the key pad and the door would open. With Hawke his uncle set in another series of tests to insure his valued prize didn't escape. No one but his uncle and the computer embedded in Hawke knew the answers. After a series of key strokes, the door opened and shut behind Hawke. Greggor placed his palm on the pad and the door opened. He and the hybrids found Hawke waiting inside the lift for them.

They rode in silence to the communications floor. Hawke stepped off first heading for the room. Greggor quickened his pace, so they arrived at the same time.

Hawke looked around for a few seconds and then pointed to a console. "I will use this one."

Greggor nodded and took the chair next to him.

An hour later Hawke leaned back in the chair and looked at Greggor. "I patched the hole and repaired the breach. If someone tampers with this again, I have placed other safeguards. The test subjects will be secure."

Greggor nodded, pleased. Hiring and training staff to work the lab would set him back a few days but he would have order restored before his uncle checked in again. "Were you able to retrieve the camera footage from yesterday, it would help understand what happened."

“Yes, but it would upload a virus to the system and open up sensitive areas. It is a simple and effective way to wipe out small areas of data. It is better to leave it alone.”

Greggor nodded and hoped his uncle would accept Hawke’s verdict.

“I have work to do,” Hawke said standing and then walking off toward the lift. Rather than follow, Greggor watched Hawke’s progression to the lower lab through the cameras. Not once did Hawke look in any other direction but straight. When the lift stopped on the correct floor, Hawke walked with military precision to his lab, and placed his palm on the security panel. The door slid open and the object of Greggor’s fantasies stepped into the lab.

Chapter 8

The cool dawn brushed against Asia's cheek, stroking her awake in slow degrees. She lay high in the trees looking out over the forest. The natural beauty soothed her and for a few moments, all life's cares and concerns disappeared. Sitting up, she rested against the tree and gazed toward the stone monstrosity.

"They have used me to do things; even now the computer in my brain is seeking this link to shut it down."

Hawke's pain and embarrassment touched her through the link and mirrored what she'd felt when the Liege held her mind hostage. There were nights when flashbacks of the men she'd destroyed kept her awake, she hadn't been a good person most of her life. Did the fact someone else controlled her mind and body cancel her foul deeds? No. How was what she did different from what Hawke had done? Both had the same oppressor. But... what if this was another trap? Her mind argued. Without the chameleon bracelet she would've been caught and caged. What if the Liege had discovered another way to link with her and use this new information against her? But how? It made no sense.

Unable to draw a conclusion that would satisfy both parts of her nature she closed her eyes to clear her mind. Last night the dream of the Black Wolf returned. As usual, he sat high overseeing a large litter of pups. Sometimes he poked a few pups, settled arguments and cleaned others. This dream left more questions than answers, and she still did not understand its significance. The Black Wolf Alpha had been legendary in the pack, and now roamed a different plane that wound up in dreams.

"Asia?"

Her eyes flew open. "*Mistress?*"

"I didn't hear anything from you and worried. Is everything okay?"

Okay being a subjective word, Asia hesitated. "*Gunnolf is dead.*"

"So sorry to hear that, I know you wanted to see him."

The sincerity in Jasmine's voice filtered through the link. "*Mistress, the black wolf spoke to me through a link. I don't understand how that is possible.*"

"*Through Gunnolf's link?*"

Asia shook her head, realized Jasmine couldn't see and then spoke. "*No, through a separate link. One that feels strange, I feel him. I mean when he talks I sense his feelings.*" She shook her head positive she hadn't explained it right. "*What I'm trying to say is I don't know how he's able to do that when La Patron and no one else has been able to link with me.*"

"*Hmmm, links fall under Silas' area of expertise. I just use them and don't know how they work. Hold on a sec.*"

Asia looked toward the imposing castle. Her wolf hadn't calmed down since she walked away. Could it be their mutual suffering compelling her wolf to ignore the danger the castle presented? Several ideas rolled through her mind, none made any sense.

"*Well... let me see how to explain this. In order for the wolf to link to you there has to be in place an intimate, not necessarily sexual, connection. Like parent and child, boss and employer, brother and sister, and mate to mate. Silas said that once you respond, the link will click in place and become unbreakable. But you can shut the person out from time to time but that has a price, but the link is permanent until death.*"

All of that, she knew. But she didn't know Hawke and he shouldn't be able to create a link with her.

"*Asia?*"

"*Yes Mistress?*"

"*What do you think of this wolf?*"

"*The black wolf?*"

"*That's right, another black wolf. Yes, tell me your thoughts, what does he say when he contacts you?*"

Asia exhaled marshalling her thoughts together. "*He is a glorious beast. Tall as La Patron, although his eyes are hazel. I suspect he is stubborn, he did not give up easily.*"

"*Good looking beast, got it. What does he say?*"

For some reason she hesitated to share his remarks, it seemed like a betrayal in a weird way. If it had been anyone other than Jasmine she wouldn't reveal his shame.

"*He asked me to help him. Claims to be a prisoner in his body, and that the Liege is using him.*"

"I see. What does your wolf say?"

Asia frowned. She hadn't communicated with her wolf other than to dismiss the whining. *"She wants to go to him,"* she said in a halting tone taking stock of her wolf 's feelings. A swirl of emotions rose from her beast, fear that they'd leave, joy that Hawke was near, apprehension over their reconnection, and aggravation that Asia ignored her needs.

"Is it possible he is telling the truth? You can scent a lie right?"

Asia closed her eyes and hit the tree with the back of her head. How could she have forgotten something so basic?

"Yes and yes. Weird but I'm operating a step behind my normal. Promise I will pay attention and revisit the messages again."

Jasmine cleared her throat. *"If your wolf is unhappy about you leaving the wolf behind, and he's created a link with you, a stranger, that could mean something significant."*

She frowned. *"Mistress? What are you talking about?"* Jasmine's straightforwardness had been one of the things she valued most about their relationship.

Through their link Jasmine's sigh sounded like a soft whistle. *"He could be your mate."*

The last word sent a shock through to her mind, freezing her in place. She didn't breathe. How? Her mate lost his head in the lab, she'd seen it. It couldn't be true.

"No, m*y mate is dead."*

"I know sweetie, but Silas thinks you got a do-over."

Asia brows furrowed at the words. *"A what?"*

"A second chance, another shot at love, mate and pups, all that. It's possible the Goddess has blessed you with another mate."

"And you call it a do-over?" The many sides of her Mistress' personality always amazed her. Jasmine could be sweet and nurturing or hard core and demanding, whatever the situation required, the woman adapted.

"Yes, it's something to consider. It would explain why you are still in the area instead of leaving with Tobias last night. Maybe you can't leave, not yet anyway."

Asia looked toward the castle. "A do-over?" She murmured allowing the words to fill her mind, and rolled them over her tongue.

"I'll think about it Mistress."

Jasmine laughed, the tinkling sound touched her. Asia smiled and waited for a comment or explanation.

"You do that, think on it. In the mean-time, Jacques says he has a virus ready to download if you need it. No more hammering with software. He says to type in the standard codes that all of you received before the Lyrill trip, it'll open a back door and the virus will download."

"What's funny, Mistress?"

"Uh... well, Rese and Rone have started a pool on how long it will take you to return to the castle for the wolf. All I'm gonna say is take your time, no need to rush. Women stick together and we don't rush."

Longing swept through her at the mention of the twin's antics, and the betting pool. She missed everyone. Strange, sitting high in a tree in the middle of nowhere, she came to realize she had a place to call home.

"What was your bet?" Jasmine laughed.

Asia chuckled as a sense of freedom and rightness assailed her. Home. Jasmine had been telling her all along, but it wasn't until this moment that it settled. Everyone in the compound and everything there was pack, home.

"I can't say, Rese is watching. But I have faith in the end you will do the right thing."

"Okay, at least a few hours or another day."

"Not that long, oops."

Asia shook her head wishing she was there. *"Got it. Mistress?"*

"Yes?"

"I'll be ready to come home after this. There is something else." She exhaled and hoped Jasmine's good humor continued as she told her about leaving the castle and the release of the test wolves.

There was a pause and then Jasmine spoke. *"What? I told you Silas said to leave the test animals alone."*

"Yes, Ma'am and I apologize, my anger at being deceived over-rode everything, but that is no excuse. I failed my mission."

"Your mission was to rescue Gunnolf who's a ghost. There's no way you could've accomplished that. But you did discover important information Silas is using, the full-blood running the lab and now you're bringing him out. Both of you will need to leave the continent at once. I'm sure Silas has a few questions for him."

Asia released a breath. Jasmine's tone spoke of her anger even as she rationalized what happened and found something redeemable in all of this. The Goddess chose well in La Patron's mate.

"Yes Ma'am."

"If you need help call me. If he is your mate, you cannot leave him behind; your wolf would never allow it. Go, and retrieve your black wolf. I will have a plane on standby."

"Is that my new mission?"

"I don't think you need a mission to carry out this one. The twins are talking about a short trip to the island with their mates. It'd be good for you to be home before they leave. If you need anything, I'm here."

Asia looked down at the ground and scented the area. She needed food, water and a bath. After repacking her bag, she climbed down and headed toward the nearest town. Pleased to be included in the group with the women, she refused to rush.

Chapter 9

Several hours passed before Asia returned to the hidden passage she'd used once to escape. She was certain they'd erased or placed an alert on Jerry's pass codes, so she avoided using that and used a code she'd picked up from the hybrid's memories. A long shot but it might buy a few minutes. The door opened into the looming dark hall. Asia morphed into Jerry again and after a quick scan, raced up the stairs and out the door toward the communications center. She moved with blinding speed across the hall, hoping the cameras didn't pick her up until safe in the room.

Within seconds of reaching the hall, four hybrids filled the area. A tall slender human male pushed through and strode forward. He eyed her up and down. Jerry called him Greggor, Lord Boris' nephew and manager of the castle. But she remembered him from Madam's Boudoir and his strange fetish.

"I can't imagine why you returned here after what you've done.

Lord Boris is furious and on the way."

Asia smelled the lie and breathed with relief.

"You better have a good excuse and it better match the cameras. Hawke was able to restore the camera footage, what was Ponce doing in that room?" Greggor pointed to the communications room.

Another lie. Greggor had no idea what happened and expected her to fill in the blanks. "He had been in the communications room most of the day and went crazy. When I heard the alarms and went downstairs to help Chuck and Tank, but got hit over the head and passed out. Earlier, I woke up in the forest and returned here." As lies went, that one wasn't all bad.

"He is lying," one of the hybrids said.

A flash of satisfaction crossed Greggor's face. The punk set this up. "I gave you a chance to come clean, to explain what happened to the Liege. Your chip was off the grid for hours and reactivated when you entered the door. Why is that? How did you disable the thing?" Greggor wasted a sneer and nasty gaze on her. Asia had been busy locating the cameras and devised ways to prevent them from recording the fight.

"No answer?"

Asia met his gaze with a raised brow.

"Jerry you have worked for Lord Boris for ten years, you know the rules and the punishment. This is out of my hands." Greggor stepped back and gave the order. "Kill the bastard."

Asia exhaled and steadied her focus as all four breeds charged. And then waited until the first one was close and dropped into a split hitting the floor. The sound of skulls smashing into one another filled the hall. And then paused a beat while they moved apart, scooted to the side to stand and slammed her fist beneath the chin of the closest breed. The hybrid's head snapped back in an awkward position, she grabbed him by the collar and threw him toward the two breeds heading in her direction.

The other hybrid behind her tried to grab hold, but she jumped and roundhouse kicked him in the chin. Next the beast spun and fell through the glass to the lower level and hit the ground hard, splitting his skull on the concrete.

Two hybrids rushed from the front. Asia leapt forward, grabbed the camera embedded in the wall and swung until the base tore from the ceiling. Hearing the hybrids behind her, she ran toward a second camera on the opposite wall, grabbed and pulled the metal away from the wall. She held the device and slammed the metal into the face of the first hybrid that reached her. Jagged metal cut through flesh and bone like a cleaver, dropping the hybrid to his knees.

The fourth hybrid leapt over the downed breed and caught the tail end of her jacket, yanking her forward. Hot breath from the beast scorched her skin. He wrapped an arm around her and squeezed. The buttons of Jerry's uniformed pressed into her skin. She scanned the hybrid for metals. There were none in his arm, just his left calf.

Asia exhaled, leaned her head on his chest so the camera wouldn't see more than she intended, and pushed his arms away. The hybrid's body vibrated with intent as he struggled to maintain the bear hold, but his muscles were no match for the metal in her arm and legs. As soon as she had leverage, she pulled her legs up and pressed against him.

Sweat poured down his forehead, yet he continued to hold on to her. When the gap widened between them, she dropped to the ground, hopped back and punched him in the eye twice in rapid succession. The second time she ripped out his chip, threw the device on the floor and stepped on the chip with the bottom of her boot. The hybrid fell forward. Asia caught him with one hand allowing his body to shield her healing arm from view.

"Jerry, I don't know how you did all that, but I wonder if you can stop this," Greggor said standing in the hall. Asia heard the whirring of the laser and leapt out of the way as it burned a hole through the breed.

She moved with lightning speed zig-zagging across the area. Greggor took aim and fired repeated shots knocking out more security cams, glass partitions and chunks of the wall.

"Stop."

Asia hid against the wall at the command and closed her eyes. That was not the same voice that called to her through the night. Damn. The computer was in control of Hawke again. Now she had to fight or die. And dying was not an option.

"You are destroying the building you imbecile."

"No, it's Jerry, he's out of control," Greggor said taking deep breaths.

She heard Hawke's footsteps and flashed to the other side. Greggor blocked her way, but he hadn't seen her yet. She punched him, knocking him to the ground.

"Mistress?" There was no answer. She'd come face to face with Hawke. He was slightly taller than La Patron and just as wide.

"What are you doing Jerry? Why is Greggor attempting to destroy you with weapons when he can push the red button on your chip?"

Asia couldn't believe the man expected to have a conversation while her adrenaline spiked through the ceiling and her wolf did flips in her belly.

"I don't uh, know." The red button wouldn't work with the chameleon, but she didn't want to go into her chameleon biology right now.

Hawke's gaze narrowed, and he crossed massive arms. "Why are you lying? I don't understand why. Logically you cannot win, and yet you have defeated superior beings. Greggor is not included in that statement of course. Your behavior puzzles me." Hawke gazed down at her as if she were a lab experiment.

"*Mistress? I need you to pull his wolf.*" Asia watched him watch her. Seconds ticked with neither of them speaking.

"Something... your scent is different. The distinction is slight but there. Did you eat onions with your meal?" Hawke placed a finger next to his chin, and continued to stare.

"No." She cleared her throat. "Curried lamb, that's what I ate, no onions."

"True, I smell no onions."

"*Sorry, we were... uh, busy. Silas is here. Ready?*"

Asia looked at Hawke, and the next moment she jumped to the left as his fist slammed into the wall where she'd been standing sending debris in all directions. Quick as a flash he was on her trail, tracking her, throwing punches.

"Mate my ass," she growled and returned a punch to his mid-section. Hawke staggered but didn't fall. *Oh shit.* She had punched him with her metal arm and he didn't hit the ground. He leapt forward.

She ducked and rolled out the way as he crashed into the wall.

"*Now, Mistress call his wolf!*" Asia gasped taking in gulps of air, while he moved slower than before but still moved. All the fighting and running took a toll. She couldn't keep running much longer. Unprepared for the blast of energy that shot through her, Asia fell to the floor. Her chest heaved as she struggled to breathe.

Seconds ticked without a sound.

"*You came back.*"

Asia's head dropped for a moment of gratitude at the sound of his voice. She looked up and stared into his eyes. "We need to leave," she said aloud refusing to use the link.

"*Please, I need to secure my research. No one needs to access those files again. You will need to do key the codes for me. Come.*" In wolf form, Hawke padded toward the lift.

Asia headed toward the communications room instead. Greggor had blown the door away with the laser and she planned to upload the virus. A few seconds later she'd typed in the code. An error message appeared.

Asia frowned.

"*We need to leave before the system reboots and locks everything down again.*"

She glanced at the intelligence shining in his eyes. *"I had a back door in this system."*

"Yes, I know, I fixed the breach. You will need to access the back door from my system, please hurry." He turned and headed to the lift.

She followed. "*Key this in,"* he said and then gave her a series of numbers which she typed. The door closed, and the lift headed down to the lower level.

When they reached his door, he said another series of numbers which she keyed and the doors opened. "*Quick, sit at the table and type exactly what I say. There is less than ten minutes."*

Asia sat without questioning him. Hawke sat nearby on his haunches watching as she typed in several series of key-strokes, some she had to re-type. Seconds ticked on the clock but he remained adamant that they complete this first. Once done, he instructed her how to upload the virus throughout all the systems, not just the one's in the castle.

"*I disabled the door but I don't know how to leave the castle, do you?*" Hawke asked when she finished.

Asia searched Jerry's memories and there was one place on this level. She had seen the door before, but if time was their enemy, returning upstairs to the staircase wouldn't work. "Yes, come with me," she said and ran to the lift. Together they reached the door, she placed her palm on the panel and the door opened. Apparently, she'd been wrong; they *hadn't* changed Jerry's security level. Hawke padded out beside her and they went down deeper into the bowels of the castle to the locked mechanical room. The other day she'd seen the steam flowing from this vent and hoped they could turn off the heat so the metal didn't burn them. After keying in the code, they stepped inside and she closed the door.

"*This is the way out?*"

"Through the ventilation system." Asia pointed to vents high on the wall and frowned. The other day it seemed as if there was one vent, now she saw three.

"*The vent is high, I cannot jump that high.*"

"Shift and climb."

"*No. I don't trust him. The computer controls his mind.*" Hawke trotted around the room seeking another way out. "*That one, the middle one leads to the outside, plus it's better insulated and won't burn. The other two are live.*"

She glanced at him and then looked at the vents. Pipes ran all through the room, a couple close to the middle vent.

Instead of agreeing to Hawke's suggestion she crawled toward the top of the pipe to reach the vent. So far he'd been right, the temperature was bearable. Leaning to the side, she pulled off the grate and climbed inside. At the end of the chute she saw outside and exhaled. He hadn't tricked her, at least not about this. But then again, he wanted to leave the castle.

"B*ehind you*," Hawke said surprising her. "When I saw your claws

I remembered *I can partial shift. If you move to the side I will go first.*"

"No." Asia scooted forward and crawled toward the opening. His claws scratched the metal making an irritating sound. She hoped there were no sound or movement sensors in the vents. The natural scent of his beast made her wolf push to shift. Asia took a moment and reminded the beast to be patient, safety first. Her beast calmed but let her know of her displeasure. Asia grabbed the iron grate and pushed. The damn thing didn't move. Damn. She'd need the power in her legs.

"Can you back up a little? I need to turn." She sensed his hesitation, and then he moved. After moving around a bit, she managed to change positions and placed both feet against the grate and pushed.

Instead of the grate pushing outward, she slid backward on the metal.

"Damn." She scooted forward again. Hawke moved close, his furry chest rested against her back. She stiffened at the contact, and pushed again. This time she had the leverage necessary, and the grate bowed forward and then popped from the concrete on one side. She pushed it open and slid forward. The drop shouldn't be too bad.

"*You should turn and look below to make sure it's clear.*" Hawke moved back, the soft warmth of his fur vanished.

Asia ground her teeth at his suggestion and jumped. It was further to the ground than she thought. The graveled walkway near the castle jolted her system on contact. Moments later, Hawke hit the ground beside her. He had partially shifted, which made for an easier landing. Their gazes met, and he returned to his wolf. She took off running into the woods, not quite sure what to do now. Once again, she hadn't thought beyond the mission, that whole act first think later thing had to change. For now, the safety of the tree beckoned. The world appeared different from that vantage point.

"*Where are we headed?*"

Asia ignored his question and continued running. Boris would send hybrids after them as soon as he realized all the test wolves were missing, including Hawke. Goddess please let the plane be on the way.

"*I need to access a computer.*"

She rolled her eyes as they ran around trees and jumped over thick roots or vines. Where did he expect her to get a computer?

"*This is important. I need to get to a computer.*" He sounded cross.

She stopped, turned and glared down at him. Two wolves slammed into his side, knocking him back, snapping at his hind legs. His inability to fight surprised her. He stood taller than his attackers and yet he didn't fight. In human form she doubted she would've defeated him. Was his wolf that much different? These wolves were getting the best of him. Asia stepped forward prepared to grab one of the animals.

"*Don't.*" Hawke said to the savior who looked like Jerry the security guard. His wolf didn't agree. He'd puzzled over the inconsistency since he heard the disturbance in his lab. Something big happened. Bigger than the destruction of the lab, the excitement of a new discovery niggled at the edge of his reason. He'd deal with her ability to alter her appearance later and focus on surviving the night.

Hawke recognized the scents from the test wolves before they attacked. Both had undergone several operations and were unwell. He refused to hurt them further. After allowing them a few nips, he batted the older wolf across the jaw with his paw, knocking him across the grass. The other wolf whimpered and ran to check on her mate.

Both wolves shifted to human. Their combined pain and sorrow and anger buffeted him.

"You travel with this scum?" the female hissed at Jerry. "He is a murderer, a defiler of innocents." She spit in his direction. "I would kill you for what you've done. Goddess strengthen me to kill this abomination." She rose, and he saw the glint of steel as she ran toward him. Hawke prepared to shift to his hybrid form, but Jerry stopped the woman.

"No, you cannot kill him. You don't know everything, and cannot judge him."

The remarks surprised Hawke.

"I know what I saw," the woman said, her chest heaving.

"That doesn't mean what you saw was real, there's always more sides to the truth. At any rate I won't allow you to kill him." Jerry stood between him and the woman.

The older woman broke down in tears. The loud sobs cut Hawke to the core. He looked away, right into the eyes of her mate. The man lay on the ground but his hate filled gaze didn't falter. The mate would gut Hawke in a split second.

"He killed my pups. Slaughtered them on the operating table

while trying to turn them into something hateful."

Hawke sensed surprise from Jerry and wondered if he'd be left alone in the woods which were more than he deserved. He had little recollection of what happened when the computer ruled his actions. His wolf hid from the horror in a small corner of his mind ignoring the outside world. At the time hiding seemed the best way to survive, listening to the female wolf now, he wasn't sure.

The older man stood slowly never releasing Hawke's gaze. "Come, the Goddess will judge him. He will not have peace or rest easy. A mark will always be on his back. One day he will sire pups and experience the pain of loss."

Hawke flinched beneath the harsh words and hoped the man spoke from anger speaking and not a prophetic declaration. The woman dried her face with the back of her hand, threw a hard glare in his direction and went with the male. Together they left the clearing.

Heavy hearted with a gut full of guilt and shame, Hawke looked at his rescuer. Their gazes locked.

"Let's go." Jerry turned and ran.

Surprised and pleased at not being abandoned, Hawke followed.

Chapter 10

Ingrid ran through the trees trying to find the way home. How long had she been a captive? Five? Ten years? The time no longer mattered, she ran free down the road. Oh, how she missed mother, and her sisters. She stopped at the cross-road and read the battered sign.

Highlands Cross. Ingrid smiled and wiped the moisture that ran down her nose in a constant drip. Home wasn't too far. Last night she'd told the others she could make it on her own and she had. Turning down the dirt road she ran. Her vision blurred, but she ignored it. Grandmother's house came into view first. Ingrid slowed down and veered toward the front porch. The house was dark. And she heard the heartbeats upstairs in the bedrooms. One moment she thought it strange she could hear their heartbeats, the next it disappeared from her mind like the morning mist.

Pain, sharp and nauseating, ripped through her head. Ingrid fell to the ground and rolled into a fetal position moaning as waves of mind-numbing needles pierced her brain. The intense pain lasted for a few moments. She tried to stand and emptied her stomach.

Dizzy, she by-passed the house and headed to the pasture where the cows lay resting. Her gums tingled at the sight of Beth, her granny's old milk cow. Hunger ripped through her belly and she bent forward again.

Something was wrong.

Ingrid knew it but didn't stop moving toward the old cow. Tears rolled down her face as she picked up the machete hanging on the tool rack in the shed. The pounding in her head ramped up as she tried to change direction. Her hand shook like a leaf in the wind but didn't relinquish the heavy blade. Not when she lifted it over Beth's neck, not when she whacked over and over again through skin, flesh and bone, and not when the cow dropped dead on the ground. The machete continued to shake in her hand in a morbid dance.

A light flicked on in the distance. All thought of family and the dead cow disappeared. Drawn by the brightness in the midst of darkness, blade in hand she moved forward.

Chapter 11

Asia ran faster, trying to escape the faces of the wolves. They'd be lucky to make it through the week. Why hadn't the wolves left with Tobias? Guilt weighed on her. She'd given them their freedom and it may cost them their lives. What should she do? Not abandon Hawke that's for sure, her wolf would never allow that. And those two would never travel with him.

"*What is your name?*"

"Asia," she said out loud without thinking and wished to could recall the information the moment it left her mouth.

"*Asia? I've heard that name somewhere. Where have I heard that name?*"

She stopped and looked down at him. "Good question. Where?" She crossed her arms, and waited. When she met Angus, he mentioned a group overseas had been asking questions and looking for clues into her past.

"*My memories are returning but not fast enough. I am getting snapshots that don't make a lot of sense yet. Some things are crystal, but personal information, pack, littermates, where I'm from... all of that is blurred.*"

Asia's heart pounded at the familiar confusion. She had experienced the disorientation, trying to bring order to chaos. "*This is the first time.*"

"What?" She had no idea what he referred to.

"*That I have been able to think clear for any length of time, to win against the computer chip in my brain. The chip doesn't have full control like before. Before it would've forced a shift, to return to human.*"

That bit of information surprised her. "That's unusual." She slipped again. "I mean... I thought nothing affected the chips after installed." She did not want him to know anything about her previous connection to the Liege.

"*Yes. I thought that as well. Where are we going tonight? I need to rest.*"

Asia blinked at the change in conversation. Perhaps he didn't

trust her either. Smart man. "I have been sleeping in the tree."

"*Tree?*" Hawke sounded surprised. "*But I need to access the database I uploaded to the cloud. If I don't log in with the correct password, the file will self-destruct and the chips in the minds of those wolves will stay live.*"

"What?" Asia hadn't heard correctly.

"*I didn't wipe out the files; I moved them into a lockbox that no one else can access. I froze the codes so that Master... damn. So that the Liege cannot activate the chips and destroy the test wolves. But that is just a delay mechanism. There's more work to be completed in the program to permanently deactivate the chips.*"

"What about your chip?"

"*I never had control of mine. Just the test wolves.*"

Asia nodded. "Maybe there will be one on the plane."

"*Plane?*" Hawke took two steps backward. "*What plane?*"

She completed another scan, no one was near. "We can talk about this in the tree. I need to rest as well." The amount of energy she'd used to rescue him cost her big time. Each step became harder to make. If she didn't rest soon, she'd be vulnerable and dependent on him. That notion stiffened her resolve.

"*What plane?*"

"To take me home."

"*I understand but I must undo the damage first, otherwise the wolves will be recaptured and tormented worse. This must be done and I need your help.*"

It was on the tip of her tongue to tell him to go do it, but Jasmine's face flashed in front of her with a warning. "Okay." She turned and climbed the tree without a backward glance. Her wolf whimpered and then stopped when he climbed behind her. By the time she reached the three branches, she realized he'd have to find limbs to support his weight. She had no intention of sharing her space.

Asia grabbed the bag from the short limb, pulled out her canteen and drank. The large meal from earlier had long gone. She pulled out an apple and dried fruit from another purchase that day. Hawke settled in the next tree on two limbs and watched her.

"Hungry?" she held up the apple and fruit.

"*No, you eat.*"

She returned the canteen and zipped the bag. Lying across the branches she gazed at the half moon and ate.

"*Mistress?*"

"Asia?"

She told Jasmine everything that happened since their last communication. "*A place to access a database? I'll ask Silas. He's meeting with the Alphas now, when he's done, I'll get back with you. He may insist this gets done before you leave. That way he can use that information as a bargaining chip with the European packs.*"

"*Yes, Ma'am.*" Although disappointed with the delay she understood it would be easier to insure damage control's successful implementation before leaving. Otherwise, she'd need to return. She waited for Jasmine to tell her La Patron's response at her disobedience.

"So how is it?"

Asia frowned. "*What?*"

"*Being mated? How does all that feel?*"

Since Jasmine didn't bring up her recent infraction she didn't either. She thought about it for a moment. Neither she nor Hawke addressed being mates or talked about Gunnolf. She needed time to re-energize for both issues. "*He's bossy, annoying, caring and is sad. I don't know what to do with him.*"

Jasmine laughed. "*His wolf and memory is returning, give the man a few days to regroup and you won't need to know what to do with him.*"
Asia scoffed. "*Sex is easy and meaningless. What I mean is Hawke throws off these emotions, like a juggler. Happy, sad, embarrassed, pleased... I'm not sure what to do with all that.*"

"*Hmmm, you have forgotten some things, nothing about mates is meaningless. But I'm not going to get into that, mating's too hard to explain. Remember when you were locked in the lab, you went through the same thing. You said you were free to feel, that could be what he is experiencing. He's lucky you're his mate, you can help, make his transition easier.*"

"*Perhaps...*"

Jasmine sighed. "*Asia. You won't win. Not if Hawke's your mate. I'm a breeder and I couldn't hold out against Silas. You're a wolf, so is he. If you take too long, your wolf will take over. I've seen that and so have you. Don't play with this.*"

"I *don't want a mate.*"

"You don't want a mate or you don't want Hawke?"

"Both."

"Tough. Deal with that. Everyone else has. Don't throw this gift into the face of the Goddess."

"I'm... I don't know what to do. I'm not you. I don't nurture. I destroy. I fight. I don't think things through and I work better alone." Asia hadn't meant to expose so many of her fears, but once released she breathed easier.

"I know sweetie. But he's your mate, both of you will accept each other's flaws and all. Once you bond he will see the strong, courageous woman you are and thank the Goddess daily for your love."

"Love... I cannot love him, or anyone. The Goddess has decreed I am his mate, but I have no love to give." Love consisted of four letters with no meaning. Nothing touched her any more. In the beginning, the killing had been hard, she'd return to the lab sick over her brutal actions. Now, she plowed her fist through flesh and bone, yanking out body parts to remove computer chips without blinking. She'd cut off a hand, break a neck, dismember anyone who stood in the way of her completing a mission and not blink. She didn't chat, or laugh, or hang around people, she had no friends, no expectations from anyone, except her Mistress. And that was new and scary. Instead of thanking the Goddess, he would curse the day he united with such a broken mate.

"I want you to be happy, you believe that right?"

"Yes, I do."

"Good, I'll contact you with information on the computer."

Asia had been so engrossed with her conversation with Jasmine she'd forgotten Hawke sat in the next tree. "I asked for help in locating a computer, we may need to travel into the city."

"I cannot shift from my wolf or hybrid form into human, going into a populated area will be risky."

"You ask me to help and then tie my hands," she snapped.

"I fear the chip will retake control in human form. I cannot risk that, not until the test wolves are free and I destroy the research information." That made sense even though it would make things difficult.

"Why destroy? Some of it may be useful. You can send the files to La Patron so he can look at them. What kind of research took place in the lab?"

"Why do you refuse to speak to me through this link? You speak to others through a link but refuse me, why?"

Asia stared at the moon and counted to ten. How could she explain her fear? According to Jasmine it would happen sooner or later. The very idea of bonding with him through their link sent chills skittering through her body. "I'm not ready to bond with you. I share a link with one other person, my Mistress."

"*You aren't ready to link with me? But it would be safer for us to communicate in silence.*" Hawke didn't bother masking his surprise.

Asia didn't bother masking her annoyance. "I'm working on it."

Chapter 12

Greggor moved slightly and held his jaw. Pain radiated through his face as he sat. The haunting silence in the building screamed his failure. Hawke had left. How had this happened? For the first time in his recollection someone penetrated his uncle's fortress and from the looks of things, shut down the labs.

He stood little by little and looked at all the damage. Burn marks from the laser decorated every wall. He winced in remembrance. Jerry had scared him before, but nothing like earlier today. The man moved as if possessed, he'd never seen anything like it, not human at least. The glass wall and door to the communication room were gone. Greggor stared at the empty space for a moment and then stepped across the debris into the area.

Gathering courage, he typed in his password with a silent prayer. When the screen normalized he smiled and clapped. Hopeful, he brushed the glass from the chair and sat. After entering more commands, he grinned as dot after dot appeared on the screen giving him the locations of the test animals and Hawke. Excited, he would take the three remaining Hybrids in the harvesting truck and retrieve his inventory. The animals could starve in their cages for all he cared, or he'd have the hybrids feed them. As long as he reported success after his failure, his uncle may forgive him. He rubbed his hands with determination, and clicked the button to download the information to the truck's locator device.

Nothing happened.

Confused, he frowned, looked at the dots on the screen again, and clicked the download button. Next, he refreshed the screen and instead of the download button appearing, one by one the dots disappeared. Mouth agape he stared horrified at the blank screen.

"Where'd they go? Where the hell did they go?" He slapped his keyboard and hit the refresh button over and over. The screen blanked. The next second a picture of the castle filled the screen. "What the...?" He re-logged and the same picture appeared. He couldn't access anything in the data base. Not the security cameras, the automatic doors, or lifts. Again, he'd fucked up. Stomach tied in knots he laid his head on the keyboard. Desperate, he searched every nook and cranny of his mind for a solution and came up blank.

"Wait." He pushed away from the monitor and stood. Hawke's system wasn't connected to the main system.

The lifts didn't work. Instead, he headed down the stairs to the lower level and entered Hawke's lab. Everything looked the same. No sign of a struggle, no blood on the floor. He searched the room for clues and came up empty. Pulling a chair in front of the key board he entered his code, the welcome screen appeared.

"Good." He still had access. Rather than search for the test wolves he searched for Hawke and found him. Next, he widened the map, wrote the co-ordinates and then printed a copy. Pressure eased off his chest as he locked down the castle, regained control of security and rebooted the cameras.

He needed to think in steps, secure his uncle's property and main investment. *Hawke left.* Greggor's mind refused to wrap around that fact. The wolf had been a staple here for over thirty years. What happened? The footage from the cameras showed more of him and the blasted laser than anything else. There was one clip with Hawke and Jerry fighting and then nothing.

Dammit, he needed more answers than questions when he talked to his uncle. He needed help. His uncle had left a number for him to use in case of an emergency but cautioned him against using it for any other reason than Hawke. This situation fell in that category and more. Rather than wait, he headed up to his office, and made the call.

"Why are you calling here?" The gruff voice said before Greggor spoke.

"I'm at the castle, Hawke is missing." There was a pause.

"Missing as in kidnapped or missing as in escaped and do not say you do not know which."

Greggor snapped his mouth closed, stopping those very words from leaving his mouth. He had no idea.

"Well?"

Since he couldn't imagine anyone kidnapping the arrogant bastard he went with the other choice and hoped he was right. "Escaped."

"Damn it. How the hell did that happen? Where is Boris?"

"In the states."

"How many hybrids do you have left?"

Greggor blessed the man for not suggesting they involve his uncle for this retrieval. "Three."

"Three? He left nine."

"The test wolves created a number of security challenges," he said in a stiff tone at the imbecile comment muttered low enough so he could ignore it.

"Have you at least tracked him?"

Greggor bristled at the derision in his voice. "Yes. I have the coordinates, he is in the forest."

"Why haven't you recaptured him?"

"I think he had help when he escaped and I don't want anyone interfering on the retrieval."

"Help? Who?"

"Looked like Jerry, the security guard. But he didn't fight like him. Something strange happened. I don't want interference when I retrieve my uncle's prize."

"Give me the co-ordinates, I will send assistance. Make sure you sedate him and keep him locked beneath the ground until Boris returns. He can sort this mess out then."

Greggor smiled, thinking of ways he'd keep Hawke confined.

"I'm going to activate the hybrids and leave within the hour."

"Sounds good. Make sure your hybrids shoot the right wolf and not any of mine. I want no casualties behind this."

Chapter 13

Hawke sat still on the limbs of the tree and watched Asia. That name reminded him of something, something significant, but every time he pressed to remember pain shot through his skull. She looked like Jerry, a man who'd worked at the lab for the last ten years, yet her real name was Asia. How had she accomplished changing her appearance? More importantly, why didn't he know something like that could be done? For decades he'd worked in the lab decoding text and solving the most complex riddles and he had no inkling such a thing could be accomplished.

Even without the computer chip controlling his mind, he wanted to study this new phenomenon yet he realized the need to protect her secret. Lord Boris would do anything to have the ability to change appearances at a molecular level. Nothing could happen to her. His wolf claimed her, and that settled matters for him. Asia was his to protect and cherish.

Hawke frowned.

But she seemed unwilling, and uninterested. Had he been a captive so long he couldn't recall bitches being so touchy, temperamental? Her stubbornness made no sense. Did the test wolves' comments about his past actions turn her sour on him? He remembered her defense, she sounded as if she'd spoke from experience.

A well of pride rose in his chest. In the past thirty hours, she'd done what others attempted for decades and succeeded where they failed. For the most part she'd shut down Lord Boris' lab. All the research Hawke completed in the past decade waited in a cloud. He'd sent a virus to Sir Boris' files and whenever the man opened them the virus would change letters in the reports at random. Once started, the virus couldn't be shut down or reversed, rendering the information inaccurate and for the most part, unreadable. A fitting end to the man's reign of butchering innocents.

Hawke had no idea how long he lay staring at the object of his desire, the longer in her presence, the stronger his mind and need for her grew. He vibrated with wanting her.

His head lifted, and he sniffed. A familiar scent hit him.

Greggor. And since "coward" described the man, Hawke knew there were hybrids nearby. He peered down and saw two hybrids circling the tree. He glanced at Asia and called through the link.

"*Asia.*"

Because she hadn't opened her end of the link, his warning didn't penetrate her sleep. He ground his teeth in frustration and scented the air to seek Greggor's location. The man hid a few feet away in a copse of trees with another hybrid.

Determination to lead them from Asia blazed through him. He leapt from the branches, and shifted to his hybrid form midair and landed on a nearby tree. The hybrids on the ground raced behind him. He continued moving deeper into the forest, pulling them away from her place of rest and didn't stop until Greggor left that area altogether.

Satisfied she was safe, he calculated the distance between the two hybrids and Greggor. He planned to kill them all. Hawke had four forms. Human, wolf, hybrid and bulked hybrid. In his bulked form he resembled a shorter Hulk standing at around seven feet. But according to Lord Boris, the metal bones in his arms and legs gave him similar strength to the green creature.

Hawke maximized the bulk on his hybrid form and dropped to the ground. Blood pumped through his veins, his wolf gloried in the freedom to release aggression against those who represented his enemy.

Ten inches, razor-sharp claws sprung from his fingertips. Sharp fangs lengthened, crowding his mouth and resting on his chin. Long toenails lengthened and curved as his feet widened. It had been too long.

The first hybrid leapt forward, and he caught him in the throat, holding him off the ground in mid-air while watching the second hybrid approach. These two were cannon fodder and not the most dangerous in the group. He tried to lock in on Greggor but the scheming man had moved again.

Hawke threw the hybrid at the large wolf that'd leapt into the clearing, knocking the animal back. With a quick dip, he jumped up and landed on a branch, missing the second hybrid's punch. Scenting the air, two full-bloods had joined the fight, his wolf growled at the dominance challenge. He leapt to the ground, grabbed a wolf and pierced his neck with his claws. Hawke backhanded the hybrid and sent him flying into a nearby tree.

The other wolf jumped on his back trying to get a grip on his wide neck. The other hybrid landed a punch to his stomach and face. Hawke picked up Greggor's location, it was across the clearing. He saw the tranq gun in his hand and knew the man waited for an opening to shoot him full of tranquilizers. Asia would be left unprotected and he couldn't allow that to happen.

With a roar, he grabbed the wolf from his back and slammed the beast onto the hybrid, knocking it off him. He snapped the wolf neck, took aim and threw him at Greggor. The man's eyes widened, and he jumped aside. The beast hit the third hybrid and knocked him back a few feet.

Hawke snatched up the hybrid and dragged him to the side as a cover, and then rammed his fist into his face in the same manner he'd seen Asia do yesterday. Bone crumpled and blood poured down his hand. He didn't recall seeing this much blood before but the deed was done. Next, he twisted the head for good measure until it broke free of the spinal cord and dropped the carcass.

He sensed Greggor crawling and sought to reach him before the man got off a shot. No one knew better than him how potent the tranquilizer was, he'd created the serum. The remaining wolf snarled and snapped but kept its distance. He suspected they were setting him up for Greggor.

Instead of co-operating, Hawke leapt forward, the wolf followed, and they clashed in the air. Hawke swiped the wolf across the neck with his claws and hearing a click dropped to the ground and rolled into the tree line. The ping of the dart hitting the ground inches from his chest pissed him off.

Enraged, he would kill Greggor first chance he got. The hybrid he'd backhanded jumped on him, pinning him down to the ground. Hawke looked into the vacant eyes of his opponent and then glanced at the metal around his neck. With little effort he moved his arm up and grabbed the necklace. Lord Boris said these were impossible to remove, but since the man was a liar and a cheat Hawke decided to test that theory. Although the hybrid's muscle's strained to hold Hawke in place and sweat poured down its forehead the eyes never changed.

Hawke waited to see if Greggor would move closer now that he was down to one hybrid for protection. He heard nothing and sensed no movement. The hybrid leaned to the side and punched him in the face. He rolled them over, grabbed the necklace and lifted the hybrid in the air. This time he slammed the hybrid against the tree so hard his skull split. Hawke knew that wasn't enough and broke his neck as well.

Breathing hard he stepped back, spun around as the dart landed in his shoulder the medicine entered his bloodstream immediately. In moments he'd be out. He took one step, then another like a Saturday night drunk. Fire shot through his veins freezing him mid-step. Damn, that extra ingredient he'd added to the formula worked too well. A tingling numbness, spread through him. Hawke fell to his knees. Footsteps drew closer and through the dimness of his vision he saw Greggor leer.

"Hello Hawke."

Too sluggish to respond he cursed the jackass in his mind and wished him a thousand deaths. In the corner of his mind, he thought there was a sound, a cry, a scream of anguish. He fell forward into the dark abyss.

A sense of unease rolled through Asia waking her. She listened to the forest while shaking off the dregs of her sleep. Deep-resting was critical after expending the amount of adrenaline and energy she had at the castle. But something woke her. She glanced at Hawke intent on asking if anything happened and found his tree empty. Alert, she scanned the area. In the distance Hawke had company.

Damn, he should have woken her instead of handling this on his own. She remembered his pitiful fighting skills with the test wolves and wondered if he were still alive. The scent of hybrids and full-bloods fueled her anger. She morphed into her hybrid, masked her scent and hopped from tree to tree. It took longer to reach the area than she would have liked. When she could get a good view, she paused.

Stunned, she watched Hawke destroy his opponents with ease. Unable to move, she kept her distance in the tree and watched. Why had she thought him inept? It became clear he didn't need her help.

A glint in the trees caught her attention. *Tranquilizer gun.* Her heart raced at the gun pointed at Hawke's back as he snapped the neck of the hybrid.

"Hawke, watch out," she called but was too far for him to hear. She searched her mind for their link but it was too late, he crumpled to the ground in the midst of slain bodies.

Pain, sharp and piercing lanced her chest. Her wolf took over, shifting mid leap running through the forest at blinding speed, leaping over roots, and ducking branches. Once in the clearing she hit Greggor in the chest, the weapon flew out of his hand and slid into a tree. The man lay on the ground, his face bleeding from a scrape of her claw.

"What the fuck are you doing standing there?" he screeched.

"Get this bitch off me."

Asia's wolf bit down on his arm until it hit bone. He screamed and tried to push her off which sliced his arm more. Sensing the hybrid behind her, she leapt across Greggor and shifted to her hybrid. Cold anger filled her at the sight of her mate lying on the ground, before the hybrid attacked; she picked up Greggor and punched him in the stomach.

He screamed.

She tossed him aside for later. The puny man would pay with his life for what he did. First, she needed to disable the hybrid and then the gun. Perhaps she'd shoot Greggor with a tranquilizer. That thought pleased her wolf.

The hybrid charged. They always charged. Asia stepped aside and gut punched him, causing him to stagger. And then she punched him beneath his chin with her metal arm. He flew backward and hit the tree. She strode to the tree where the gun rested and grabbed it. One dart left, she watched Greggor rolling on the ground holding his belly, pointed and pulled the trigger. His eyes widened and looked down at the dart protruding from his leg. He grabbed at it with both hands and removed the tranq. The look of hatred he sent her would have scorched the sun. Pleased, she nodded her appreciation, broke the gun in half and went to finish off the remaining hybrid.

"I'll kill you for this," Greggor said, his words slurring.

Neck broken and chip removed, Asia tossed the hybrid aside. She couldn't talk well in this form and didn't bother.

Instead she went to her mate and removed the dart. Anger, pain and sadness filled her chest. Breathing became a major challenge. What if she'd remained asleep? They'd found him by his chip and he'd led them miles away from her to protect her. The realization stunned and shamed her. Something alien tugged on her heart, followed by guilt. If they had shared a link, Hawke would have heard her warning.

Asia scanned the area, Greggor alone lived.

Tempted to kill him, her wolf urged her to care for their mate first and return to kill the bastard after finding a secure place for Hawke to recover. She stared at his hybrid form in awe, the man was massive, she'd need to remain a hybrid to lift him and even then she hoped she could carry him. Caves hidden in the foothills of the mountains beyond the forest would be her first choice. It was a distance, and she risked exposure with the sun rising. But she could defend them better in the cave. For now, safety ranked highest.

"Hawke," she whispered and touched his brow.

His head rolled in her direction. The next moment his body morphed to human. She thanked the Goddess.

Lifting him, she settled his weight in her arms and headed in the direction of the mountains. The sun had just risen when she arrived at the base of the mountains, and she'd seen no humans during the long trek. That didn't mean none of the locals saw them, she was certain the few who saw her carrying a large man like a baby created wild tales to be retold later. She re-scanned the area, and then shifted him in her arms a bit before trudging upward to the low entrance she had discovered by accident on her way to Lord Boris' castle.

After stepping inside, it became clear she wasn't the only one who recognized the merits of the cave. Leftover food containers, cigarette butts, clothing items and a roll-out bed greeted their entry. She laid Hawke on the make shift bed and went to explore deeper. A small, child sized opening led into a larger cavern.

Asia debated whether to break through the stone or continue her search for another entrance. Thoughts of others with easy access to the cavern made the decision for her. She continued searching for another way into the cave and after a series of dead ends, shifted into her wolf and squeezed through a small slit between stones. Her breath caught at the jagged rocks and smooth plateaus lining the sides of the large cave. She stepped over gravel and looked around, searching for water and game if possible. Water, she found and drank her fill. Her stomach grumbled. She needed to get Hawke situated and then go for supplies.

How would she get him into this cave? She'd deliberately chosen a place impossible for humans to access, but in his present form, he couldn't access it either. She retraced her steps and watched him sleep. Out of options, she sat near the entrance to defend her mate.

Chapter 14

The sun set low in the sky when Hawke moved. Asia looked at him over her shoulder and then refocused on the entrance. Two drunks had wandered near earlier but sobered quickly when she growled her displeasure. The men ran, tripped and rolled a good distance down the hillside.

"What happened?" Hawke said, his voice deep and harsh.

Asia turned; prepared to defend herself she stood and watched as he took stock of the surroundings.

"Asia?"

The huskiness of his voice caressed her skin. She shook off the effect and continued staring at him.

"Goddess, you are so beautiful."

Her wolf whimpered at the awe in his voice, but she remained vigilant as he sat up and scooted back against the wall. He tilted his head in the same manner when he looked at her in the hall at the castle. "I'm in control," he said with a puzzled look staring at her. "Did you do something?"

Still in wolf form Asia stared, looked away and unable to stop looking at him, stared again.

Hawke frowned. "Something is different. The computer is muffled, like a hum." A spark lit in his eyes, stealing her breath, and confusing her. "The chip's not controlling any more, it's there but not strong like before."

Asia's wolf whined, pushing her toward him, urging for the connection between mates. Stepping out on a symbolic limb, she opened the link. "*Good, that's good.*"

His eyebrows shot up. A moment later a smile appeared. "*Thank you, Asia. Thank you. Such a long time... so long since...*" his eyes closed and a rush of warm wind flowed through the link, brushing against her mind as if tasting and caressing every nuance of her essence. Asia's body tingled beneath the onslaught. This mingling was unlike anything she'd ever experienced which made no sense, she'd been mated before.

A soft breeze carried the aroma of his craving, filling places she never knew existed. Her wolf whined and stepped closer, taking in more of his scent, licking his hand and face.

"You are so beautiful," he whispered. The deep huskiness in his voice left her panting and defenseless. Resisting him never entered her mind. Warm tendrils of need arced between the links, binding and tying them together. Hot coils of desire wrapped tight around her as an embrace.

"Asia," he whispered. "Let me see you."

The raspy hunger in his tone slid into a crevice of her mind she hadn't known existed and filled the space with something akin to hope. Could she? Fear, the parasite in her mind, rose swift and strong, urging her not to trust this man, not to release everything, not to allow him access to her dark secrets and shame, not yet.

Allowing Hawke to see her wasn't the same as giving in, plus her wolf would take matters into her own hand if she backed out of this mating dance.

Asia shifted into her true form.

Hawke's gaze softened as he pulled her forward and cupped her cheek. She touched the scar on the side of his face with the tip of her finger. His gaze roamed her face, as if imprinting her on his brain. "So damn beautiful." The heat of his words brushed against her cheek. Unprepared to share everything her eyelids lowered beneath his steady gaze.

Hawke fisted her hair pulling her head back and kissed her hard. Her wolf purred. The noise slipped through her lips. His movements quickened as if the unchecked sounds were a fire accelerant, inflaming him further.

Long licks of his tongue danced with hers. Intoxicated with pleasure, he tasted like a life-altering liqueur. She'd never thirsted to this degree and pressed into him for more.

He growled, lifting her onto his lap. The length and width of his cock set off a happy dance with her wolf, they were both pleased.

Hungry for him, she rocked against his hardness.

Lips parted, he gasped. Images of them in a variety of positions crowded her link. Turned-on, she ground against him.

"*You're wet, ready for me. Thank you, Goddess, I cannot wait.*" Hawke flipped her onto her back, snatched the meager cloth covering her and thrust one finger inside her pussy. Tight muscles clasped onto his digit, greeting him properly.

He groaned and shoved his pants down with the other hand. "*Goddess, I can't take any more. Your scent is driving me crazy. I can't decide what to do first. Sample this delicious nectar...*" He removed the finger from her and sucked. He smacked his lips and smiled as he replaced the finger in her pussy. "*So sweet.*"

Asia moved beneath his talented fingers needing more.

"*You want me?*" He asked through the link. His hesitancy hid his insecurities and shame. He knew about his baggage but not hers. His woman hadn't opened to him completely.

"If you want me," she whispered.

Hawke crushed her against him, giving her another one of those mind-boggling kisses.

If she were a better person, she'd tell him the type woman he'd take as a mate so he could make a quality decision. But the closeness of their bond worked its magic on her, watering dry places in her soul and filling an emptiness she never thought possible. Mating him without full disclosure was selfishness personified. She knew and didn't care. This time she'd grab the brass ring and end the dusty road of loneliness she'd traveled far too long. Instead of confessing her past she held onto his broad shoulders as he moved between thighs and with one powerful thrust, initiated their mating.

Asia's breath locked in her throat. Thank the Goddess he moved. She feared he'd stop or worse, talk. Before she could voice her objections, he thrust back into her again, and again. Rain, no a torrential downpour fell inside her. What other explanation could there be for the wellspring of giddiness sprouting in the barren landscape of her heart? Pockets and crevices of a lifetime worth of debris were swept clean or replaced by the fire of their mating. She had no idea which and didn't care as they spiraled higher together, consumed with each other's heartbeat. First separate and with each thrust they synced, closer and closer together until one was indistinguishable from the other.

Her body tightened like a locked spring and then exploded into millions of pieces as they crested. The braided bond of their mating kept her grounded, a sense of security spread through her limbs and settled in her mind. Bit by bit, the shudders wracking her frame ceased. Her heart slowed to a normal pace and her limbs went limp. Air flowed through her nostrils assuring her she had survived the life changing moment.

Hawke's palm cupped her cheek, and he placed a soft kiss near her mouth. It was such a simple thing, but the gesture touched her in ways she couldn't explain. Rain, comprised of his gentle touches, soft words and even softer kisses watered every dry, dusty, dirty place in her being. Perhaps that explained her blurred vision when his lips brushed against hers, not seeking anything, but for the sole purpose of touching her.

"Amazing Asia, beautiful inside and out," he murmured.

She snuggled closer, and sent a silent prayer to the Goddess he was right.

Chapter 15

The sunset marked the end of their quiet time. They'd spent hours exploring each other's bodies, and easing the itch accompanying the mating.

"*Mistress?*"

"*Asia. Everything okay?*"

"*Yes. Has La Patron decided anything?*" She didn't want to rehash her disobedience, but she needed to know if La Patron planned to remove them now or later. She hadn't mentioned anything to Hawke yet, and waited until she knew the plans for certain.

"*Yes, Silas is sending you to an old associate of Angus. Chacal. The man lives on the outskirts of Odessa and has arranged transportation.*" She gave Asia the co-ordinates to pick up the vehicle. Grateful for the solid plan she nodded at Hawke. He kissed her cheek, and earned a smile.

"*After you finish and verify the problem's corrected, plan to catch a flight to London so we can bring the two of you home.*"

"*Yes, Ma'am.*" Excited by the prospect of assisting Hawke and spending more time with him, Asia shut down the link with Jasmine without further thought.

"*Well?*" Hawke squeezed her hand.

"I'm going with you to take care of this problem. We have a vehicle waiting on the way and then we drive to a place where you can use a secure computer." Embarrassed of her botched mission, she didn't mention she had no choice in the matter or that his project became her assignment. The most important thing was to make the deadline and reset the switch. She refused to fail again.

Hawke nodded and looked around the cave. "It's getting late, but I'd like to get as far as we can tonight and pick up the transportation. Maybe grab a change of clothes and alter my appearance a little." He gazed down at her, taking in her smooth brown complexion. "Is this you? I mean, is this your true form? Not like Jerry or Tate? I'd like to know what my mate looks like."

Whisky colored eyes stared up at him. "Yes. This is my base form. I can't discuss my ability to change forms, not yet. But this is who I am." Asia found a pair of sunglasses and a cap in the cave and gave them to him.

Happy, he wrapped his arm around her small waist and pulled her close. Asia smelled natural, like the earth and all things good. Long, dark brown curly hair fell down her back. He loved her curves and full hips. Bending forward he brushed his lips across hers. "I don't need to know anything other than this beautiful woman is my mate. Everything else is extra." Her eyes widened and he read the uncertainty. In time he'd prove himself worthy of her and wipe that look from her gaze.

Together they walked down the hill headed to the forest to find and dispose of Greggor. Hawke wanted to find a computer but Jasmine hadn't responded with a location yet.

A small group of six men and women met them on their way to the forest.

"Seen anything suspicious round here?" the farmer leading the group asked.

Hawke's grip tightened on her hand. "Suspicious? Like what? We've taken an early stroll and haven't seen much of anything other than each other." He gazed down at her upturned face and thanked the Goddess again for a sexy, strong, compassionate mate.

"A couple of gents said there are wolves in the mountains, said the animals chased him down the hillside." The farmer peered at Asia and then at Hawke. "Sure you haven't seen or heard anything?"

Hawke removed the sprigs from Asia hair before answering. "No, I didn't hear anything."

The farmer smirked, a look of male understanding passed between them. The other men nodded. The faces of the two women reddened. Asia remained stoic and silent.

"Okay, be careful. There's reports of wolf sightings."

"There's always wolf sightings," Hawke scoffed. It was no secret wolf packs roamed the area.

"True, well good day to you." The group continued in the direction they'd left.

Hawke waited a second. "*Please tell me you were the one who scared the gents.*"

"Yes, I scared off two drunks."

"Good, let's grab a bite to eat and search for a computer. Greggor has long gone; there is no scent of the creature."

Hawke nodded. Holding hands, they walked in the opposite direction of the castle at a brisk pace.

The next few hours they moved at a steady pace toward the small hamlet where the vehicle awaited. Hungry and tired after a long day, Hawke and Asia stopped on the outskirts of a town. Asia changed into an unassuming male and left to buy food and lodging.

A half hour later, Hawke pulled his cap down and pushed his glasses up as he walked through the lobby of the hotel where Asia secured a room for the night. She opened the door before he knocked. Once inside they embraced and all the neediness from earlier returned full force.

"I didn't sense anything, did you?" she asked helping him take off the jacket they'd stolen.

"Just humans." Hawke looked at the table filled with food. "That looks good; did you order anything for you?"

Laughing, she pushed his shoulder, grabbed a piece of meat and sat on the chair while he ate. During the meal, he kept sneaking peeks at her and the bed. Before the platter cleared, she stood and walked into the small bathroom. A few seconds later he heard the water and his imagination went into over-drive. Hawke tamped down his libido, finished the last of the meal and patted his lips.

Asia. Her name rang a bell the first time she mentioned it. Today as they traveled, more of his memories surfaced from the quagmire of the locked chip in his mind. Over a decade past, he remembered Lord Boris' excitement over finding a test subject whose body didn't reject metal implants. According to the reports he'd read, Asia was a walking miracle, a deadly assassin, brilliant spy and almost impossible to defeat. In retrospect, her test results sparked the renovation of his laboratory and the insertion of the metal in his legs and arms. Lord Boris didn't want to use him as a test subject initially but after tests failed on so many other wolves, Hawke convinced him to use him.

The test worked better than everyone suspected. The computerized chip in his brain took complete control of his arm and leg implants and in turn his actions, relegating his wolf to a single role as breeder. Hawke shook his head in disgust. He'd been their bitch, a willing bitch stepping up for every new test. Some worked, others didn't. But he'd been insatiable for knowledge, and pushed the envelope until he reached Frankenstein status. After all he put his body through the true miracle was his wolf survived.

Asia walked out the bathroom drying her hair. Hawke stopped thinking. Stopped breathing and stared at her perfection. He couldn't reconcile the Goddess standing in front of him with the femme fatale in the reports he'd consumed through the years. She still held the record in the Liege organization with the highest kill count, and successful missions accomplished. Her exploits reached legendary status and over the years he'd lived vicariously through her exploits.

Now she was his. His to love, protect and serve. Humbled by the Goddess' gift, he rose on his knees, pulled her close and brushed his lips across hers, hungry for a small taste.

She pushed against his shoulders. "You need a bath, go wash."

He laughed, laid his forehead on her breasts and rubbed them back and forth. She laughed, and he didn't think he'd every tire of the sound, and pushed him away.

"Ugh. Go shower before all the hot water's gone."

The thought of a cold shower galvanized him into action. He sprung from the bed and headed into the small room. "Don't get dressed," he said stripping off his clothes. "I'll be right back."

Arms outstretched, Asia flopped on bed, scanned the area out of habit and settled. They'd made great time and should reach the vehicle by noon tomorrow if they left first thing in the morning.

Asia listened to the shower in anticipation. Yesterday in the cave she'd seen lust, passion and admiration in his gaze. He hadn't faked it either she seen enough to know the difference. Hard as she tried she couldn't remember if the first time she mated came close to now, but doubted the possibility. Her blood rushed through her veins at his nearness. Despite what she'd told him, every part of him smelled delicious and right. All day she touched and brushed against him. Inside she burned to get as close as physically possible and then she'd want more. She sensed the same fire burned in him, especially when he didn't balk at spending the night in a hotel rather than far from everyone.

They weren't safe, not by a long shot. Not as long as the computer chip remained lodged inside his brain. She'd listened to the sound on and off all day.

Wait. On and off?

Asia sat up to think. Had she stopped listening or had the chip blinked on and off? She wasn't sure. Excitement coursed up her spine. She had to be sure. The water stopped. Inching back in the bed, she pulled both pillows behind her as props.

Naked, Hawke stepped into the room drying his hair. Need to be one with him gut punched her. Without thought her hand rose beckoning him to her. His gaze widened and then drooped to a sexy, slumberous half-mast. Hawke took her hand, placed a kiss in the middle of her palm and then licked that same spot.

Asia trembled as fire licked the nerve endings in her hand, raced up her arm and settled in her core. "Hawke," she murmured on a shaky breath.

He looked up at her and crawled forward. "I've wanted to do this all day." He leaned forward, and placed kisses all over her mound. His fingertips pulled her lips apart, his tongue slid up and down and then wiggled inside her opening.

Asia's head fell back as he worked magic with his tongue. She tangled her fingers in his thick black hair and pulled sharply moving him where she needed him. He pressed his lips to her clit and sucked the tiny bundle of nerves into his mouth, alternating with rough lashing with his tongue.

"Oh God," she screamed as she humped his face to a beat in her mind, lost in desperation to cum again. He caught her clit with his teeth and bit down on it. She tugged his hair pulling him closer, telling him her enjoyment without words, and begging for more. He scraped her clit over and over again.

"Yessss," Asia said moaning, and rocking against him. Close... her body lifted higher and higher. Her legs locked around his back and she erupted in orgasmic bliss. Her body shook beneath the force of her release. Floating back to reality, she pulled his head back, bit her bottom lip and winked at him.

"Beautiful," he whispered sliding up her body, his hot flesh scorching her as he brushed against it. His hardness landed between her thighs, superbly positioned for entrance. He stared down at her. An inner light burned in his gaze as he studied her. Uneasy, she lowered her lids to protect her secrets. She wasn't ready for him to know the real woman he'd mated; it was nice being accepted for the moment.

Hawke placed a finger beneath her chin and lifted her face. "You are beautiful mate."

Her heart tugged at the sincerity of his gaze and the ring of truth in his words. His mouth pressed against hers, his tongue swept across her lips and pressed for entrance. She moaned in pleasure as he deepened the kiss.

Caught up in his taste, his masculine wood scent, his sudden thrust into her caused her to buck upright and gasp with pleasure.

"Mmmm, so tight, so wet for me. You have no idea how that makes me feel," he murmured while thrusting steadily with deep strokes. The sound of slapping flesh filled the air, peppered with their grunts and moans.

Asia slapped his ass and widened her legs, urging him deeper. He quickened his movements, the music of their coupling took on a rock and roll tempo, lifting her higher. She growled in pleasure at his primal taking.

Her body was on fire as he pounded into her relentlessly. Waves of pleasure rippled through her as she splintered in bliss a second time. He thickened inside her. His cock pulsed as he slammed into her again and again. He stiffened, shuddered and released a low growl into the pillow next to her head as he spilled his seed deep inside her body.

Chapter 16

Asia lay in the bed, listening, watching and wondering. Once Hawke stepped into the room, all thought of the chip in his mind died beneath the sizzle of the mating call. She owed Tyrese and Danielle an apology. During their last mission the newly mated pair slowed everybody down because they couldn't keep their hands off each other. At the time, she didn't fully understand how overwhelming the mating dance could be.

Her skin tightened and ached for his touch. The heat and deep low throb in her core became unbearable. It's a miracle they were able to travel as far as they had without throwing each other to the ground and fucking like minks. With a soft smile she glanced at him asleep next to her. She traced one of the many scars on his arm and chest. Whatever surgeries they'd put him through shouldn't have left this many scars unless they were recent. Asia had noticed scars and bruising on the test wolves as well.

"What did they do to you?" she whispered glad he was asleep and re-scanned the area. Greggor hadn't regrouped yet, but he would and there'd be hybrids after them, if not already. She frowned. Why the delay? They could find Hawke... she listened for the tick of the computer chip.

Asia's heart beat so loud she swallowed and listened harder. Nothing. No ticks and she would know that sound the rest of her life. Was it possible the chip no longer worked? What happened? She'd never been able to stop the chip that had been lodged in her brain until she'd been buried alive, died and rebooted with a clean slate. How had Hawke managed to stop the chip?

She closed her eyes and sought their link. A surge of warmth greeted her. Even asleep he welcomed her presence. She was swept away on a tide of colorful ribbons that wrapped around her waist holding her close as moments of his life unfolded. If she could stay in that position always she would. It would be nice to know a little more about him, she thought. The second the idea crystallized snapshots flew before her eyes.

"Whoa, slow down. I can't see anything," she said more to herself than the pictures. But they slowed, almost to a crawl, and she remained still as her mate's life passed before her eyes. The slide show went in reverse from present to his past. There was no sound, and some things, like books, files or reports he read, she couldn't make out. Asia recognized the cold eyes of Lord Boris Lancaster, the sarcastic twist to his lips, and evil sneer. One snapshot showed him patting Hawke on the shoulder as a comrade, another talking down to Hawke who kneeled in front of him, another he raised and cane and then a whip and beat Hawke without mercy.

Horrified by the brutality a young Hawke suffered, she understood why he was priceless to the Liege. It took years for Lancaster to break Hawke's wolf, and banish his spirit. The men had burned, starved and beaten a young Hawke to the point he should have died. That he still lived; the answer to how he survived was a secret somewhere that she'd love to know. When it came to the end, the picture shuddered and repeated itself again and again as if bumping against a wall, preventing the slide show from going forward. Had the Liege locked Hawke's memories as they'd done her?

"I'd like to see what's hidden." The picture slowed and the next frame came into view. A younger Hawke in Lancaster's castle. Hawke being handed to Lancaster. Shock raced up her spine. "What?" Handed to Lord Boris? What the hell? The pictures continued but her mind remained on that one snapshot.

Hawke as a pup running behind a much larger black wolf. Hawke in human form with a dark-haired male and other men nearby.

Her breath caught. Gunnolf. The images she'd seen of Gunnolf matched the image of one of the men sitting in a large room with Hawke and possibly his Alpha. The vision struck so hard she tumbled from the link gasping for air. Images continued to swirl in her mind.

Someone gave Hawke to Lord Boris, someone in his former pack. No wonder someone wanted those memories blocked.

Did Hawke know? How much of his memory was he able to access? She ran a fingertip across his brow. Both of them were victims of the Liege but for some reason Hawke was sacrificed. Damn, it was inconceivable that someone would give away a pup to humans for experiments.

Hawke stirred.

Indecision lodged in her chest. Should she tell him what she saw? What did he know about Gunnolf? Certain what she saw were highlights or important markers in his life, there were hours, days, months and years of living she hadn't seen. Did he have memories of Gunnolf? Had she met him as a child and not remembered? So many questions.

First, they had to deactivate the kill chips in the test wolves, and then they could sort out the rest of this stuff. Asia slid from the bed and went to use the restroom. Her mind refused to release the images she'd seen through the link. What to do? Time refused to slow down so she could filter all the information. They needed to pick up the car and make it to Chacal's. Lord Boris would never allow Hawke to just leave. And if they knew she was in the country, her life would be in jeopardy as well.

She morphed into the male she'd been last night when she rented the room and then woke up Hawke.

He opened his eyes. The familiar tick restarted, and she waited to see what he'd do. And then the ticking stopped. He blinked and stretched.

"You let me sleep." He stood, brushed a kiss against her lips and headed to the bathroom.

"Yes, you were snoring." Asia teased while waiting for him to finish.

"I do not snore. I've watched too many vids of myself sleeping." Hawke stepped into the room and pulled his shirt over his chest. She itched to touch him. It took everything within her to walk to the door.

She spoke over her shoulder without looking at him. "I didn't scent anyone, I'll go down first, and head out. Give me a ten-minute start and then follow."

"*Are you sure you want to go first? The chip's in my head, and if we're followed, I can lead them in the opposite direction.*"

Asia turned to look at him. "*And if they go in the opposite direction from our transportation what am I supposed to do? Go to the car? Go the Chacal without you?*" Hawke didn't respond.

"*Hawke,* we *do this together, it doesn't work with you heading in a different direction.*"

"*Okay. Ten minutes.*"

She left the room, headed down the stairs. No one was in the lobby and she was glad. Once outside she walked at a brisk pace in the direction of the vehicle. When she cleared the village, she cut through the trees and ran at a comfortable pace.

Hawke caught up with her. They ran in silence and stopped at the next crossroad. "It should be straight ahead."

He nodded, and she hoped he wasn't sulking from this morning. Asia took off, and he came up behind. When the truck came into view, she scanned the area.

"That's it," she said as they slowed and approached the Jeep.

He headed for the driver's side. She exhaled at his presumption but didn't argue since he was a native. Hawke started the car and pulled onto the road. She scanned him for his chip and it ticked again.

"*Your chip goes on and off, did you know that?*" she asked through their link.

To his credit he didn't run off the road even though she sensed his surprise. "No. I did not. How do you know?"

"I can hear it."

He glanced at her and then back at the road. "You can hear it?"

"Yes, it ticks. While you slept there was no sound. The sound restarted when you woke, but went off again before you went into the bathroom. Something is short circuiting it."

He didn't say anything for a while. "The disruption must be our mating. That's the only thing different. When I'm with you, I'm stronger. My beast is stronger; we have taken my body back."

Asia didn't say anything. He could be right. The next time she talked to Mistress she'd ask. Meanwhile, she scanned the country side, and tried to keep her mind clear of what she'd learned this morning.

"Do we turn right or left?"

Asia glanced at the instructions she'd written from memory, and then at the map she had purchased last night when she checked into the hotel. "Left." She pointed in that direction.

He turned, and the ride continued in silence, each of them locked in their own thoughts.

"How did you learn to drive?" she asked curious about how much freedom Lord Boris allowed, especially after what she had seen.

"I don't remember the exact situation." Hawke frowned in concentration. "I saw a vehicle in an article somewhere, inquired about it and requested permission to learn to operate one. Lord Boris approved and I've known how to drive since then. It's been a while since I've sat in this seat." He glanced at her, winked and then smiled. "I like driving."

She nodded and looked out the window suppressing a yawn. The short nap she had taken last night after sex wasn't enough. Asia should have slept but couldn't. Not in an unfamiliar place with so many strangers. There were too many variables beyond her control to sleep easy. The lull of the ride pulled on her. Her eyelids grew heavy.

Hawke glanced at Asia and smiled. Based on what he'd seen on the map, from this point on, it was a straight drive. A hundred miles or so, another left turn and then a right turn would place them on Chacal land. He took in the scenery; so much had changed in the past decades. But then again, so had he. By a quirk of fate, the Goddess mated him with Asia Montgomery, a true mystery in the scientific community. For years, Lord Boris tried everything to replicate the success they'd found in her and for the most part failed.

They had tried to embed the camera behind his eyes and failed. Hawke recalled reading a report after they embedded a computer chip, and a locator chip in her brain, it had been a miracle she survived the surgery. Not only did she survive, the mechanical devices worked better than they imagined. Lord Boris bragged of the twenty-four-hour access they had to everything she saw and heard, which made her the ultimate undercover operative. According to the data he had received, Asia Montgomery represented the crème de la crème of Liege research and yet she sat asleep next to him. They had lost her. Somehow, she'd been able to outsmart them and went off the grid.

He could imagine the scene between Lord Boris and his cronies over her defection. They would be rabid, foaming at the mouth. For whatever reason the Goddess gifted him with this unique creature, he would be forever grateful and would protect her with his life. Perhaps everything that happened to him in life was preparation for this new chapter. Hawke grinned liking the sound and simplicity of that plan.

The road ahead narrowed a bit as they crossed a small bridge. A sharp, blinding pain lanced his skull. He pushed the accelerator. The car shot forward, crossed the bridge and hit something solid.

Chapter 17

The jeep skittered to the side. Hawke turned the steering wheel hard. The car spun and hit something again and then stopped. Before he could speak, Asia still in male human form, hopped out the jeep and took on two full-blood wolves.

Enraged at the sight of his mate under attack, Hawke jumped out, shifted to his hybrid, pulled one of the wolves off her, and broke its neck. Another wolf leapt on his back and bit his upper arm, hitting the metal bone. Hawke reached over, grabbed the beast and used it as a bat to hit two other wolves who raced out the woods at them.

He stepped aside, picked up another wolf and slammed it into the ground breaking its bones before tossing it into the trees. Another wolf leapt at his throat, he ducked and then punched the beast in the side sending it flying into a tree.

More wolves raced toward them. The more full-bloods they destroyed, others took their place. Tired of the game and aware of their time constraints, Hawke bulked his hybrid, roared and swatted the wolves with his longer claws. Most lost their heads, others bled out through slit necks. He turned and watched Asia jump high and land on the back of a wolf with her elbow. The loud snap of broken bones settled the matter. The wolf dropped to the ground, dead.

Breathing hard, her chest heaved as she looked around the area. Hawke followed her gaze. This wasn't a random attack. Not this many wolves.

"I counted eighteen," she said in between breaths. "These aren't from Greggor, someone else joined the party."

He tossed the carcasses of the wolves to the side of the road so they could drive through and then returned to his normal size. "Am I ticking?" He looked at her.

Asia stared at him a few seconds before answering. "Not right now. Why?"

"A sharp pain hit me right before they attacked. I think they pinpointed me and that's what I felt. Hurt like a bitch."

She chuckled. "Watch it, I'm a bitch."

He winked and slid into the driver's seat. "I know."

She closed her door, looked out the window at the dead wolves as they drove down the road. “Perhaps we will be there before noon if we don’t have any more company.”

“The pain hit right before they did. I couldn’t give any warning, sorry about that.”

“The way you swerved the car worked fine. I knew something was wrong. Who do you think sent those wolves? Did you recognize any of them?”

Hawke had been too busy destroying them to learn much. “No, I should’ve paid more attention, gathered information to help untangle this puzzle instead of killing them outright. My beast is operating in primal mode and doesn’t think rationally when you’re involved.”

Her brow rose. The feminine gesture looked strange on the face of the man. “Yeah?”

“Yes. We’re mated. For us, your ability to beat a pack of wolves or hybrids or soldiers with guns does not matter. If there is a threat to our mate, the threat must be destroyed. There is no gray area, none at all.” He glanced over to see how she took his confession. She wore a thoughtful expression, but hadn’t made light of the situation. That was a good sign and a good start for open communication.

“Mates protect each other. Not just one watching out for the other, this goes both ways, Hawke. I feel the same as you.” Asia looked at him. “Can you understand that?”

On one level he did, but his wolf balked. “Yes, I hear you, but as an Alpha male wolf, my beast will never allow you to be in danger and not react on primal instincts. I will destroy any threat to you and cannot change that Asia.”

“Well, I’m a fucked-up bitch with my own way of handling things. I protect mine as well. We’ll find a balance to work together.” She looked at him with a wry expression. “Because there is no way I can allow Lord Boris and the Liege to take you again. My wolf and I cannot allow that either. In this we are in agreement. No one fucks with our mates.”

Warmth filled his chest and eased the tension he’d sensed when they started this discussion. “I agree with you. My wolf will never allow anyone to take control again.” Hawk would rather die first.

Asia nodded, and he knew she understood. Death was preferable to captivity. They drove the rest of the way in silence until she pointed to a side road.

"Turn here."

Hawke made the turn down the paved road and continued forward.

"I wonder why your chip goes on and off," she said with a thoughtful expression. "Is there something we can do to keep it turned off?"

He shrugged. "Is it on now?" He couldn't hear the ticks as she called them.

"No. Which means right now they can't lock onto you. I'd prefer to keep them away from Chacal's property. The man is an associate of La Patron and is allowing you to use his computer system as a courtesy. I don't want anything to happen to him or his home because of this visit."

"Yes I agree, but I don't know how or why the chip is short-circuiting. The thing never has before, not until you came along anyway. Maybe it has something to do with our mating. When you showed up in the castle, our link burned in my mind dragging my wolf forward."

"Burned in mine too. Perhaps it's the link?"

"Could be, or the sex, or just being close or all of it. I don't know." "We'll do a simple experiment. The next time you're ticking I'll link with you, maybe tell it to stop ticking or something like that to see if it works."

Hawke nodded. "Is this the turn or keep going straight?"

"No, turn here and press the intercom at the gate, then say our names."

He followed her instructions and then drove through the gate after it opened. The voice instructed them to follow the cobblestoned pavement up to the house. After driving another mile up the winding road, a large white contemporary structure came into view.

Hawke's hand tightened on the wheel as they reached the drive in front of the house. He stepped out, went to assist Asia, but she stepped out before he rounded the car and headed up the stairs. They needed to work on how to approach unfamiliar areas because his wolf gave him fits over her walking ahead into possible danger.

"*Asia.*"

She stopped and looked over her shoulder.

"*Let me go first.*" He had explained as much as he could and hoped she didn't fight him on this.

Asia stared at him a few seconds and then nodded. Exhaling in relief, he took her hand, and walked to the door. The door opened before Hawke knocked. Surprised at seeing the tall distinguished looking gentleman with golden brown eyes wearing a deep purple long sleeved shirt with ruffles at the cuffs and a drawstring around the collar that reached the top of his thighs, Hawke nodded.

Tight, dark brown pants stuffed in black knee-high boots completed the unusual attire. An angular shaped face with a long thin nose, pointy chin and blackish-brown hair falling straight from a widow's peak to his shoulders reminded Hawke of a model Renaissance man.

Chacal didn't speak, or smile, or invite them inside the house. Instead, he stepped back turned and walked down the hall. Hawke stepped inside and looked back at Asia when she didn't follow.

"*That man smells different. I don't think I've ever smelled a wolf like him. Mothballs, he's real old.*"

Hawke touched her mind with urgency. "*We can discuss that later.*

First, I need to get to the files in the cloud before time runs out." Asia exhaled and followed.

He picked up Chacal's scent and followed the trail to a wood covered steel door which blended well with the interior wall panels. The house was much larger than it appeared from the outside. Chacal stood nearby watching them.

"*Chacal thinks you're a man.*"

"*Yeah, I know. Does it bother you to hold hands with a man in front of him?*" He heard the laughter in Asia's voice.

"*No. I'll hold you anywhere in any shape or form.*" She chuckled and squeezed his hand.

They waited for Chacal's instructions. He pointed to the door. There was a clicking sound, and the door slid open. Hawke peered inside and then looked at his host. "Is the system down here?" Chacal nodded.

"*Thoughts?*" he asked Asia while looking into the well-lit area.

"I'm not sensing anything other than equipment."

Hawke led her through the door and down the stairs. Organized electronic equipment filled the well-ventilated room. Hawke rubbed his hands together in pleasure. True, he had been a prisoner for decades, but he loved learning and the knowledge he had acquired over the years had been his narcotic of choice.

Eager, he strode to the long table with keyboards situated in front of three thirty-five-inch sized monitors. He typed in a few codes to prepare the system for what he needed. The system accepted his codes. Next, he ran a few tests to see what traps, if any, were resident.

Hawke sensed Chacal behind him as he continued creating a system within this system so that it couldn't be traced to this location. Entering the cloud took longer than he planned but after thirty minutes he accessed his files in the cloud.

"I'm in."

"Good." Asia sat in a chair next to him.

First, he concentrated on the test wolves, pulled each file and deactivated every kill chip. Some were already dead by other means, but most still lived. Once their chips shut down, so did the tracking beacons. Greggor wouldn't be able to locate them any longer; Lord Boris' power over the wolves was now dead. Exhilarated over righting that wrong, he eyed Asia and smiled.

"The wolves are safe, thank you for this. At least one weight is removed from my conscience. It will take years to lighten the stain of blood from my hands; this is a good first step."

Next, he encoded his research files so that no one other than him could read or understand the documents. A lot of the research came from prior studies of his mate. For a split second he wondered how she would feel about that backdoor connection, and decided to wait until much later to discuss his exact duties in the lab. Once she understood his thirst for knowledge, his actions should be seen in a better light. At least he hoped that would be the outcome. One never knew with Asia.

Hawke's primary role had been to duplicate Asia's experiences and modify the techniques so that a broader range of wolves could accept some of her changes. To date, the chip implants were his only success. None of the wolves, other than him, could accept metal bones. If he could destroy the research files he would, but Lord Boris set the protocols and Hawke hadn't had the time or clearance to change those yet. Instead, he settled for coding them so the records would have no value in their present condition.

It took several hours to make all the changes, to close all the doors, to erase his footprint and to clean up the system he'd borrowed. By the time Hawke finished, hunger and fatigue lay heavy on his shoulders. Asia had sat quietly next to him the entire time. Chacal remained nearby seated in a chair.

When the system accepted Hawke's last command, he laced his fingers, stretched, and smiled at Asia. "Done."

She grinned, but he read the weariness in her gaze. They both needed to regroup before heading toward the pickup point. Hawke stood and offered his hand. She accepted and stood. Leaning forward, he brushed his lips against hers, pleased by the flash of desire in her eyes.

He winked and turned to their host. "Thank you for the hospitality and the use of your system."

Chacal nodded and rose and headed toward another door on the same floor. Assuming it was another exit to outside, they followed. Instead of outside, they entered a luxurious dining and living room combination.

Hawke's gaze bypassed the sparkling crystal chandelier, the thick Persian rug beneath the long mahogany polished table, exquisite signed artwork gracing the walls, statutes and statuettes on various surfaces all of which he knew denoted certain points in history.

Instead, his stomach growled in appreciation of the table laden with bountiful aromatic meats, steaming vegetables, stews, and platters of sliced cakes or bread.

"Smells great," Asia said as she dropped his hand and headed for the table.

Hawke met Chacal's gaze, and nodded. "Thank you. Is there a bathroom I can use?"

The older man turned and moved in the opposite direction. The movement was so smooth Chacal appeared to float down the hall. He stopped and pointed to a door. Hawke nodded, and stepped inside the large, space.

Asia took a plate from the sideboard and placed slices of medium rare beef, a turkey leg and other goodies on her plate, scanning for danger the entire time. She didn't trust anyone who refused to speak. Chacal's random heartbeat mystified her. The entire time Hawke worked on the computer she'd monitored their host. *"Mistress?"*

"Asia."

"We are at Chacal's. Hawke has disabled the chip. The test wolves are free."

"Okay, I'll tell Silas. How are you and Hawke doing?"

"Good. Somehow our mating interrupted the chip in his brain, have you ever heard of that happening?"

"No, I'll ask Silas. That's great if it works out that way. Because as long as he has the chip, they can track him and you're not safe. You're still using the chameleon to disguise yourself, right?"

"Yes and I appreciate you looking into that for us. If we can figure out how to short circuit it more, then we should be able to neutralize it completely."

"Good point. I'll ask Jacques and Matt as well, some things may have come across their desks while doing research that can answer that question."

Asia ate while listening to Jasmine and monitoring her link with Hawke. "*Chacal is old.*"

"*Huh? Why do you say that?*"

"I'm reading him. And he's old like La Patron, maybe older. It's obvious in the way he moves, and doesn't speak."

"What do you mean doesn't speak? He talked to Angus."

Asia stopped eating and placed the fork on the table. *"The man has not spoken an audible word since we arrived. Is there a way to verify he is Chacal?*" She exhaled to calm her beast. Hawke was taking a long time in the bathroom. If he didn't surface soon she'd go find him.

"*Angus says he will talk when he chooses and yes he's old, an eccentric. He may not speak but he will watch everything and make his own decision how to interact with you. Chacal has already contacted him with an update. Right now, you should be at a table eating, are you?"*

Asia drew in a deep breath through her nose and swallowed. "*Yes, it's really good. Thank you. We will leave after we eat."*

"Why?"

The question surprised her. She assumed Jasmine had a plane on standby someplace near to whisk them out of the country. Chacal and Hawke returned. He met her gaze, smiled and took a plate.

"Why? Because the job is done here."

"I understand but why not rest before you head out tomorrow?"

Asia coughed to avoid choking. Her eyes watered and she sipped the fruit flavored beverage. "*Head out where?*" Had her Mistress changed her mind about wanting her to return to the compound?

"*Chacal made arrangements for you to fly out of Odessa on his private jet tomorrow morning. You took longer than we thought to reach his place, and he sent for the pilot when you arrived. The pilot should reach there in six hours, you'll leave then.*"

Asia released a breath. "*Okay, that's good, we'll leave from here if Chacal allows us.*"

Chapter 18

Lord Boris Lancaster sat at the table with Sir Roderick and Lord Gordon in an underground lab in northern North Dakota just south of the Canadian border.

"Well?" Sir Roderick drawled. "How bad did Greggor fuck up this time?" He and Gordon chuckled at Boris' misfortune of being related to such an inept soul.

Warmth rose to his cheeks, but he quickly banished all expression from his face. "Seems he lost the tests animals and Hawke."

His comrades stopped laughing and sat straight in their chairs. "How is that possible? Hawke? Gone? After all these years?" Roderick asked, confusion lining his voice.

Boris had been just as confused until he watched the footage from the security cams. Some areas were blotchy but between the fight with the hybrids and the dead lab workers he recognized Hawke had helped. Help they needed to identify and exterminate. If someone, anyone could shut down a computer chip as powerful as Hawke's, then all of their experiments were at risk. They would be back to square one and that was unacceptable.

"Yes. Greggor thinks the security footage is destroyed, he doesn't know I have backdoor access to all the cams in the castle. These secret cams are the main reason I don't need to return often." In reality, Boris could run the castle via his remote program. Often he turned off the security beams on the roof, doors and windows when one of their allies needed supplies. This particular setup happened outside of the normal security cameras that Jerry monitored. One place he did not have full control was Hawke's lab. The full-blood constantly altered everything he installed, after ten years he stopped. Now it came back to bite him in the ass.

Boris pressed a button. "Watch this and tell me what you think."

The screen flickered to life. With each slide his fingernails dug into his palm. Someone dared to violate his sanctuary, robbed him of his test animals, and killed his staff. Pain ripped through him from the deep gouges he'd made in his palm. Blood ran from his hand and dripped to the floor and then his skin re-knitted, removing all signs of his anger.

"I didn't know Jerry's lover could fight like that," Roderick said leaning forward, watching the small male drop kick and destroy a hybrid.

"He didn't. I have no record of him being trained for anything other than computers," Boris said, watching the slides. "Watch close, right here." This part seemed off to him. Not that Jerry killed Ponce that would have happened regardless. But that Jerry ran off instead of killing himself as well.

"Your point?"

Boris withheld a sigh. Griffith had been dense so his demise was no great loss, not in Boris' opinion. But he expected more from Roderick and Gordon. "He didn't self-terminate, instead he ran." Neither man spoke.

"There is a kill chip in his brain, and he ran," Boris ground out.

"Do you have anything else?" Roderick said.

"Yes. Hawke and Greggor in the lab talking and then the idiot had Hawke reset the computers." Boris had no footage on what happened in the entire castle after that point but he would never admit such a huge breach. There were a few things he kept to himself, like the destruct button which would detonate enough explosives below ground to blow the castle out of the woods.

"That caused a problem?"

"Yes, Hawke closed me out from that point without knowing. I have a few images after that, but they're sketchy."

"What are your plans?"

Boris grinned and looked at his partners. Both men stared at him for a moment and then smiled.

"I plan to recapture my property and kill the bastard who rescued him. First, I'm going to throw some fuel on the fire, and send the dogs after my dog. We need to know how someone entered the castle and

why Hawke's chip is not responding."

"Yes, I will inform the doctors in the lab to hold-off on installing the implants until we know more."

Boris batted down his embarrassment for this glitch and hoped project Lobo would not be impacted. The recent test results on

Hawke's pups had been excellent.

"Ask questions. See if anyone knows of anything in the Black Clan biology that would impact the chip. If this is unique to the black wolf, it may not affect other test animals and we can make our schedule."

"I have discussed it with a few people already." "What do they say?" Gordon asked.

"Mates. A mate can and will cancel out anything that impact or impede the wolf. Nothing can stand between the two. His body will reject and destroy the chip without any help from the man."

"Mate? How did Hawke come in contact with a mate? Was there anyone new in the castle?"

Boris nodded. "Greggor hired a new lab tech, Tate Green. But he's dead along with the others. The only person, other than Greggor and Hawke, who left the castle alive was Jerry. Jerry worked for the castle for ten years."

"What do they suggest?"

It grated Boris that they should defer to outsiders but he held his council. Thanks to his nephew he sat in the hot seat of irresponsibility and he did not appreciate it.

"Hawke headed to Odessa, I assume to leave the country from there. Our allies set up a surprise attack and lost every wolf. None survived."

Boris let that sink in so they would realize how serious this matter could become. "Hawke has control of the chip and is able to bulk to enormous sizes, we've all seen him. Thanks to spending years in our research department the man's a master strategist and with metal in both legs and arms, he'd be tough to bring down."

"We know all of this," Roderick snapped. "He's the second, possibly first, most volatile experiment. Asia's in the wind and now Hawke. What's the plan to get Hawke?"

Boris grinned at Roderick's outburst. "I've sent a team of specialized hybrids to capture Hawke and his mate."

Roderick rubbed his chin. "The bluebirds haven't passed all the tests. What if something goes wrong? You should have cleared that with us first."

Boris knew he'd taken a risk sending their newest fighters to recover Hawke. That's why he showed everything they stood to lose before dropping that bomb. "Time's of the essence. Plus, there's another reason I moved quickly." Boris paused, grabbed their attention. "I suspect the help Hawke received was someone using the chameleon bracelet."

Roderick's eyes narrowed as he leaned forward. "Angus? You think he returned?"

Boris nodded. It was a stretch, but he'd rather they think of the Black Wolf more than his use of the Blue birds for what amounted to personal reasons.

"Yes, it's possible," Gordon said. "Both men are from the Black Wolf clan, we forget that about Hawke because of how long the sod's been around. If anyone could neutralize the computer chip, I'd say it would be Angus. That dog won't die."

"He won't have a choice once the Bluebirds reach him. Even Hawke will have a hard time defending against the birds."

"We want Hawke captured, not killed," Roderick said eyeing him. "And the companion as well. This may be Angus and I want to unwrap him personally."

Boris nodded but didn't respond. Accidents happened all the time. He'd preferred Hawke dead than working against him. Even now, he had a hard time decoding Hawke's files.

Chapter 19

Stuffed from a large tasty meal, Hawke rose from the table and nodded thanks to their host. Now that he'd fed his hunger, his wolf pressed to mate. He glanced at Asia, hoping she would morph into her true form, he needed to hold her.

Chacal pushed back from the table, and waved them forward. Hawke took Asia's hand and rubbed the middle of her palm with his thumb.

Asia shivered.

Hawke winked and continued following the older man until he stopped in front of a set of double doors. This time Chacal didn't open the doors; instead he stepped aside, turned and walked in the opposite direction.

Hawke opened the door and stared at the opulent suite. The cherry and cream décor in the living area was soft and inviting. He tugged Asia's hand and walked across the threshold. A slight tingle ran across his skin.

"It's warded," Asia said before he did.

"Yes, I felt the vibration. Hope that means it's safe for you to change." He allowed his feelings to roll through the link so she understood what he needed. Ignoring her scent all day kicked his ass, he and his wolf wanted to be buried between her thighs. His balls ached with wanting. Hawke had kept his wolf locked down all day by promising serious play-time tonight.

"First, I need to scan for cameras. Although anyone who doesn't eat and wiggles fingers to open steel doors may not need cameras." Asia walked around the room, assessing.

He agreed and headed for the bathroom. The first door he opened was a large walk-in closet filled with robes in various sizes and colors. The second door led into a large bedroom with a super king-sized bed at the far end. A large flat screened TV took up a significant part of the wall, speakers, a wine cooler with several bottles and a mini-refrigerator were spread across the room.

"Nice," he murmured, walked further into the room and opened another door. "Oh yes." This was the room he'd been seeking. Four people could fit comfortably into the large glass enclosed shower. Hawke's gaze landed on the centerpiece of the room. Smiling, he strode toward the middle of the room where an over-sized circular tub rose as an offering to the Goddess in cream colored marble and gold trim.

Chacal may not talk but the man had class. Hawke turned on the water, checked the temperature and filled the tub. Looking around he found a glass cabinet filled with various scents. Medium sized, gold rimmed jars contained unique flavors, he sniffed each until he came across one his wolf noticed and poured a liberal amount beneath the flow of water. Tantalizing aromas of lavender and vanilla filled the room. Pleased with the fragrance and the atmosphere, Hawke ran to the shower, turned it on and washed fast. Once dried, he dimmed the lights, turned off the water in the tub and went to find Asia.

Eyes closed, she lay across the bed.

Unsure if he should press or allow her to rest, Hawke remained by the door battling his wolf and his conscience. Last night she hadn't slept much, and then the fight against a pack of wolves. Plus traveled a great distance. He pushed down the disappointment, and rationalized this was all a part of being mated. Some days like tonight, her needs came first. Asia needed rest, and that was okay. He would be okay. Turning, he headed toward the shower.

Asia's laughter stopped him cold, and he spun around to see her leaning up on her elbow. "Wow, you should've seen your face when you walked out of here. I thought you'd start crying any minute you looked so sad."

"What? Don't tease your mate like that. I'm operating on fumes here." Hawke strode to the bed, picked her up, and placed kisses all over her face.

Asia laughed and pushed him back. "Tickles... your whiskers tickle. Let me down so I can undress."

"No." Hawke headed to the bathroom. "I'm going to undress and bathe you. Tonight, I plan to pamper and feast on your lusciousness."

Her soft gasp made him wonder if anyone had ever treated her as the special woman she was. Hopefully not.

"Pamper and then feast... hmmm, sounds like a contradiction to me," she murmured sliding down the front of his body.

"Trust me, it's not and I'll show you." Hawke pulled off her pants and removed her top. She stood bold and beautiful in front of him. He leaned forward and captured her dusky nipple into his mouth.

Asia moaned and held his head in place for a few seconds. When her legs shook, he picked up his prize and walked to the tub.

"That smells great. What is it?"

"Some scents I combined, glad you like the aroma." Hawke lowered her into the water, pleased when her eyes fluttered close and she rested on the bottom. After releasing her, he kneeled on the side, cupped his hand into the water and poured the warm liquid across the top of her breast. Her nipples pebbled beneath the water.

"Ummm, nice."

Hawke removed the wash cloth from on top of the stack of towels, swirled the cloth into the water and with deliberate strokes ran the wet towel across her legs, thighs and stomach. Asia moaned and widened her legs.

The look of bliss touched deep places inside and he prayed to the Goddess for strength to last a longer. Those small sounds slipping from her mouth sent his beast into a tailspin. "Like that?" his voice dropped to a husky whisper.

Asia nodded. But that wasn't good enough. Not any longer. His mate hid from them and his wolf refused to accept that any longer. Even though she didn't block the link, there were limits on where he could go, what he could see and learn about her. That frustrated his beast and slowed their mating. Hawke intended to break through her walls with love and affection, two things missing from most of her life.

Hawke started at her feet, massaging first, rotating each foot, pressing his thumb into pressure points for relaxation. "If I haven't told you how much I appreciate you finding a safe place last night, I need to correct that right now. The dregs of the serum from the tranquilizer hit again last night, and I crashed, leaving us vulnerable to attack." His hands moved up to her calves while appreciating the small sounds of delight escaping her mouth. Hawke doubted she was aware of the purring noises.

"Thank you." He opened the link so the full force of his pride in being her mate, his commitment to their bond and his gratitude for her care filled the space to bursting. Hawke would never be able to verbalize the wellspring of emotions Asia set off in him and didn't try.

Her eyes opened, and their gazes locked. First, he massaged one thigh and then the other while holding her gaze, promising her with every touch that he'd be there for her. Next, his fingertips brushed between her legs. Asia opened her mouth without releasing a sound.

And then Hawke placed his palm on her flat stomach absorbing her tremors. Moving behind her, he started at the base of her neck, massaging tight muscles until they loosened beneath his hand.

"Mmmm," she murmured dropping her head forward to her chest. He placed a kiss to her neck, feeling her pulse, and then watching it jump beneath her soft skin. Next he massaged her shoulders and then each arm. By the time he dragged the washcloth over every inch of her body Asia was boneless.

"Are you okay?" he asked more to hear her speak than to answer. "Better than okay. That was... can't really describe how good that felt."

Hawke turned to pick up the towel when he heard her voice catch and gazed over his shoulder. Asia's eyes squeezed tight, and she laid ramrod stiff. Concerned, he tested the link to see if she'd left it open enough for him to make sure she was okay. Stunned didn't begin to describe his feelings over the battle she fought with her emotions. He'd never seen anyone so conflicted over a kind act. That explained her rigid posture, she fought for control and he didn't want to interfere. Hawke eased out of the link, picked up the towel and waited for her to acknowledge him.

He could wait. He *would* wait as long as it took for her to work through her demons. The moment Asia walked into the lab, she'd set him free, allowed him to face and deal with personal demons every day without judgment. They were two of a kind.

Asia opened her eyes and met his gaze. Hawke stood in front of her holding a large towel. "Ready to get out?" he asked without acknowledging what just happened. One day she'd share her past, and allow him to help banish the darkness. Until then, he'd stay close without pushing.

Asia wet her lips and pushed. "Yes, thanks. That was great. Didn't realize how tense I was."

Hawke picked her up, wrapped her in the towel and walked into the bedroom. When he reached the bed, he stood her in front of him and towel dried her from bottom to top with brisk strokes, spending extra time on her clit and taut nipples. By the time he pulled her close for a hard kiss she trembled in his arms. He took her hand and placed it on his rock-hard cock. "Feel that?"

She nodded.

He pressed his hardness into her. "No, say the word. Do you feel this?" he asked more demanding this time.

"Yes." She leaned against him, resting her head on his shoulder.

Hawke cupped her ass and squeezed.

"Lay down."

Asia glanced at him, turned and crawled to the middle of the bed, giving him an eye full. His dick hurt it was so hard. He followed and nipped her thigh from behind. She spun around laughing. Hawke caught her around the waist, pushed and held her in position. He placed small bites all over her ass while she squirmed to be free.

"Settle down, feisty bitch." Hungry, he licked her ass all over and kissed the places he'd bitten. One finger slid between her legs and played in the moisture. Blessed the Goddess she was ready for him, he couldn't wait another second. Admiring her round butt, he pulled her up on her knees and spread them apart. She wiggled her ass and looked over her shoulder at him.

Hawke smacked one cheek and for good measure the other. Asia tried to scoot forward, but he pulled her close and with one thrust slid inside her tight sheath. Tight, vaginal walls pulsed around him in welcome. He pulled out and then slid back, in and out, faster with each thrust. Goddess she was hot and snug around him. But he needed more and lifted her off the bed for a deeper angle. Faster and faster Hawke thrust inside her. Her walls tightened. Wanting to fly over the wall with his mate, he drove deeper and then like a four-wheeler, pleasure slammed into him. Unable to stop, his fangs dropped and he bit into her shoulder prolonging bliss filled spirals of color and weightlessness.

“Mistress was right,” Asia said later.

Too tired for a full discussion, Hawke limited his words. “About?”

“Oh... she said sex with a mate was different. There’s no way to prepare anyone for mating. There are no words.” She stretched, yawned and curled into him.

“That’s true.” Hawke pulled her close and drew the cover over them.

Chapter 20

Early the next morning before the sun peeked over the horizon, dressed in beige khaki's, Asia and Hawke strode across the tarmac to the sleek jet parked on a far corner of Chacal's land. They would fly to London, and catch another flight to New York. Excited that Hawke fixed the problem with the test wolves, Asia was ready for him to meet Jasmine and La Patron. She hoped Hawke would work in La Patron's lab to help her pack win against the Liege. Besides, she wanted Jasmine to meet Hawke. Dr. Passen would be in heaven with all the information her mate stored in his brain.

The large hangar held another jet, and a helicopter sat on a pad nearby. They didn't come into contact with anyone else other than Chacal this morning when he joined them for breakfast. Asia wondered who cooked the two meals they had eaten since arriving. Did the odd man live alone? When breakfast was done, Chacal placed a tablet in Hawke's hand and left the room. The tablet held instructions for them to reach Chacal's private airstrip.

Although grateful for the hospitality, the food and much needed rest Chacal creeped her out. The old man's silence and stealth-like movements were the stuff of spy movies. Returning home sounded better than ever.

The tablet held a picture of the plane, captain and one-person crew. Those individuals met them as they approached. Asia suspected Chacal had done the same for them.

Hawke greeted the two males while she scanned the area. A stiff breeze brushed the back of her neck. She couldn't get a handle on what made her skin itch. Her beast stood, sniffed a few time before releasing a low, rumbling snarl. An elusive scent tickled her nose.

"*Tell them to leave the plane and walk away.*" Asia told Hawke, trouble headed in their direction.

"*Done. What's coming?*"

"*Don't know, yet.*" She sensed Hawke move in the opposite direction of the hangar. Good thinking, they didn't want any damage to

Chacal's property. They still needed a ride out of here.

"*Incoming.*" Hawke bulked into his hybrid and ran to the left away from plane into the nearby woods. He moved so fast Asia turned and for the briefest second saw the tattered ends of his shirt flapping in the wind.

A burst of air blew past her almost spinning her around. "What the..." She jumped back as something ran by her in blurring speed. Worse, she hadn't picked up anyone or thing on her scan. A loud thump and then crunch came from behind her. Two blue spotted... huge beasts attacked the plane, rendering it useless in a matter of seconds. And then jumped to the other plane, repeating their motions. Before she could react, they leapt forward and headed in the same direction as Hawke.

Hawke. Asia took off at a run.

"Don't... shift. They... have cameras... Liege will see... you."

"Dammit, you have to stop doing this. Stop trying to protect me. I'm La Patron's warrior. This is what I do."

"Argue later."

Hawke's short response sent a shaft of fear rolling through her. What were those things? How did she kill them? She increased her speed and followed the trail of broken limbs and fallen trees. Her eyes widened at the bloody sight.

Hawke fought like a man possessed, his movements so fast she could barely make them out. The sound of flesh hitting flesh, bones breaking and rearranging, bodies flew in all directions, but they didn't stop, they came back at him like a fucking Duracell battery.

Three of them piled on top of him and her wolf flipped. Running forward, she morphed in a hybrid. Asia's twelve-inch claws plunged into the face of the nearest... whatever it was. While impaled, she lifted it from the pile and rammed it into a tree. She placed both hands on its face to twist off his head but the damn thing wouldn't move.

"What the..."

Something, a sledge hammer perhaps, hit in the back of her head, she released the beast and stumbled a few steps. The thing she had held shook its head a few times as its flesh repaired.

Oh shit. What the hell had the Liege created? The beast behind her took a few steps back like a bull, and charged. At least that hadn't changed, these things always charged.

Asia stepped aside and slammed her steel fist into his stomach sending him flying forward into a tree so hard the trunk cracked. The beast slumped to the ground, rolled to his side, the back of his head split open like a melon.

Asia jumped in time to miss a punch to the face and rolled across the ground. There had to be a way to knock these things out, at least long enough for them to get away. She picked up a fallen limb and brandished it like a spear. The beast snarled, and she had a strange feeling he laughed at her makeshift weapon. She glanced at Hawke. He held his own but his movements had slowed, he favored his right side.

Two of these creatures weren't moving, but the two that were, had an unholy light in their eyes. Asia suspected Lord Boris channeled his excitement through these beasts.

Filthy bastard.

The beast in front of her charged, again. She side stepped him, but this time he changed directions, following her.

She leapt into the air and jammed the sharp point of the limb down through his skull. The tip of the stick came out at the end of his spine. Claws outstretched, he staggered a few steps. The glow in his eyes dulled and then he fell. Asia picked up another limb and speared the beast on top of Hawke.

The loud howling sound coming from the defeated thing sent chills down her spine. For a moment, she thought Lord Boris screamed his frustration. Enjoying that image, she kicked the beast a few more times, moving it off Hawke and stooped to check his pulse.

The strong, steady beat eased her concerns, even though his eyes were closed. There were marks all over his body where they stabbed and cut him with their claws. Asia frowned. The wounds should be healing instead of oozing blood.

"Hawke?" She slapped his face.

"*Don't talk, use the link. The cameras are still live.*"

Asia closed her eyes, grateful to hear his voice, even if he insisted on telling her what to do. "*What happened? What were those things? I need to move you, but you're bleeding and it's not stopping.*" She tried to keep the panic from her voice and failed.

"*Their nails were dipped in the same serum used in tranquilizers, sent traces of it into my system. Everything's slowed. I'll heal, it'll just take longer.*" He turned, opened his eyes and looked at her. "*Smart.*"

Hawke laughed and then started coughing. "*Genius, you copied my hybrid. Boris and the others probably thought they were seeing double. That's genius.*" He returned to human.

Warmth from his compliments warred with concern over his condition and their open location. "*You're the genius, at least that's what the rumors say. Can you stand? I want to get you out of these woods before the tranq drags you completely under.*"

Hawke rolled to the side, held his head a moment and then pushed. She helped him stand and stabilized him. "*When you're feeling better, we're going to talk. You ran off –*"

"*I needed to know who their target was.*"

Asia didn't know what to say, she'd thought he tried to keep her safe.

"*There... There was a project...*" He coughed and almost fell. She bulked a bit more and held him steady. "*Bluebird, it wasn't ready, far from it, but it looks like... like it had a test run today.*"

"*Bluebird? Is that why their skin looked funny?*"

"*Funny?*" He glanced at her and then at the forest floor, picking his steps carefully.

"*Speckled. They had blue speckles.*" Asia frowned in concentration.

"I saw something like that before... where?" The memory teased her.

"*At the lab*?" His steps faltered.

"I *think so. But not in the lab, afterward maybe. In the forest with the others.*" Trying to remember, she shook her head and held him tighter. Their movements slowed. She didn't think he'd make it out of the forest. "*Let me carry you.*"

"*What? No. I... can make it to the hangar. I'll lay down there and then...*" He stumbled.

She grit her teeth and held onto his waist. The only way they would make it to the hangar before night fall was if she carried him. Asia doubted he'd last five more minutes.

"*Hawke.*"

He stiffened and continued walking without answering her.

Hawke stopped. "*Someone's coming.*"

Asia morphed into the male from this morning but retained the extra strength needed to help her mate.

The scent hit her the same time he spoke. "*Chacal.*" Hawke straightened.

A few moments later the older male stood in front of them dressed in a white ruffled blouse, black tights and matching boots reminding her of a painter from a bygone era. Asia didn't sense any emotions from him. Not anger, curiosity, fear, nothing. No one spoke. She wrapped her arm around her mate's waist in preparation to walk past the man. Hawke needed to rest not stand in a staring match.

Chacal waved them forward and turned.

Relieved they had someplace for Hawke to sleep and heal, Asia tightened her hold and walked him out the forest. A large golden-brown Mercedes was parked not far from their exit. Chacal surprised her and sat in the driver seat. She opened the back seat for Hawke, assisted him inside and climbed in next to him. Next, she wrapped her arm around him and held him close. Chacal glanced at them in the rear-view mirror and drove.

The drive took them pass the hangar. The damaged planes looked like a toddler had thrown a tantrum and broken his toys. How would they leave now? Once she got Hawke settled, she'd contact Mistress and give an update. The silent return drive to the house took less time than she remembered. Had it been a two hours ago they'd prepared to board a plane and leave. So much happened in such a short period.

Asia couldn't believe the Liege was still creating monsters.

"*Damn Liege.*"

The car stopped. Instead of parking in front of the house, he entered an area she assumed was the garage. There were at least six vehicles, and room for more, of different styles and functionality parked in spaces.

"Thank you," Asia said grateful while opening the door. Mindful of Hawke's injuries she pulled him out the car and lifted him in her arms. Her knees buckled beneath his weight. Inhaling, she grabbed energy from her beast, and hefted him higher in her arms. Chacal stood watching until she met his gaze.

Chacal nodded, turned and walked toward a door, did the strange thing with his fingers. The door slid open. She followed him inside the building. Nothing looked familiar. Uncertain which way to go, she looked into his golden gaze and waited for a hand sign, or grunt or head tilt to point her in the right direction.

After a few tense moments the last morsel of her patience vanished, another door opened, and he stepped through. She exhaled, shifted Hawke in her arms and followed. The bracelet required a lot of energy and she'd expended quite a bit this morning already. Fatigue bombarded her. But she needed to get her mate settled and check his wounds. She hadn't seen any blood on the seat of the car, hopefully the bleeding stopped.

Chacal stood to the side and stopped in front of what appeared to be the same room they'd occupied last night. Tired, she nodded her thanks, and stepped across the threshold acknowledging the ward. With Olympic worthy strides she headed for the bedroom and lay him across the mattress. Head bent, hands on her knees she took a deep breath and then stood arching her back in a slow stretch. Asia's arms and legs ached along with her head and shoulders. She twisted her neck and rolled her shoulders while watching him sleep.

The bleeding had stopped.

From where she stood, the wounds appeared red, inflamed, but, not as bad right after the fight. She pulled off his shoes, socks, and pants. A few strips of jersey material remained from his tee-shirt, so she left it alone.

Confident she had done everything she could she morphed into her true form on the way to the shower. Standing beneath the steaming water her mind drifted to the events of their morning.

Bluebirds... the Liege must have zeroed in on Hawke's chip. The damn thing turned on, and she missed the ticks. Not that she could monitor the ticking in his mind all the time, but she'd become accustomed to listening for the soft sound. What were Bluebirds?

Her skin chilled in remembrance of their thick padded necks and off color flesh. Those things had been difficult to slow down, and she wasn't one hundred percent sure they were destroyed, not with the cutting-edge technology the Liege now utilized. Hawke said the cameras were still live which meant those beasts were still on-line. No telling what Boris and his cronies were able to do with those computer chips embedded.

Asia couldn't help but marvel at the new equipment. Her scan did *not* pick up the beasts. Those things moved so fast she didn't see the first two. When the two leapt from the top of the jet it looked like they were flying, the distance had been that great, before the bottom of their feet hit the ground.

Hawke said they were new, in the test phase. That meant there were bugs, things that could be used against those things to their advantage because she was certain they would see the bluebirds again.

"*Mistress?*" Asia stepped out the shower and wrapped a towel around her.

"*Asia, are you and your mate alright? Chacal told Angus you guys were attacked before you boarded the plane.*"

"*Yes, Ma'am.*" She walked into the bedroom, dimmed the lights and crawled into bed. "*Have you heard any more on the mating stuff? Hawke's' chip goes on and off. Lately, it's more off than on. But that's how they're tracking us, when his chip is live. He thinks the reason it's off at all is that we're mates.*"

"*Yes. Jacques and Dr. Passen had a lot to say. When you come home, they can tell you all the finer points. Bottom line, the stronger your bond, the less any outside influence. Get closer, merge in the inside, through his link. According to both guys, that'll fix the problem. But you already linked with him, right?*"

"*We linked.*"

"*But?*"

"*There are some areas I'm not ready to share.*" She recognized how defensive she sounded.

"*Is he open?*"

Asia thought of her trek down his link the other night. "*Yes. Yes he is.*"

"*Based on how Jacques explained it, and I'm repeating him so bear with me on this. There's an imbalance if the two of you aren't linking the same. At this point you can't share energy or complete the mating process until you give all of yourself, like he's doing. I'm not judging you, just passing on what I've been told. But... if you want to shut down the computer chip, finish mating, seems like that'd solve the problem.*"

Asia thought of everything Jasmine said. "*Okay, I'll talk to Hawke about it. Next thing, the Liege has new toys. Bluebirds. Speckled blue tinge to their skin, necks you can't twist or snap, and strong computer chips. Could you have Jacques or Matt check to see if they have anything on these things? They were hard to shut down and I don't think we destroyed them. Those bastards will be back.*"

"Bluebirds? Interesting name. Are they the beasts that wrecked Chacal's new plane?"

Asia winced at the mention of a new plane. "*Yes, sorry about that. Two of them bounced on it a few times and then ran after Hawke.*"

"Chacal's rich, he already ordered another plane. Plus, he sent footage of those things in action. I'll tell Silas they have a name and what happened when you fought them."

Asia squeezed her eyes shut as heat radiated from Hawke's skin warming her. "*Someone gave Hawke to Boris, someone from his pack. I saw it in his memories but I'm not sure if I should tell him*," she said in a rush. The words left a bitter taste on her tongue.

"*What? I... I don't... I didn't think they did that.*"

"Someone did, Mistress. When he's found it's an automatic death sentence."

"Good. From the pack?"

"*No Mistress from me. I plan to kill the son of a bitch when I find him. I have a part of his name but that may have changed through the years. I saw half of his face. Should I tell Hawke?*" The silence stretched, she thought Jasmine chose not to answer.

"*Mate with him completely and everything else will flow from that. You saw something and made plans based on that, while refusing him the same courtesy. After you mate, the bond will be strong enough to handle anything that comes rolling your way. Ask me how I know?*"

Asia sighed and glanced at Hawke. She liked him, a lot. Respected him and could see a future with him. But the idea of belonging to anyone so completely... being enslaved to the Liege for decades left its scar. On an intellectual level, she knew mating with Hawke was one hundred percent different, but her freedom was too new. Being in control of her mind, her actions and decisions... she wasn't ready to give it up yet.

"*Gunnolf sat in the room.*"

"What? Your Gunnolf? He knew Hawke? Wait... hold on. Are you saying Gunnolf was in the room when Hawke was given to the Liege?"

Mistress had a way of cutting to the crux of the issue. "*Yes, I believe so.*"

"*No Asia. Don't be wishy-washy on something like this. Silas and Angus sang this guys' praises. Something's off with all of this.*"

"*Yes, I agree.*" Asia waited for Jasmine's response, hoping for a plan or directions.

"Angus will leave today. Should be there sometime tomorrow, things are ballooning and may blow up in our face. Angus knows that area, the packs and Alphas. According to Silas, if somebody's giving Black Wolf pups to the Liege, that's a serious problem, he wants to make sure we understand who we're up against. Black Wolf clan or Liege or both."

"I understand." She hadn't thought that far, but it made sense.

"Mate with Hawke so you can get a clear picture, I do not want Angus or you to walk into negotiations with the Alpha's over there blind." Asia swallowed hard but didn't speak.

"Do I need to make that an order? I don't want to, but I will. Don't test me in this, Asia. This is too important."

"Yes, Ma'am."

"Yes, I need to order you to mate, or yes you understand how important this information is?"

Asia pressed her fingertips to her forehead and rubbed. *"I understand how important this information is. I will mate with Hawke,"* she said in a low tone hoping it was void of emotion.

Jasmine laughed. *"I wonder if I'll hear from you at all after you finish mating. Anyway, Silas needs me and you need to get busy."*

Asia bit her lower lip at Jasmine's strong suggestion and closed their link. Drugged, Hawke couldn't take part, so she had a little time to hug her secrets. She snuggled closer, listened to him breathe and fell asleep.

Chapter 21

The command for a conference rang in Greggor's head. The sound had the effect of having his ear pulled, dragged into the office and pushed into the chair facing the monitor. Accustomed to this particular brand of humiliation he assumed the position, arms on armrest, back against the back, feet flat on the floor.

Intense waves of pain rolled through him from the top of his head to the soles of his feet as steel manacles slid from their compartments. Cold steel wrapped around his wrists and ankles. Greggor's heartbeat raced as the room dimmed and the screen expanded. Dots formed everywhere blurring his vision from the pain.

Something major must've happened for his uncle to exert this much pain and pressure. The bastard knew what he was doing and didn't care about the trickle of blood running from Greggor's nose. He shook his head to rid his face of the evidence of his discomfort. Fastidious son-of-a-bitch had no problems shedding blood but couldn't stand to look at it.

The temperature in the room rose. Sweat beaded his brow and ran down his face.

Minutes ticked, his chin dropped to his chest to ease the shards of pain in his head. Hate rose, ripe and ready to destroy the bastard for toying with him.

After what may have been an hour, or longer, the display flicked on and Lord Boris stepped in front of the camera, a sneer on his pinched face.

"What do you have to say for yourself nancy-boy. You gutless whelp, you failed me. Thirty years, it took me over twenty-five years to break and mold Hawke into something useful and you lost him," Lord Boris said in a clipped tone.

Greggor winced at the insults. "Something happened to him, he wasn't himself that day. Couldn't put my finger on it, but he hadn't shifted after the tranq shot. He was out of it."

"That's different? No."

A buzz escalated in the base of Greggor's neck and radiated up his head. "Please uncle," he screamed as a drilling sensation pierced his skull.

"You lost everything and dare ask for mercy?" Greggor screamed as a jolt of energy hit him.

"My test wolves, my employees, my files and security compromised because of your incompetence."

Another jolt lanced through his body singeing his nerve endings. Greggor's arms and legs shook like leaves in the wind. "Please uncle..." he gasped for breath. Sounds of his labored breathing filled the room. After a long pause his uncle spoke.

"What have you learned so far?"

Greggor struggled to swallow. "Based on his last signal, he's in the vicinity of Odessa. I just need a team to pick him up," he said pleading his case with his uncle. He hated these video chats; no matter what he did it was never good enough. If it weren't for the kill chip in his brain, he would've left years ago.

Lord Boris laughed. The cruel sound left no doubt the man thought he'd said something ridiculous. This sound had been honed into a cutting weapon to humiliate and demean. "Why would I give you more merchandise when you already lost nine hybrids?"

Greggor didn't defend his actions or what happened. The old bastard knew everything and still blamed and punished him. Anger simmered beneath his skin while he remained still. The old man would pounce on the smallest tick in his jaw or eye movement, and make a monumental case. Experience taught him to minimize his words and expressions.

"Have you no answer?" his uncle yelled.

"The beasts fought Hawke and lost."

"No. Not Hawke. They lost to that idiot you hired. Jerry. Or his lover Ponce. Which was it?"

Greggor hesitated. His uncle knew both men destroyed the hybrids. "Jerry used the laser you sent and I haven't seen the footage and don't know what Ponce did yet." Afraid something would set the older man off again he kept his tone neutral, yet reverential.

The screen changed. The fight between Ponce and the hybrid filled the display. His eyes widened at Ponces' fighting skills and then his death at the hands of his lover. Greggor sat in disbelief when the screen flickered back to his relative.

"Were you aware he could fight like this?"

"No, Sir," he said with feeling. Where had Ponce learned how to disarm a hybrid, even he didn't know that information and he'd searched.

"So... something else happened beneath your nose and you're clueless. Hmm, wonder why you are there... you are worse than the three monkeys who make those silly signs... you know nothing, you see nothing, and you hear nothing."

Greggor's jaw clenched but he remained silent.

"Be prepared, I have sent you two hybrids, you will track Hawke down with the tranq gun. When he is down, contact me and I will oversee his collection."

"Yes, Sir. Thank you for the opportunity to redeem myself." Greggor swallowed hard.

"Do not fail this time. I have tolerated much from you because you fall somewhere down the line in my family tree. But no longer. If you cannot do what I demand you are of no value to me or my cause. Things of no value are waste and all waste is tossed aside. Do you understand?"

Greggor squeezed the arm rest to stop the tremors. "Yes, uncle." The computer screen blanked. Five to ten minutes later the steel restraints released his wrists and ankles.

Shaking, he stood, walked out the office, down the hall to his private rooms, and emptied his stomach into the toilet.

Boris watched the boy run out the room and snickered.

Chapter 22

A loud thud followed by the shuddering of the bed woke Hawke. Eyes open, he remained still, listening. The sound, like a wrecking ball hitting a building, came again. Curious, he rolled to the side of the bed, the room swirled and then righted. How long had he been asleep? Goddess, he had no idea. Moments ticked before the fog disappeared in his mind.

The sound came again. Chacal hadn't knocked or sent a sign that anything was wrong. But Hawke's beast said different.

"Asia." He placed a hand on her shoulder, allowed it to rest there for a moment and then pushed. The building shuddered again.

"What's going on?" She rolled to her back and blinked. Taut nipples stood at attention and he wished he had time to salute each. But his wolf urged him to locate the threat to their mate.

"Am I on or off?" he asked instead.

"On. Shit." Asia jumped from the bed naked and morphed into the male form she'd been using.

"How do we kill those things?" she asked pulling on clothes.

"I'm not... wait a second." He rifled through information in his mind, there were many flaws in the design. Bluebirds were unstable and not in full production.

"The chips aren't behind the eyes or embedded in the skulls. They have sensors... but the control is external. Lord Boris directs, and repairs the thing from his location. That's why the cameras are so strong. One of the problems was the sensors didn't always work and Lord Boris couldn't always control them. They're more machine than human, my advice – separate the head from the body. It'll send the right message. I don't know how they replenish the poisonous tips, just in case protect against their claws." Hawke pulled on his clothes and boots.

"The neck is thick, is there another way?" Dressed in gray cargo pants, a matching long sleeved shirt, and combat boots, Asia strode toward the door.

"Go for the heart. You can't just pierce it though, it has to come out and that won't happen easy. The skin has a thin layer of metal on top, which causes the blue coloring." Hawke strode out the door and stopped. In the hall leaning against the wall were medieval weapons. A battle axe, long spear, and two swords.

"These will do nicely," Hawke said lifting the axe in one hand and the spear in the other. It had been a while since he'd used either but each would allow him to cleave the body of his opponent in half. Asia tested each sword and settled on one. They turned, jogged down the hall following what amounted to a well-lit path until they came to a steel door.

Hawke pushed the exit open, stepped outside and shifted into his hybrid. Asia stood next to him and shifted into his mirrored image. He grinned and ran forward to lead the bluebirds away from Chacal's property.

"He has a barrier like La Patron uses," Asia murmured when they reached a shield around the property.

Hawke pointed at the three bluebirds concentrating on one point of the barrier. "There, you see them? I think you terminated one with that limb yesterday."

Asia nodded. "Could be, they all look the same to me."
"*Kiss me*," Hawke said.

She stepped closer, wrapped her arms around his neck and kissed him. "*Am I ticking?*" he asked through their link.

She deepened the kiss, and he almost lost his train of thought.

"*No.*"

"*Good. Let's gut these bitches. We tear them apart to send those bastards a serious message.*"

"You had me kiss you to see if you were ticking?" Asia asked when they broke apart.

He glanced at the bluebirds, they hadn't seen him yet. "No. It seems the closer we are the less the chip works. That's not as close as I want to get with you, but it'll have to do for now." Hawke stepped away from the embrace and tested the barrier with his fingers, pleased when one passed through with no problem. "Good, we can leave,

they can't enter." He glanced at her. She hadn't moved. "You okay?"

"Just thinking."

Hawke hadn't told her about the bluebird composition to scare or worry her. There were ways to destroy these things, and once he had access to all of his memories he'd research for a better answer. "Okay, I'll draw them away from the house, maybe back into the forest."

"Sounds good. Once they follow you, I'll bring up the rear and start taking them out."

A tingling sensation traveled down his back when he walked through the barrier and looked at his opponents. His beast howled in anticipation. Hawke took off running. Increased his speed, and then raised the spear in one hand and the axe in the other. When he reached the hangar, he threw back his head and released a howl, a challenge.

Amazed at their speed he sensed the beasts' right behind him. Hawke leapt upward just in time to miss the dive of the first bluebird. The beast hit the ground so hard, it created a trench with mounds of dirt on both sides. Hawke landed a few feet away, raised the axe and swung the sharp blade across the creature's thick neck while it tried to stand.

The whiz of the axe stopped the bluebird's movement. Hawke met the blank gaze of the bluebird in the split second before the head separated from the body and flew into the forest. The force of Hawke's swing spun him around and he pitched forward into a nearby tree.

He had just gotten his balance when another bluebird slammed into his side knocking him back. He dropped the spear from the collision. Hawke tightened his grip on the handle of the axe, ducked the next blow and jumped over the headless bird lying on the ground to land on the other side of the small clearing.

The other bluebird ran toward him with lethal claws. Hawke swung the axe removing half the outstretched arm which fell to the ground. The beast continued fighting as if his arm was still attached. Hawke ducked the next punch but miscalculated his opponent who compensated for the loss of one arm with a high kick to his mid-section, knocking him onto the ground. Hawke dropped the axe and rolled to his side.

The beast leapt forward to pin him.

Hawke rolled to the left. The bluebird hit the tree hard making a loud cracking noise on impact and then fell to the ground covering Hawke's weapon.

"Asia?" He hadn't heard from her since Chacal's. It took a moment to catch his breath. The beast lay on top of the axe. Hawke rose slowly, walked to the other side and picked up the spear. The bluebird's head healed as Hawke watched.

"Asia?" Concerned, by her lack of response, he left to find his mate.

He'd cleared the tree line. Asia and the bluebird fought doggedly in the clear area a short distance from the hangar. Hawke stepped aside prepared to help but angled himself in a way to see when the bluebird in the trees arrived. He rubbed the smooth wood of the spear, determined to gut the bastard.

Asia's movements were jerky, mechanical and Hawke wondered if she'd ever fought with a sword. The beast never eased up; kept her on defense punching and kicking. If they had merged fully, Hawke could share his skill set with sword play. Although he understood her reluctance, to a point anyway, situations like this caused major frustration. Regardless of what anyone wanted if the fight took a nasty turn, he'd jump in and tear the bird apart before allowing serious injury.

Hawke sensed the arrival of the bluebird before the beast landed in two feet in front of him. That was one of the flaws in the design, despite the incredible speed an enemy would always know the large creatures were coming and could prepare for their arrival.

Hawke jumped up, did backward flip and landed a few feet away. The beast carried the axe and ran toward him with the handle gripped in its' remaining hand. Hawke bent forward, holding the spear and waited to the last second before stepping aside. He turned and kicked the beast in the ass sending it crashing to the ground.

He glanced at Asia. The beast still had her on defense. The thought of her injured or scraped by a claw sent him in her direction. Hawke grabbed the bluebird from behind and slammed it into the ground.

"*What are you doing?*" Asia asked looking at the beast on the ground and then at him.

Hawke pointed at the bluebird and watched the other one out the corner of his eye. "*Don't play with the thing. Destroy it so we can get the hell out of here. Everything is being recorded. By now they know there are two of us and suspect there's a reason we're doing this. The less they know the better.*" He turned in time to block a blow from the bluebird.

The beast swung the axe and missed Hawke by a hairs' breath. Asia gasped. He shut her out and took his own advice to destroy this beast. He suspected Lord Boris used Hawke's old training tapes as blueprints for the hybrids, and perhaps these as well. Holding the length of the spear with both hands, Hawke tested his theory and parried the blow by raising the weapon high.

The axe broke the spear with a loud crack. No, that was not one of his moves. Hawke would never split a pole in half, and give his opponent two weapons instead of one. Holding the two jagged pieces of wood in each hand, one with a sharp protruding blade, Hawke jumped back to avoid the next swing of the axe. He spun, kicked his opponent on the chin and watched him fly backward. The moment the beast hit the ground, Hawke slammed the blade into its chest staking him in the heart. The tip of the spear penetrated the metalized skin with ease. Next Hawke rammed the jagged edges of the wood into the bluebird's forehead, pinning it to the ground. Both halves of the spear held the beast immobile for now.

The bluebird grunted and growled. It swung the axe at him, lifted its back and legs to break free. Hawke waited a beat and then wrestled the axe from its grip. Once in his hand, he separated the bluebird's head and body. This time he grabbed the feet of the beast and dragged him to the headless body of the other bird and pulled off the fabric covering its upper body. As he expected, the beast's body went into repair mode but the damage was too great. There were no heads.

Hawke pulled out the stake, and wrapped the head in the fabric to take with him. Glancing at the grisly scene, he'd return later and bury the remains but he needed to go to his mate. The sight that met him stopped his heart. Asia on her knees, the beast hovering over her with outstretched claws. He released the head in his hand and ran toward them.

"*No. Merge with me now,*" Asia said her voice strong, confident.

He opened himself completely, and met her vibrancy on a plane created for them alone, intertwining with her essence. Hawke's breath caught as snapshots of her life flashed before his eyes, on and on it went. Her energy brushed against his. He opened his knowledge, displaying his knowledge of the sword. He lent her his strength, while informing her he'd step in if he felt the need. It took seconds to complete yet the impact was for a lifetime.

They merged.

On the battlefield, in the midst of combat he mated with his wonderful, unique bitch. Her fears touched him. He swore to hold them close to his heart. He received small snippets of the things she had suffered, but they were more than enough to strengthen his resolve that she'd never be anyone's victim again. He waited to see if her knowledge would turn the tide of battle in her favor. If not, he'd destroy the bird.

Asia remained in her position on her knees and opened the link between her and Hawke. Light touched dark areas of her being. She sensed his awe, his compassion and his pride. That surprised her but she couldn't take the time their mating required to analyze everything going on inside right now. They would finish the intimate process later.

Bluebirds tweaked her curiosity. She'd spent time fighting this one finding its weaknesses, testing its agility, its strategies. For the most part its offensive measures were similar to the hybrids. Their enhanced speed made the hybrids appear like old clunkers, the metalized skin was tough to penetrate but not impossible. Asia had punched it in the face and got no different response than when she punched it in the gut.

She appreciated the video clips of sword play from her mate; it had been years since she used a sword. Hawke waited, and she knew he'd step in if she didn't finish. "*I'll explain later*," she said through their link as she did a split with her legs, dropped to the ground, and rolled away from the beast.

The bluebird charged.

She side-stepped it at the last moment and kicked it in the ass. It hit the ground with a loud thump. Moving quickly, she jumped up, holding the sword with both hands and rammed it through his back, piercing its heart. Breathing hard, she stepped behind watching it try to push up and free itself.

Asia grabbed the handle, moved it back and forth in a sawing motion. The beast tried to grab her but could not. She added a twisting motion, shredding anything in that area of its back and chest, not stopping until its' arms fell limp to the side. Removing the sword, she moved to the side and with two blows separated the head from the body.

She took several deep breaths. Hawke grabbed the beast by its feet and dragged it away. At the moment she didn't care where. Asia's body throbbed to complete the mating. One moment her skin itched to be with Hawke, the next, tingled. Hot and then cold. The signals all pointed to one thing, they needed to complete what they had begun.

Now that the immediate danger passed, her wolf pressed her to mate. She gazed in the direction he'd gone. They had a lot to discuss. His memories threaded with hers but didn't overwhelm. A sense of rightness replaced her normal parasitic fear. The constant shame she carried for decades, disappeared like a fine mist in the morning sun. The weakness she feared never materialized, instead a sense of empowerment spread through her mind and body.

She sensed his return, morphed into her familiar male persona and wondered at the bundle he held in his hand.

"*It's their heads. Those three won't rise again.*" He picked up the last one a few feet from her and extended his other hand to her.

Holding onto the sword, she took his hand, and they returned to Chacal's.

Chapter 23

In the distance Asia saw Chacal standing on the veranda watching their approach. His billowing cream colored ruffled blouse and tight pants seemed out of place against the backdrop of the contemporary structure. She wondered what he thought of all of this. His property destroyed, home attacked, and he never said a word.

"Chacal ever say anything to you?"

"No. You?"

"No. That's weird."

"Why?"

"There's been an attack, his plane's gone, those dead things are on his property... I thought he would talk, help...."

"We have a place of refuge, food, water, a bed. That's help. Everyone's strengths are not on the battlefield."

Asia knew that but the man made her uncomfortable. "*Can't put my finger on it but he creeps me out.*" She squeezed Hawke's hand as they stepped beneath the portico. Chacal turned before they reached the porch are, she glanced at Hawke and they followed. Chacal led them down a different hall until eventually reaching the suite of rooms they had been using. Before Hawke could say thank you, the man turned and disappeared like a specter or something of that sort.

Once inside Hawke wrapped his arms around her waist, lifted and spun Asia around chasing Chacal from her thoughts.

"Mmmm, I want to see you," he murmured as she clung to him.

Holding tight, Asia morphed into her base form and slid down his chest. His fingertip outlined her nipple, causing the dark bud to tighten. He pulled the gray shirt from her body and stared.

"So beautiful," he whispered before bending to pay homage to each nipple. The press of lips on her skin ignited a simmering heat. Her legs trembled when his mouth closed around her nipple. Liquid fire, scorching in intensity, raced through her system, building her need to a fevered pitch.

"Hawke..." she groaned holding onto his shoulders. "Stop teasing." Her fingers curled into the fabric of his shirt, and pulled hard. The material ripped apart at the seams.

"Oh yeah, you want this?" Hawke stepped back removing the material while holding her gaze.

Asia's vision narrowed onto his lips. At that moment nothing else mattered. Her skin itched from the heat. Like an addict she craved his particular touch, his smooth taste and his sexy scent. The howl from her wolf escaped through parted lips, surprising them both. She pulled off her boots and two quick moves.

Hawke's eyes lit with an inner glow when she wore nothing but a come-get-it-smile.

He charged.

Asia pivoted and dove for the bed. Hawke caught her legs, widened them and pulled her toward him. Her wolf took exception at such an easy conquest and kicked him. She leapt over the side of the bed and peeked in his direction.

He remained by the bed with arms across his chest, clearly unbothered by the kick to his chest. The longer Hawke stared at her, the harder her pussy throbbed with need. But her contrary wolf demanded he conquer first before getting the goods.

She glanced toward the bedroom door, then back at him and scooted to the side. Before she could blink he'd leapt across the bed, pulled her in his arms and they rolled across the floor. Without thought, her beast took over and she pushed at him with both feet. Hawke moved at little but didn't move enough for her to break free. Asia tried to grab his hands, to push him off. Nothing worked. He was just as fast, and stronger. If she could have broken free, she would have.

The certainty of that knowledge stopped her wolf. Hawke proved worthy on every level. She couldn't win against him in a fight. On a subconscious level she had realized that back in the lab when she called Jasmine to pull his wolf. He leaned forward, and she turned to the side, offering her neck. Hawke groaned, placed small kisses along her shoulder before his incisors scraped against her skin.

"Yield?" She sensed his question held a deeper meaning. Sharing bodies was one level, but mating required the joining of everything.

"Yes."

Hawke touched her chin and turned her face to meet his gaze.

"I yield." The words came from a place deep inside she hadn't visited in decades. The place where hopes, dreams and to-do lists were hidden from those who would destroy every part of her. At that moment, she released them for the dark, remote corners of her mind. Freed them to enter the light of commitment she read in his eyes so they could take root in the fertile ground of their mating.

He pulled her into his embrace, and opened his link and bit down on her neck. They joined on a different level than on the battlefield this time. Hawke brushed against her purple essence, wooing her to his deep red. Then the two, her essence and his, danced.

Cught up on what happened on their spiritual plane, she hadn't realized he'd entered her until her walls tightened around his cock in welcome. Arms loosely laced around his shoulders, Asia faced him on his lap, riding him like a seasoned cowgirl.

Pleasure arced up her back as he lifted and slammed her back down on his steel rod. Their essence twisted and intertwined in harmony with their movements. Lightheaded she clamped her knees to his waist as he increased the speed. Colors exploded behind her eyelids robbing her of breath. The two-links merged into one and then separated, this time both bore traces of the other color. The merged again and her world burst into a thousand pieces as she spiraled high and lingered while waves of orgasmic bliss rolled through and over her.

Asia couldn't see until Hawke appeared and wrapped his arms around her tight. They remained suspended in their links, absorbing each other's energies. Nothing in life prepared Asia for this moment. Her thinking realigned. Her vision sharpened. Her hearing clarified.

The slow ticks caught her attention, and she followed the trail of the sound to the chip embedded in Hawke's brain. Asia tried to pull out the device and couldn't. "*Stop ticking.*" The sound stopped. Surprised and pleased, she told Hawke what happened.

"*Tell the thing to shut down permanently, see if that works.*"

Sounded like a good idea. Asia instructed the chip to stop working permanently. "*Since it stopped ticking I can't be sure about the permanent part.*" Now that they were linked, the chip carried a foul odor, or her dislike of all things Liege conjured a scent. Either way, the damn thing had to go. "*Can I tell it to dislodge and flush out through regular channels? Would that be safe for you?*"

"*I don't know. Go ahead and try, if anything goes wrong, you're here.*"

Asia had forgotten he held her on a spiritual plane and sexually they were still connected. Humbled and emboldened by his confidence, she spoke to the chip. "*Dislodge and pass through as waste, leave no traces or damage.*" She waited and nothing happened.

"*Everything okay?*"

Asia repeated what she said, and he tightened his hold. "*You are wonderful. I'm doubly blessed by the Goddess with a beautiful and smart mate.*"

She grunted.

"*What?*"

"*Nothing.*" But thoughts of past transgressions, mistakes, and shortcomings flew fast and furious across her consciousness. Embarrassed, she tried to break free of their embrace.

Hawke would not release her.

Instead his memories brushed against her, slow at first, as if testing the waters. Asia saw the blood on his hands, not from war, but as a vessel for the Liege. Surgery after surgery, scalpel in hand Hawke sliced, implemented, and ran tests on innocents.

Year after year, atrocity after atrocity he butchered his people at the bequest of others. The sheer weight of his shame eclipsed hers and she wondered how anyone could survive the heaviness of such a load.

"*After everything I've done... all the blood I spilled, bad choices I made... the Goddess gave me a gift... you. There must be something worth saving, redeemable, since you're my mate.*" Hawke's voice cracked as his wolf turned from her.

Asia's wolf trotted after him and rubbed against his side, and licked his muzzle. She understood. In light of what he dealt with, her challenges were insignificant, at least in his mind.

"*Few people could know or understand what you went through. The feeling of being a puppet and manipulated and used. Seems we're both worth saving because the Goddess gave me you.*" Asia placed a kiss on his chin.

"But unlike you, I was a coward. After a while my wolf hid like a pup sucking on his mum's tits. I should've fought harder against them, done more to help the others –"

"And you would have died." Her voice rising to gain his attention, and derail him from this train of thought. "*They would have killed you,"* she said, her tone full of conviction remembering how Lord Boris broke a younger Hawke.

Frowning, he met her gaze. "*You sound sure of that. Why*?"

Asia closed their link and rested her head against his shoulder. The solid beat of his heart offered comfort. She listened for the chip.

"The chip's quiet. I'll check tomorrow to see if it moved."

Hawke stroked her head twice and cupped her cheek with her palm. "Why are you so sure the Liege would've killed me? You shut down our link so I can't see. What do you know?"

"I saw what happened when you were younger. The things Lord Boris and a few others did to break you. Your wolf held out a long time and didn't stop until they replaced the metal in your arms and then later your legs. I guess the computer chip was installed around that time?"

"No. The chip came first. But after the surgeries were successful, the computer controlled the metal bone structure. You're right, that's when my wolf stopped fighting." Hawke stared at her. "What else did you see?"

Asia frowned. "You can't access your memories?"

"Not yet. They're blocked and I can't push through. Why? Can you see yours?"

A kernel of hopeful excitement rose in her belly. "No. Mine are blocked or missing or fake because the Liege tampered with my mind and gave me different identities through the years. That's why I tried to rescue Gunnolf; he knew things about my past."

"Blocked? Gunnolf? You knew Gunnolf? How?" Hawke leaned back against the bed holding Asia in position.

"Like you I guess. It used to hurt when I tried to look inside my memories. Now, I get nothing. I finished a job and was on my way home when Gunnolf spoke to me." She told him about the conversation and her later adventure.

"Gunnolf used to be around; I think any way, in the beginning. It is possible I killed him, but I'm not sure." He pressed his forehead to hers. "I'll search and share your memories if you want."

Asia swallowed hard glad they had worked around to this point. "I'd like that."

A loud pinging noise shot through the room. Hawke's arm tightened around her. Neither moved. The sound came again, this time with a voice.

"Asia, I need you and Hawke out here. We have a lot to do with a short window."

"Who is that?"

"Angus. La Patron's litter mate. Jasmine, my Mistress and mate to La Patron told me he was on his way but I forgot with everything going on."

He nodded, lifted her from his hardness, causing them both to groan at the separation. "*Both of us need to shower and get dressed.*"

Feet now flat on the floor, the vee of her thighs were mouth level for him and he kissed her mound. The warmth of his tongue slid between her wet lips and brushed against her clit reigniting her flame.

The sound reverberated in the room again and then Angus spoke. "You've got ten minutes, Asia."

She moved forward and widened her stance. His tongue and fingers moved in and out, pushing her closer and closer to her release. Hawke's teeth grazed her clit and then he sucked hard. She bucked forward, arched her back and exploded against his mouth. Her body shuddered and her legs buckled. Holding onto her hips and thighs, he held her in place.

"I love how you respond to me," he said in a low growl.

Weak, she nodded and stepped back so he could stand. He took her hand and led her to the shower. Small tremors continued to race through her while using the cloth, cleaned her from top to bottom. Asia took the cloth from him and traveled the breadth and width of his body, discovering what made him gasp, or laugh or moan. By the time they stepped out the shower and dressed, forty minutes passed. Perhaps the mating bond obscured time, and made everything else unimportant, she didn't know.

But they hadn't rushed, and even as Hawke entered her again in the shower, she didn't want to stop feeding the hunger for him.

Hand in hand, they left their room wearing goofy smiles, definite byproducts for the newly mated.

"A video of two test wolves, mongrels chasing a small kid down the road hit the internet. A few mongrels refused to follow pack protocol and were terminated. Others ran away. We need to prevent a war." Angus' growl burst the bubble she'd floated in and kicked her off her cloud.

Chapter 24

"What?" Asia said staring at Angus.

His emerald green gaze flicked from her to Hawke who continued holding her hand. "War. The mongrels you released from the Boris' lab have attacked humans all over the countryside. The local Alphas are blaming La Patron and seek to have you punished for placing all wolves in jeopardy."

"There is no avoiding war; it can only be postponed to the advantage of others," Chacal said entering the room with a tray filled with beverages.

Asia shook her head at the rich baritone of Chacal's voice. "You're quoting Machiavelli? The first time you say anything, and it's a quote?" The man confused her.

"Quote?" Chacal glanced at Angus who turned aside with a small smile. "I suppose you would think that. But the words are appropriate." He placed the tray on the table and sat in an arm chair.

"Asia?" Angus said drawing her attention from Chacal who sipped his drink. Angus' gaze swept from her to Hawke and then back again.

She squeezed Hawke's hand. "This is my mate, Hawke."

Hawke nodded, picked up a drink, handed it to her and then picked up another. They sat on the sofa and waited to hear what happened to turn her good deed into a nightmare.

She spoke first. "I don't understand... Hawke turned off their computers."

"True. But what was left of their minds when he did that? No one knows the true status of their mental state after years of abuse. A much older breeder, Arianna, had been abused for centuries; she didn't know how to handle being free. I think freedom scared her. In the end she flipped, and caused a lot of damage," Angus said.

Angus was right. The test wolves were prisoners inside their minds as well as the cages that held them for decades. She had messed up, disobeyed a direct order.

"Hawke, may I ask you a few questions that may clear up a few things," Angus said.

"Questions?"

"About the nature of the experiments in Boris' lab," Angus clarified.

Hawke tensed and then relaxed. "Yes, of course."

"Alpha Fredrick, from England, claims he lost pack members during the return trip to his pack lands. His beta, Tobias, claims one of the mongrels from the lab attacked when they prepared to board the plane to return home. Frederick's claim is the most harmful, carries the most weight given he assisted La Patron with the last mission."

Shocked, it took a few seconds to process the information. "They looked... fine. Sounded fine. I didn't know." And she hadn't. The older test wolf admitted he didn't know where to go or what to do. Asia hadn't wanted the responsibility, had nowhere to put them, her thoughts had been on the black wolf she had left behind. She should have thought things through.

"*Calm down, we will fix this,*" Hawke's quiet words stopped the mental rant.

Angus continued. "Alpha Verrick, we are in his territory now, is calling for your death. Claims your ignorance is fueling police investigations that will expose full-bloods to the world. Of course, he did not say that to La Patron, he's saying things along those lines behind closed doors to ramp up support."

"No enterprise is more likely to succeed than one concealed from the enemy until it is ripe for execution," Chacal said earning him a frown from Angus for using another Machiavellian quote.

"Not this time, my friend. You have never met Silas, more importantly you haven't met Jasmine, his mate and Asia's patroness. The moment Jasmine heard whispers of unrest over here; the good lady put me on a plane, not to fix things. Asia and her mate are more than capable, but to act as mediator and serve a warning that no one harms one of theirs. When Jasmine says something is wrong with a picture, everyone has learned to take another look. It's uncanny how she's able to see things we missed."

Chacal looked at Asia and then Hawke. "Who are you today?"

She met his gaze and then looked at Angus. It was his call what to tell his friend about the chameleon.

"Who my mate is today will not solve the problem we are facing. I take exception to any threat to her life. Angus asks your questions," Hawke said dismissing their host.

Angus snorted. "Quite right, some people are too nosy for their own good."

Chacal shrugged but remained silent.

"What type of experiments were you working on when Asia entered the lab? What I should ask is why are the mongrels attacking humans? What kind of tests would make that happen?"

"Through the years, many tests took place on different, what do you call them?"

"The Alphas refuse to call them wolves and refer to them as mongrels. Another test. Over time they overlapped."

"Overlapped?" Angus asked.

"Yes. The metal in my arms was done first, separate operations of course. When I handled that, they did each leg. When I handled that they'd add or remove something else. That's overlapping."

Angus nodded. Asia appreciated the explanation because she did not know that term either.

"What do you think is causing them to attack people?" Angus asked.

Hawke shook his head. His brow creased. Asia could hear him thinking.

"I don't know. They do not know the kill chips are deactivated, maybe they are reacting to that lack of knowledge."

"Could be," Angus said sitting forward. "But I think there's more. I cannot name it, but something is not right."

"*Should we tell him about the black wolf giving away pups?"*

"Do you think it's related?"

"I freed test wolves from a life of slavery beneath the blade and I'm the bad guy. Yes, I think everything is related. No one seems to care about the test wolves. They went missing for years and now that they're free, all the Alphas can do is call them insulting names... after the hell they went through in Boris' castle?"

"I'm sorry."

She sighed. "*Hawke you can't become embarrassed or offended when I or anyone talk about what happened in that place. I saw how hard your wolf fought for freedom. You are a victim like everyone else. Lord Boris and those assholes stole your youth and Goddess given talent for their foul purposes. They stole mine too. That is the past. Focus on the present. How do we stop this?"*

Seconds passed before Hawke responded. Even though Asia suspected what happened to him was an important piece of this puzzle, he needed to be okay with sharing his personal information.

"*Tell him.*"

"*Okay, but Chacal will hear as well. I can't link with Angus.*"

"*Good. I like that you link to me and your Mistress. I don't care if Chacal hears, he may be able to shed light on things.*"

"I may have something," Asia said into the silence and took the next few minutes telling them what she saw in Hawke's memories. When Chacal and Angus looked at each other instead of saying what she saw was impossible, or pointing out how disgusting Hawke's former pack behaved, she knew the shit happening was deep.

"What is going on Angus?" Her tone made it clear she did not appreciate being left out of the loop.

"There have been rumors dealing with this issue for a long time now. I have had my suspicions but never... this is disturbing on many levels." Angus looked at Hawke. "Do you know the name of your clan? I mean within the Black Wolf Clan."

"No. I have not been able to access my memories yet."

Angus leaned forward. "I have never mated and could not shed light on the problem you were having regarding his chip. Is this another side-effect to mating? The ability to break through your mate's barriers even when the mate cannot?"

"I think so." Hawke said. "That is not something I know much about either. We intend to study the phenomena later. Back to the problem of those wishing to harm my mate. Does any of the information she just gave help?"

"Not sure yet. I need to think through some things. It's possible it's all connected since it's been going on for so long." Angus looked at Asia. "Remember I mentioned this may be the next assignment the Goddess has for you?"

She nodded, recalling the conversation at the air pad before he returned to the States leaving her to rescue Gunnolf.

"If what I think is happening, then this is your next assignment. You won't be able to leave until balance is restored."

He shook his head and looked at Chacal. "You hit this one on the head."

Chacal's brow rose. "Men are so simple and so much inclined to obey immediate needs that a deceiver will never lack victims for his deceptions."

"What is this? Machiavelli day?" Asia snapped and glared at Angus. "Explain. And no more damn quotes."

Angus met her gaze and then looked at Hawke. She wasn't sure what he saw but it must have been okay because there was a subtle shift of energy in the room.

"I left the Black Wolf clan, joined La Patron because the current Alpha and I disagreed on certain fundamental things. But before that, I noted several inconsistencies amongst the Black Clans."

"Like?"

"Like our bitches have always been fertile and produced healthy litters, but our pack numbers dwindled. That did not make sense. So I asked questions and was assured everything was fine –"

"Or you were sent on an assignment for a significant length of time. Do not forget that," Chacal said.

"Yes, that is true. I... had forgotten."

The look Chacal sent Angus called him a liar, but neither argued the point. For a brief second Asia wondered what happened during those side missions.

"To hear black pups are being sold or given away, explains a part of the mystery. The larger mystery remains to be answered. Why? What would make an Alpha betray pack to the point of extinction? There is no explanation for that. It simply does not make rationale sense. And is the reason no one has moved against the leaders." "Leaders?" Asia hadn't heard there were leaders.

"Yes. The Black Clan is the oldest recorded pack. We have a separate Council who meet from time to time. From what I understand they are not as involved now as before. They are the keepers of history and are tasked with maintaining records so that the mistakes of the past are not repeated. Therein lays the dilemma. There is no reason for the Council to be involved in this."

"Why does it need to make sense?" She looked at Chacal who she now suspected was someone else from a previous life. "A wise man once said, men rise from one ambition to another: first, they seek to secure themselves against attack, and then they attack others." Chacal's eyes glowed for a second before nodding at her.

"Chances are the beginning started noble, for the good of all, and over time deteriorated into whatever it is now. I bet whoever agreed to this in the beginning never thought things would turn out this way," Asia said thinking of Gunnolf.

Angus rubbed his chin and then spoke. "A good point. But to stop whoever is behind this we need to strike at the heart of motive. Otherwise the problem will mushroom like a hydra with many heads."

"Do I need to reverse the kill chips? Push the red button to shut the test wolves down. Will that fix the problem?" Hawke asked in a neutral tone.

"*Hawke no.*" Asia knew the cost to his soul for the blood he already spilled. To do that may break him.

"*If this saves you, I will destroy each one all without a second thought.*"

"*We'll find another way. I promise you.*"

"That's an idea," Angus said.

Asia frowned. "How does multiple sightings of humans dropping dead solve this problem?"

"Hawke can stagger the drops, kill some every few hours. No need to push the button all at one time," Angus said.

"What if they aren't all involved, and it's just a few. Hawke said there were different tests. Maybe some tests affected these... test wolves who are attacking and not the others."

"Hawke doesn't know which tests –"

"It is in the files. If I knew the names of the guilty wolves, I can cross reference to see which tests the wolves had in common," Hawke said, looking down at Asia.

"Then you can find any others in those groups," she said, pleased they had found a way to avoid useless bloodshed.

"And then what?" Angus asked.

"Eliminate them," Hawke said before she spoke.

"Or we could track them to make sure they are out of control before pushing the button," she added. All three men looked at her as if she had spoken a foreign language.

"That's a good idea," Hawke said squeezing her hand and then looking at Chacal. "May I use your computer? I would like to get started on this."

"Wait." Angus raised his hand. "Alpha Fredrick scheduled a meeting in an hour and a half, we must leave soon." He looked at Asia. "You cannot look like that. The bounty on your head increased to eight million. Dress as the one from the Lyrill mission. We may need to kill that face soon, it depends on this meeting."

Asia nodded. "What is your plan for meeting with Frederick?"

"He asked for a meeting once I arrived. Officially, I am here as Patron's Ambassador."

"What's the real game plan?" she asked. Angus did not need to come across the world to defend her, everyone knew she could morph into another person and leave the country at any time. What was so important to bring Angus here?

"Silas is concerned about Black Clan pups disappearing. With the Liege opening labs in the United States, and a limited supply of Black Wolves, he wants to know everything about this plan. More importantly, he wants the operation shut down."

Asia's head reeled at the implication. Jasmine gave birth to a litter of black pups for La Patron. Asia had worked security detail and spent time with little David, Renee, Jackie, and Adam. The idea that the filth of the Liege would touch those pups fueled her with blinding rage. Asia would gut them first. Hawke squeezed her hand.

"Asia?"

Lost in the grip of indignation, she couldn't speak or think past the killing frenzy in her mind. A curtain pulled to the side, and she saw it clearly. The Liege connected with the human breeders early on and used their pups as test wolves. At some point they realized black wolves were better test subjects. Angus said someone had been seeking answers on her but what if they truly wanted answers on Black wolves and concocted a plan to use them. They had taken Hawke decades ago.

"Hawke, when did they operate on you?" She looked at him. "Your arms, and legs."

"After your operation was a success."

She nodded. "So I was the guinea pig, and they tried to repeat the experiments in your lab?"

He nodded. "Yes. That was the reason they modernized and refitted it. I read all the reports of your surgeries. Lord Boris and the others wanted to find more like you. But you are unique; there is no one else even close."

Asia heard his sincerity, and it warmed her. "The Liege has been doing all of this for centuries. Operating on wolves, testing new technology, trying to improve nature. Why?" she looked at Angus and then Chacal. "Why are they still doing this? Why haven't they been stopped? Just as you noticed the discrepancy, others had to notice as well. Especially the bitches who birthed them. Who in the wolf nation is benefitting from their research?"

She looked at each man with growing certainty. "I have pledged my life and service to Jasmine Knight, La Patroness to Silas Knight and their four pups. I will know the answers to those questions and stop any threat to my pack."

Hawke lifted her hand and kissed the back. "I pledge to undergird, and support your pledge with my life." They stared into each other's eyes for a few moments until Asia nodded.

Armed with purpose, she stood. "I'm not in agreement with blind killing of wolves, no matter what the Alphas call them. The test wolves are victims and deserve pack support, not death. Hawke will research and cross reference the test wolves. Whoever still lives we will seek out and make a decision at that time." She met Angus' gaze.

He wasn't happy but if it were him or someone he cared for, he would appreciate justice in any form.

Angus nodded. "Alright, we have a short window of time and need to prepare for the meeting with Frederick. Silas has made his position clear, there is to be no attacking you. He said that three times in front of Jasmine to keep her calm." Angus shook his head. "I hope that continues to work."

Asia nodded. "I will talk to her now that I have a better understanding of my mission."

"That would help. The way her mind works... she sees to the heart of the matter and will be an asset as we go forward," Angus said.

"We?" That surprised her. She assumed he'd be leaving after meeting with the Alphas.

Angus met her gaze. "Yes, we. You didn't think you'd get to have all the fun by yourself, did you?" He smiled. "Leon and Brix wanted to come, but Silas did not want what he's doing to seem obvious. Don't be surprised if they show up sooner than later."

She smiled thinking of the newly mated pair. "I won't." Asia looked at Hawke and then Chacal who sat quiet during their conversation. She didn't know anything about him and would trust Angus' judgment that he was an ally in the matter. "May we use your computer?" Hawke had asked but Angus interrupted before Chacal responded.

"Yes, whenever you would like. I have already changed the passcodes to allow you to enter at will. Angus has asked to use my home as a point of operations and I have agreed. There is food in the dining area if you wish to eat before you depart."

Relieved that they had the resources they needed, Asia nodded. "Thank you."

Chacal waved his hand but didn't speak.

She and Hawke stood and left to eat. Their mating robbed them of calories and left them on empty. Once they cleared the room,

Hawke pulled her close.

"*Are you okay knowing I used the research from your operations?*"

Asia thought about it for a moment, checked her emotions and nodded. "*I think so. Right now, I don't have feelings one way or another.*

You knew who I was from the beginning?"

He released her and they continued walking. "*After you told me your name, I watched you and figured things out. Yes, close to the beginning.*" He looked down at her and grinned.

"*Why didn't you say something?*"

He frowned. "*Like what?*"

"*I didn't want you to know all the awful things I've done or my limited memories. Who wants a person with no past? I thought it was unfair to mate with you and not tell you. I thought you would be angry, feel slighted."* Asia stopped at the table, picked up a turkey leg and bit into the succulent meat. "*You could have saved me from going through all that.*"

Hawke bit into his meat and looked at her. She met his gaze, saw the hint of laughter in his eyes and relaxed.

"*I suppose I should apologize, but I'm feeling too good about what you just said to do that. You mated with me because you wanted me. That's music to my ears and food for my ego. I want you, Asia. All of you. We will discover your past and mine, together."* He took her other hand and placed a kiss in the middle of her palm.

"*Together,*" He emphasized.

She nodded. "*Together.*"

Chapter 25

The old building where they held the meeting with Alpha Frederick was situated in a warehouse district. Asia wore the face of the male the European pack recognized. Upon entering, she scanned the area; there were twenty full-bloods in the building. She glanced at Angus. His brow rose as they waited for the Alpha to appear.

Hawke stood on her left. To save time and get ahead of the situation she had suggested he stay behind to work on the files. His lack of verbal response, coupled with the disbelieving look on his face spoke volumes. In hindsight, she would not have stayed behind either. Together, he had said, and that's how they would handle things from here out.

"*There are too may full-bloods here for a peaceful meeting. If they attack, we destroy them. No teasing, no feeling bad, no prisoners. I do not know your Patron, but if we are attacked it must be done in such a way this Alpha cannot retaliate. We will set the precedent now that your Alpha is not to be trifled with; Machiavelli is right in that regard.*"

"*Okay. I counted twenty inside the building. Not sure how many outside. Any hybrids?*"

"*No. Not yet. Do you suspect this Alpha works with the Liege?*"

"*I don't know. I want to be prepared.*"

"Well, *I think this Alpha brings a show of force for his pack. As long as they do not attack, allow him his bluster.*"

"*Hawke, I cannot allow him to disrespect my Alpha or my Mistress.*"

"*Yes, understood. What I suggest is this, leave Angus to speak on behalf of your Alpha. The reason for the meeting is to deal with a complaint, which makes this a tense situation. He is Alpha as well and must appear as a strong leader to his pack. It is a fine line he dances; allow his bluster to pass as long as he makes no moves to attack. He will be a better ally in the future than if we shame him by destroying his pack members.*"

Asia thought on his words and agreed. "*That makes sense. I must remember there are other Alphas and treat them with respect.*"

Alpha Frederick walked in, Tobias stood behind him. The beta nodded, and she returned the gesture.

"Greetings Angus Black Wolf," Alpha Frederick said moving forward to shake hands. "It is good to see you. I appreciate your return to deal with this problem." The Alpha removed his sunglasses and glanced at Asia. His dark gray gaze flickered over Hawke but he did not address either of them. The alpha was impeccably dressed, suit, shirt, tie, shoes and leather overcoat, all in custom-fitted black fabrics to fit his large bulk. His dark brown hair brushed against his collar.

"We arrived on time and would like to get started," Angus said.

Alpha Frederick stared at him for a moment and then nodded. "Yes, my apologies for being late. Two Alphas wanted to attend and security took longer clearing them. I hope their attending will not create a problem."

"They are here?" Angus asked.

"Yes."

"Then why ask if their presence creates a problem? I am here in good faith on behalf of my Alpha as you requested. We must start the meeting soon or reschedule."

Asia applauded Angus' handling of the Alpha. The man had been late and rude and Angus called him on it.

"Yes, we shall." Alpha Frederick turned and walked to one of the chairs placed in a clearing. There were two other empty ones.

"*I do not like this,*" Hawke said in a dark tone. "*They think we are weak and defenseless. I will show them differently.*"

"*Wait. Diplomacy, remember? I want to see who sits in those other two chairs,*" Asia said.

Angus looked at his watch. "Alpha Frederick you have two minutes to begin or we leave." His comment charged the atmosphere.

"*When Angus turns to leave, shift then,*" Asia added after Angus threw down the gauntlet.

She glanced at Angus, he continued to look at his watch but she knew he was aware of the movement in the room. A second later they were enclosed in a sheer bubble. La Patron had used this when they were under attack in Lyrill; it helped them escape without losses.

"*What is this?*" Hawke asked. Asia explained and heard his gasp of surprise.

"*Can we be heard outside the bubble?*"

"*I don't know,*" she said. "Angus?"

"Yes? And La Patron did not provide the bubble, I did. He taught me how." Angus continued watching his watch.

"That's great, can they hear us?"

"No."

"What's the plan?" Asia asked.

"If they do not start in thirty seconds, we leave."

"Do we destroy them?" Hawke asked.

"Only if they try to prevent us from leaving. More full-bloods just arrived, should be interesting," Angus said.

"I will shift to hybrid and lead the way," Hawke said.

"They may have darts," Asia said. "That's what I would use to capture us," she said when both men glared down at her.

"As much as I hate to admit it, you may be right. Stay in the bubble. Chacal is waiting to pick us up when we are done."

"Can Chacal be trusted?" Asia asked wondering why Chacal remained outside the lines of conflict.

"He has been involved with many governments over his lifetime, and has been on the losing side often. Now he chooses to remain neutral. He will not fight, or get directly involved. Trusted? We have been friends for centuries. I understand him and never ask for what he cannot give. Within those parameters, yes, Chacal is trustworthy."

Just as Angus turned to leave, Alpha Frederick spoke. "One of your pack members released mongrels from a secure location into the public where they have attacked humans violating the most important rule of secrecy. Human authorities are looking into the matter and each day becomes harder to keep our presence quiet."

Asia noticed two men sat in the other chairs. "*Do you know any of those men?*"

"On the right, the bald one is Alpha Verrick of the Southern Ukraine. I do not know the other," Hawke said.

Verrick's height and breadth mimicked Hawke's and she wondered if he had been altered as her mate had.

"How do you respond?" Alpha Frederick asked.

Angus crossed his arms. "Respond? My pack member discovered the enslavement of full-bloods, something no wolf should ever experience. You call them mongrels now, but they were not mongrels when they were captured and enslaved. These men and women were full-bloods then and are full-bloods now, worthy of respect for surviving their time in captivity. Yet you continue to persecute your own. A secure location, does that mean you knew of this group who stole full-bloods and ran tests on them? Alphas in this country allow this?" Angus looked around the room at the wolves.

"I am Alpha Verrick of South Ukraine. You change question to hide pack member's crime. He released wolves without place for them. Irresponsible act caused this problem."

"So he should have left the full-bloods in cages?" The man's face reddened as his jaw clenched.

Angus turned toward Alpha Frederick. "What La Patron is trying to understand is this. Are you upset because a member from his pack rescued full-bloods which should have been done years ago? Or is this a common practice, allowing full-bloods to be abused as guinea pigs? That notion is alien to him and as such, he approved the release of full-bloods when he saw their condition."

Alpha Verrick scoffed. "He saw their condition? How?"

"The same as he is watching this proceeding, through my eyes, and the eyes of his pack." Angus pointed in her direction. No one spoke after that declaration.

"Greetings, I am Alpha Andrei." He executed a graceful bow. "My territory is Bucharest and Southern Romania. I assure you, no Alpha approves the abuse of any innocent wolf. The situation at the castle has recently reached my ears and I agree no full-blood should be imprisoned for experiments."

Asia applauded the man's reasonable approach.

"Two problems. How to stop humans from discovering our existence and how we stop... test wolves from attacking humans," he said.

"Destroy them," Alpha Verrick said.

"Why are you so quick to destroy a group of full-bloods without full knowledge of the situation," Angus said in a dangerous tone.

"I saw tape of mongrel chasing small girl. No one lives after that," Alpha Verrick leaned forward, his bald plate glistened beneath the lights.

"Yes, I agree. But does that mean all those full-bloods should die because of a few?" Angus looked around the room. "Does it?"

Asia sensed the tide turned again in the crowded space. Angus' constant use of the term, full-blood worked like magic. None of these men wanted an Alpha challenge because they did not protect pack. Asia hoped Angus sealed the deal without anyone discovering her mate's address for the past three decades.

"No. We cannot assume all mongrels are bad," Alpha Verrick said his tone heavy. "How do we stop this? This must stop."

Angus nodded. "I agree. La Patron has agreed to locate the test wolves, if they are out of control, they will be destroyed. If not, they will be left in peace."

"I do not like others killing in my territory. You find, I decide," Alpha Verrick said.

"No. That is unacceptable." Angus did not explain further.

"I should allow this? Why?"

"It solves the problem. But La Patron will do it his way or not at all. You choose. The clock is ticking." Angus looked at his watch and then at the three men.

Asia bit the inside of her jaw to keep from smiling. The other two Alphas appeared relieved to have the situation handled and out of their hands. Verrick would be voted down.

"Patron started the problem, he should fix," Alpha Verrick said before the other Alphas spoke.

"I agree and accept La Patron's offer. I pledge to be more vigilant of my borders so that this evil thing never happens again. If any test wolves wish to move to my territory, I will accept them. They will find a haven in Bucharest." Alpha Andrei leaned back in his chair and looked at the full-bloods crowding the room.

Alpha Verrick snarled but remained silent.

"It is settled then. Please thank La Patron on our behalf, and if we can offer assistance let us know. Many of the test wolves have been resettled. Angus made a good point, not all are bad. Those unaffected should be allowed to live. My area is open to them as well," Alpha Frederick said standing.

"The charges against my pack member must be dropped," Angus said.

Alpha Frederick looked at the other two Alphas and then at Angus. "The charges are dropped."

Chapter 26

Clap. Clap. Clap. The sound bounced around the room. Hawke looked around the building to locate the noise even though he recognized the scent. Greggor. Did the man have a death wish?

"Well done, you have pardoned the person responsible for breaking and entering as well as theft," Greggor said walking further into the clearing. Two large hybrids stood behind him.

"You accuse my uncle of enslaving wolves but he has not been to the castle in over a decade. Who enslaved the full-bloods?" He looked around at his audience. As performances went his was not bad.

"*Be calm, Hawke. Let Angus handle this. La Patron is furious and may blow the room,*" Asia warned.

"*Blow the room?*"

"*Wait.*"

"The man standing with Patron's Ambassador, Hawke has been the lead researcher at the castle for the past thirty years." The mood shifted in the room as everyone stared at Hawke.

"I have watched him with my own eyes do the things Patron claims to despise and –"

"Silence," Angus roared. The room expanded and then righted as Silas released a wave of energy. The Alphas hung onto their chairs and the full-bloods looked at each other in shock.

Hawke stared at Asia.

She shrugged. "*I told you.*"

Angus walked toward Greggor, she and Hawke followed and stood at an angle to watch the crowd.

"Why is a human here? Who allowed him into this room?" Angus looked at each Alpha, his green eyes blazed with indignation. "You complain of humans knowing of your existence and no one stopped this human when he entered?" he growled.

No one spoke.

Greggor glanced at Alpha Verrick and then at Hawke.

"He came to me to explain. I thought we should all hear," Alpha Verrick said into the silence.

Angus glared at the man. "Do you see those hybrids standing behind him? Those were full-bloods once. You allowed him to bring wolves that his uncle experimented on into a meeting to discuss the foulness of test wolves?"

Alpha Verrick's gaze swung from Angus to the hybrids and then to the Alphas staring at him. "He says the big one do tests, not his uncle."

Angus grabbed Greggor by his shirt and lifted him. The hybrids moved. Asia and Hawke stepped to the side and faced them.

"Why are you here?" Angus growled through lowered incisors.

"My uncle wanted me to tell his side," Greggor stammered looking around.

Angus looked around the room and called a wolf over. The full-blood looked toward the Alphas and then obeyed.

"Are you a full-blood?"

"Yes, Sir."

"Can you smell a lie?"

"Yes, Sir."

Angus looked at Greggor again. "Why are you here?"

Hawke smelled Greggor's fear. The man never thought beyond the moment. He had lived in his uncle's shadow for so long, the idea that someone was not afraid of Boris never occurred to him.

"My uncle wanted me to tell his side," Greggor whimpered. Angus looked at the full-blood who said. "He's lying."

"Why are you lying?" Angus asked Greggor.

When he didn't respond, Angus shook him. The hybrids started to move.

"*Wait, don't shift. Not yet,*" Asia said.

"If they move again I will rip your head off before they reach you," Angus said in a hard tone.

The hybrids stopped.

"Last time, why are you here?"

"Hawke. I'm here for Hawke."

"Why? Why do you want him?" Angus pressed.

"My uncle wants his property back..."

Hawke could not believe Greggor said that. But then again it went a long way in clearing his name.

Growls filled the room.

"If he ran the lab, why are you here?" Angus shook Greggor once more.

"Because the chip in his brain isn't working. We can't control him anymore."

The room erupted in howls and growls.

"I did not know. I swear I did not know," Alpha Verrick said shaking his head. "He come to me, ask to tell his side."

"How did you know of this meeting?" Angus asked.

Hawke stood at an angle watching the three Alphas, none of them blinked at the question. Each seemed curious for the answer.

"I was told to go to Alpha Verrick and tell him what I needed. He told me to come to the meeting."

"He lies. He asked to come to meeting. He knew when he came to me." Alpha Verrick stood and took a step forward.

Angus looked at Greggor and then Alpha Verrick. "You are right, he is lying. Which means there is someone other than his uncle he fears more than you, and more than La Patron who holds his life in his hand."

"What?" Greggor squeaked.

"You challenged my Alpha. I accepted the challenge on his behalf."

"I... I... I did not. I talked about Hawke."

"But you noted he was with a member of La Patron's pack. Any challenge to a member of the pack is a challenge to the Alpha." Angus looked at the Alphas seated. "At least that is how we operate."

Alpha Andrei cleared his throat. "We do as well. I do not know this human. I cannot believe his uncle sent such a one to represent him. He had to know what would happen when in the presence of so many wolves. I suspect there is more afoot."

"Such as?" Alpha Frederick said.

"Some sort of trickery to gain information," Alpha Andrei said standing and moving closer to Greggor. "*Trojan horse?*" Hawke said to Asia.

"*Could be. I will inform Mistress.*"

A few moments later Angus dropped Greggor and stepped back, the three of them formed a triangle inside the bubble.

"Gentlemen, I suspect Alpha Andrei may be correct. Dismiss your packs and leave this place. We have seen incidents where explosives were carefully hidden to avoid detection."

"I smell nothing," Alpha Andrei said as he moved toward the exit.

Angus walked toward the double steel doors. The hybrids remained in place. Greggor lay gasping on the floor like a fish out of water.

"Hawke! Wait. I need to talk to you." Greggor stood and walked in their direction.

"If he shoots you with another dart I swear I will kill him," Asia said as they cleared the building.

"I appreciate it. Although I think he is his own worst enemy. He had to be crazy to walk into that place."

"Or someone assured him he would be safe."

"Hawke, wait. I need to talk to you," Greggor said moving faster.

Asia stopped and turned. Hawke sensed her frustration with Greggor and decided to allow her to handle things.

"Chacal will be here in a few seconds," Angus said.

"Hawke?"

"What do you want?" Asia asked Greggor.

"I need to talk to Hawke."

"He is not returning to the castle, and he is not talking to you. Go home before I break my promise not to kill you for what you did to him."

Greggor frowned, looked at her and then Hawke. "Why would he kill me? We were friends, kind of. I never hurt him. My uncle just wants him back, that's all."

"Go home, Greggor. I'm never returning to that place and we were never friends," Hawke said over his shoulder.

Greggor's face whitened and then his eyes narrowed. "But..."

"Go. Leave, I want nothing to do with you," Hawke said hardening his tone.

"You'll regret this, Hawke. I will make sure of it." He turned and headed back inside.

He should kill Greggor and destroy the hybrids to keep them from returning. He stepped backward as Angus moved forward in the bubble. Asia grabbed his arm.

"We need to go."

"Greggor is cancer that needs to be destroyed."

She nodded. "*Yes. But not by you, not today. Today we represent La Patron, vengeance is done in his name alone.*"

Hawke had not thought along those lines and nodded. He looked over his shoulder and met Greggor's hate-filled stare.

"He had a crush on you."

"I know. How did you know?"

"Remind me to tell you how I entered the castle, it all started with Greggor."

Surprised, he slid into the back seat of the Hummer next to her.

"That sounds interesting. I can't wait to hear about it."

"What do you think, Asia?" Angus asked as the Hummer moved forward.

"These Alphas would not last a week under La Patron."

"True, they answer to no one and are constantly defending their position within the pack. It is one reason they cannot organize."

"And why they fear and hate La Patron. They do not want him to touch down on their shores," she said.

Angus shrugged. "It is the way of the world. Someone bigger comes along. Do you think one of the Alphas work with the Liege?"

"No, I did not sense deceit, did you?" She asked.

"No. If they want to survive they need to band together even if it's just to share information."

"Greggor was too confident when he walked into the room. No one questioned him, makes me think he has done that before. I found that strange," she said.

"True. Silas was furious. I thought he would kill the Alphas on the spot. Makes me wish Leon and Brix were here to challenge the bastards. They are weak and that's not good." Angus looked out the window as they drove through the countryside. "How many following?" He asked Chacal in a casual tone.

Hawke scanned the area and sensed full-bloods following the car which didn't surprise him. The Alphas were right to be nervous after that small display of power.

"Eight to ten on all fours and two cars behind the bend."

"We need to get started on tracking down the test wolves," Angus said looking over his shoulder. "I don't trust any of those Alphas to go out of their way to help them. Plus, I need to make a formal request to speak to the European Council. They may require both of you to stand before them to explain what happened."

"Angus, I am after answers of missing pups. Will speaking to the Council help me with that?" She asked as their vehicle picked up speed.

"It could. But it would be rude not to appear." He shook his head. "Not that you care about that one way or the other. We will play it by ear and make decisions as we go along. I am here to help with your mission not hinder."

"We will leave tonight to track down the nearest test wolf." She looked at Hawke. "How much time will you need to cross reference the files?"

"Ten to fifteen minutes. I need to build a mobile device to activate the kill chips."

"Why? Why not break their necks or something?" Angus asked.

"It will be harder to explain. The chip should dissolve at death and it will look like a heart attack not murder," Hawke said.

Angus nodded. "How long will that take? To build the device?"

"An hour or two, no more."

"Good," Angus said.

"We are coming to the curve of the bend, it is the only place for an ambush," Chacal said in a bland tone.

"Okay," Angus said straightening in his seat.

On both sides of the road trees crowded the land. Hawke took Asia's hand and squeezed. She turned from the window to their joined hands. A moment later she met his gaze, some of the shadows were gone but not all. It was his duty to remove each one. They swerved and missed a car in the middle of the road. The Hummer drove along the narrow shoulder bypassing the vehicle.

A hybrid ran forward and slammed into the front of the heavy vehicle. Chacal did not press the brake. He pushed the accelerator. The hybrid raised his hand revealing long claws and jammed them into the hood. They broke in half without penetrating the metal and flew off in the wind. After driving side to side the hybrid lost its fragile grip and fell onto the ground beneath the rear tire. It screamed as the heavy vehicle cracked its bones leaving it rolling on the ground.

"They never attack alone, there should be one more," Asia said just before a loud thump hit the top of the hummer. Next a series of pounding on the roof of the vehicle announced the next hybrid had joined the fray.

"Can't you get rid of him?" Angus said to Chacal. "That noise is annoying."

Chacal stepped on the brake, hard. Hawke and Asia both wore seat belts. Angus did not and went flying forward just like the hybrid. Unlike the hybrid, Chacal's arm shot out breaking Angus fall. The hybrid rolled on the ground a few feet down the road and shook his head. Chacal pressed the pedal; the Hummer shot forward and ran over the downed beast crushing its skull in the process.

"Is that good enough for you?" Chacal said, adjusting his rear-view mirror.

Angus pulled the straps for his seatbelt and snapped it. "Thanks." His tone said the opposite.

They continued toward Chacal's property with the knowledge they were still being followed. Once they crossed over the property line, they drove through the security shield and slowed the vehicle.

Chacal parked in the underground area and they went inside.

Chapter 27

Asia changed her persona to another male, neither her mate nor Angus trusted the Alphas to keep their word about the charges being dropped. Earlier, they had reached the first test wolf on their list. The poor beast had whittled down to skin and bones, his skin had a blue tinge which signified he had been a test subject for the blue bird project. That project tied all the mongrel wolves together. Nine lived.

After the wolf attempted to attack Hawke, he pressed the red button, putting it out of its misery. They buried the tormented beast quickly to avoid the full-bloods that followed them from the Alpha meeting earlier. Once they discovered the dead wolf, they would pick up Hawke's scent and be on their trail.

The next person on their list was Henri, the male of a mated pair. Asia was interested to see if the mating bond diminished the effects of the test experiments. If so they could cross four others from their list and make it back in time to Chacal's to meet with the Council.

Angus informed her that two of the members wished to meet her and Silas wanted her to attend the meeting.

They crept closer to the small wooden hut, deep in the forest not far from Lord Boris' castle. When Asia and Hawke noticed the location on the electronic map, they were surprised. Why hadn't the test wolves moved on? At least headed further in the opposite direction? The hand-held device Hawke created blinked and showed movement. They knew she and Hawke were there and were on their way to meet them.

"You," the woman hissed at Hawke. Asia recognized Alise as the same woman who attacked Hawke after their release. She stepped in front of Hawke.

"Yes. But I don't have time to change your mind about anything, we have a few questions and then we'll be on our way."

"Who the hell are you?" the woman snapped, looking at her and halting mid-step.

"I was sent by my Alpha to help Hawke. A lot of the test wolves were infected and are attacking humans. We zeroed it down to those exposed to a specific test. Your mate is infected. Where is he?"

The woman's eyes widened and then narrowed. "I do not know. He left and I have not seen him."

"I'm a wolf, bitch. I can smell your lie. Either he comes out here and talks to us or he dies. Your choice." Asia crossed her arms and waited. She scented the woman's fear, but they didn't have time to play nice.

Hawke was too damn close to the castle for her peace of mind.

"He's not well. He cannot come outside."

Asia exhaled. "You are his mate, you can speak to his body, demand the poison to leave."

The woman's eyes lit with hope. "Truly? Been so long since we used mating benefits for anything other than remaining sane or stopping pain, I have forgotten much." She stared at Asia and then closed her eyes. The three of them remained frozen in position far longer than Asia wanted, but one look at Hawke's determined gaze to right a wrong kept her silent.

The female opened her eyes on a gasp and smiled. She turned and looked toward the hut. The door opened slowly and the male who had cursed Hawke stepped out the shack.

His movements gained strength with each step he took. By the time he reached them, he stood upright and wore a small smile. He grabbed his mate and kissed her hard.

Hawke nodded, and they turned to leave.

"Wait," the man called. "Thank you. We will be leaving this place now that I can protect my mate. There are bad things happening in the woods. Be careful."

That piqued Asia's interest. She turned. "What kind of things?"

He looked at his mate and then Hawke. "People are still disappearing. You're not in the lab anymore and somebody's still taking full-bloods. My mate overheard some people talking about it in town the other day. We're leaving, heading south as soon as I'm at full strength, heard there's an Alpha down there accepting new members."

Asia wondered if he referred to Andrei but didn't ask. They needed to keep moving, and she knew which town the female visited. "Thank you, we will be careful. My advice to you is to leave now. Take whatever you have and go. The Alpha of this area may change his mind about allowing you to live."

The female's eyes widened, and she ran to the hut. The man nodded and followed at a slower pace. Before he reached the door, the female was out the door carrying a bundle. Asia looked over her shoulder at them one last time before she and Hawke took off running to the next wolf on their list.

Chapter 28

Greggor paced back and forth in front of the monitor, waiting. Hawke rejected him. He couldn't believe it, but he had no choice. Everyone heard him. How could he have been so wrong? They had spent hundreds of evening discussing new research, and possible implementations.

He had listened to Hawke rave over that bitch's surgeries and the new technology to the point he had wanted to scream. But he hadn't. Because friends listened even when they didn't give a damn.

He ground his teeth in aggravation.

All those years thinking there was something... how could he have gotten it all wrong? He shook his head as water filled his eyes when he remembered the look in Hawke's eyes yesterday. Hatred, anger, even pity he could deal with, but indifference? That ripped his heart out and left it pumping on the ground. Indifference left him with nothing to build on, or tear down. Nothing he could do mattered.

Heart sore he sat in the chair and placed his head on the desk. What could he do now? For years his days revolved around watching Hawke work and visiting him in the lab. All of his fantasies were of the large, handsome full-blood. Many of his dreams centered around Hawke returning his affections and them living happy together in the castle.

"What are you doing?" His uncle said.

Greggor didn't bother to respond. It didn't matter anyway, he had failed... again. His uncle would punish him... again. It was a never-ending cycle, a horrible way to live but it was all he had.

"I asked you a question," the older man snapped.

"I'm sitting down." He couldn't drum up the energy to be afraid or respectful.

"I see that, what I want to know is why?"

Greggor sat back in the chair and assumed the position. He closed his eyes to hide his pain while waiting for the metal cuffs to strap him in.

"Something is different, what happened?"

"I went to the meeting as you required, said what you told me to say and ..."

"And?"

"He left with the team from La Patron as you suspected. I couldn't get close enough to Hawke to complete a scan. But there was no sign of his chip being active."

"They have discovered a way to deactivate the computer chips. How did he seem to you? Alert? Sluggish? Any overt affects from the removal of the chip?"

Greggor snorted. "He was very alert. Too damn alert."

"Did I miss something?"

Greggor looked at the monitor for the first time and met his uncle's gaze. "Hawke refused to return. I sent the two hybrids after him. One is completely destroyed the other has a crushed leg and is out of commission. I failed. Completely. Utterly. I'm a failure."

After a long silence his uncle spoke. "He played with your affections and left you behind, is that why you are upset?"

Greggor's gaze slid to the side of the monitor. "What do you mean? We...uh, we never did anything."

"That makes it worse, doesn't it?"

Greggor closed his eyes and leaned back against the chair.

"You think he didn't know how you felt about him?"

Greggor's eyes snapped open. "I never said... never mentioned anything."

His uncle waved his hand, cutting him off. "You may not have said anything verbally, but he knew just like I knew. Like everyone knew the two of you had something special."

Frowning, Greggor sat forward. "Special?" Hope rekindled in his heart.

"Yes. Everybody thought the two of you were a couple. In fact, I'm sure Hawke mentioned you to me a few times over the years."

Greggor gasped. "He did? When? What did he say?"

The older man shrugged. "I cannot remember such inconsequential things. But it did make me think your feelings for him were being returned."

"Really?" Greggor frowned trying to pinpoint when that may have happened. "He never seemed interested. Never spoke of anything other than work."

Boris ground his teeth in frustration. The incompetent sod could not be of his blood. He refused to believe anyone could be so stupid.

"Well if that's the way you remember it, okay. Why are you so down?"

Boris tapped his fingers against the metal collar and glanced at the pitiful boy through the monitor. Hawke had never been interested in anyone other than his thirst for knowledge. That gleam in his eyes had sparked Boris' initial interest. Even without the computer chip, Hawke's mental perception had been off the charts, the full-blood was indeed a genius.

His nephew never realized Hawke cared only for knowledge, and as long as the crush did not interfere with Hawke's production, Boris didn't care. Now he needed to re-channel that dismal emotion into something useful.

"Pity he used you that way. Got your hopes up, had all of us believing the two of you had a future." He waited for the boy to leave reality behind and step into the land of fantasy.

"You thought we had a future?"

"Of course, that's why I allowed you to spend so much time with him. I just assumed... well you know."

"If we did, it's over now. He doesn't want anything to do with me anymore."

"That pisses me off that he would treat you that way. It's not right. He should have broken things off first, given you an explanation. That's the least he could have done after all the years the two of you spent together."

Greggor straightened and stared. Boris could see the tiny wheels turning. It wouldn't be long now. He picked up the shiny collar fresh from the factory and smiled.

"You're right uncle. He should've done that. He dismissed me without a backward glance. As if I were nothing, not even an ant."

"How did you feel when he did that?"

"I hated him. In that moment I hated him and wanted to hurt him." Greggor's voice had risen to an irritating high pitch but the emotion was what Boris needed to see. It would not matter if the boy changed his mind later, the neck band would not allow the mission to change.

"I sent you a box, do you have it?" Boris saw the box sitting on the desk but preferred to have Greggor engaged in each part of the set-up.

"Yes, it's here." Greggor picked it up and returned it to the desk.

"Open it." He waited until the box was opened and then booted up the program to activate the neck band.

Greggor frowned. "A necklace?"

"Neck band. Rub your fingertips up and down the metal." Boris waited until the neck band came online and received Greggor's fingerprints. When the last print was stored into the database, Boris unlocked the device.

Greggor looked at him and then at the neckband. Boris remained silent and waited for the boy's curiosity to kick in.

"What does this do?"

"It will give you the strength and cunning you need to make Hawke talk to you, and maybe apologize. That way you can break it off and have closure." He shook his head at the gullibility of the boy who snapped the neck brace on without asking any other questions.

"That is what you want, right? To make Hawke pay for the way he treated you?" He typed in a few keys.

Greggor's eyes went from sad and pathetic to angry hunter. "Yes. He needs to pay for that."

Boris clicked a few more keys. "What if he won't talk to you? What will you do?"

"I will hunt him down and make him talk. He won't have a choice."

Boris nodded and added the final keystrokes.

"You may have to hurt him, can you do that?"

Greggor's eyes bulged and darkened. "I will kill him if he resists. He will never treat anyone else the same as he treated me."

Boris sat back in his chair with his hands clasped across his stomach. "Finally I have emotions from you I can use." He pressed the final button to begin the change in Greggor's mind and body. "Welcome to the Liege."

Chapter 29

The sliver of moon crested the mountain providing minimal light in the inky black night. After three days, Hawke and Asia completed the first part of their mission. According to a message they received from Angus, there had been no recent killings, this part of the problem was solved.

Bone weary, they decided to stop at the next hotel, sleep and start fresh in the morning. The vehicle Chacal loaned them had been a godsend but her eyes blurred and she had zig-zagged across the road too many times.

"There should be a hotel ten miles up the road," Hawke said yawning. The last test wolf didn't fight, he ran into a crowd of people. It took two hours of following the wily beast before he wandered into a place where few would notice him falling to the ground. After Hawke pushed the red button, the wolf screamed drawing attention as he dropped dead. Instead of burying him as they did the other six, they left him for the authorities.

Tomorrow afternoon they were scheduled to meet with the council. Asia wasn't sure why, but La Patron required she attend, and she would.

"I see a light ahead." Hawke pointed.

"I wonder if our tail will spend the night or go ahead." She glanced at him. The past few days they had been shadowed by no less than four full-bloods. They never approached but she sensed them every time they searched out a test wolf.

"Probably. Wouldn't be surprised if they took a rest as well, they've got to be just as tired."

She turned into the well-lit parking lot, pleased there were not a lot of cars and popped their trunk. Hawke stepped out, grabbed their bags and met her in the front of the car. She locked the car with the remote and they entered the lobby together. When they reached the counter, it was empty. "No one's here?" She looked at Hawke who looked around the large space.

"No. Let's go."

She frowned at how quick he wanted to leave. It might be a while before they found the next hotel. "Go? You don't want to look around, ring a bell for service?"

"Scan."

She scanned the area and sensed movement in the direction of the hotel. It wouldn't be empty for long. She shook her head and met his gaze. "Can't we have one night in peace? I just want a shower and you."

His eyes glowed. "Then that is what you will have. Let's go."

They turned to leave and three men, full-bloods, walked in. Asia recognized their scents. These were the men who had been trailing them. They looked familiar but she wasn't sure. Hawke stepped in front of them, pushing them backward so she could walk behind him to the door.

"One moment, please."

Hawke looked over his shoulder at the man behind the front desk. "You wanted a room?"

"Not anymore." When he finished speaking men and women walked through the front and side doors, pushing them back.

"Come with us please." One of the men who had been following them said.

"No." Hawke did not explain and neither did she. Instead she stood behind him prepared to fight from the rear.

"We simply want to talk," he said looking around the room at the growing crowd.

"Talk but make it quick as you know we have had a long day," Hawke said.

"We must wait, just a few moments, please have a seat." He pointed to a chair in the middle of the room.

"No." Hawke said and Asia knew he grew tired of the delay.

"Why do you need to wait?" she asked.

The male looked at her and then at Hawke. He didn't immediately answer. That was a big mistake. Hawke bulked to his hybrid, and picked the male up by the neck. There were several growls in the room but no one moved to intervene.

"Answer the question," Hawke growled.

"They waited for me. My apologies for being late," a newcomer said walking into the well-lit part of the room.

"Please, put him down. There has been enough violence already against our people, don't you agree?"

Hawke stared at the man for a few seconds and released the male before returning to his normal size. "What do you want to talk about?"

She sensed Hawke's wariness and looked closer at the small male. He was full-blood, but the creases in his skin and thin hair, she would guess him older than Angus and La Patron's three hundred years. Was he another Alpha? Had they trespassed?

"Are you here to help? Friend of the wolf or enemy or neutral like Chacal?"

"Help? Help with what?" Hawke asked.

"Our people are disappearing. La Patron is aware and that is why he sent Angus Black Wolf. But we do not know where he stands on the issue. We have followed you since the meeting with the three stooges and have seen how you treated each wolf. You gave each an opportunity to prove they would not be a threat to us all. You took time to help those you could and terminated those you could not with humble dignity. That is rare."

Asia thought the image of the three stooges appropriate and funny, but remained alert and quiet.

"They were victims, none of them deserved to die for something beyond their control but they could not control the need to destroy." Hawke shrugged and she knew what it cost him to appear as if it didn't matter. It did. He did what was necessary but she felt his pain each time he pushed that button.

"True. My questions have gone unanswered with the council. I have been shunned and labeled a trouble maker. The Alphas you met with yesterday hide behind their titles and do nothing as their pack shrinks. They challenge any wolf who questions them or points out the truth. I am surprised they were so... malleable at the meeting. But then I am told your Alpha is not one to be trifled with. So again I ask, are you here to help?"

"You are?" Hawke asked.

"Radoff, Alpha of the Red Clan. You are north of my lands."

"I am Hawke, this is Orion." He pointed at her using the name they'd given her new persona. "We are tasked to hunt down the test wolves and settle the matter. I don't know what La

Patron's plans are or how long we will be here. We are not the enemy of the wolf, we are full-blood. But I cannot say if we are here to help because I don't know what is required."

Radoff stared at Hawke for a few moments and then looked at Asia. She met his gaze for a few moments and then looked at the men standing behind him. Two had been at the Alpha meeting. Had Radoff been there?

After a lengthy silence, Radoff spoke. "You are entitled to your secrets, of which there are many. But what happens to our people affects you. You will not be able to avoid becoming involved. That time is coming sooner than you think and I am glad. We have waited a long time, and suffered many losses over this matter. It is more than you think and goes deeper than you know. It brushes against the fabric of who we are as a people. Certain things, natural orders, should never be toyed with."

Chill bumps rose across her arms as he spoke. His words reminded her of La Patron and his battle in the states. Within the past few years he discovered human females bred half-breeds for full-bloods and it rocked their nation. In certain areas, half-breeds still had it rough even though La Patron's pups were all half-breeds. He had made a comment similar to Radoff about someone messing with the natural order of things.

"I agree," Hawke said.

Radoff nodded and stood. "When you are ready to learn more, return here. This is neutral grounds run by members of my pack. I would caution you to be careful. Your Alpha is powerful; there is no question about that. But no one is infallible, and there are those who would take what is his by any means possible. Tread carefully and keep your Council to a few."

Hawke nodded. "Thank you, that's good advice." He looked around the room at the crowd. "Have you lost members of your pack?"

Radoff stared at him for a moment and Asia would swear his eyes blazed gold for a second before settling. "Yes. Yes we have." He turned and left the lobby. Within seconds the lobby cleared leaving them and the male behind the desk who waited for their decision.

Asia looked at Hawke, leaving it up to him.

"Thoughts?" He gave her his back while looking around the room.

"He is old. The first mated pair said something similar a couple of days past. We may need to talk to him and I am tired."

He glanced at her and walked to the front desk. She sat in a nearby chair and waited. Why couldn't this be easy? Just point out the bad guy for her to fight or destroy, and it would be over. A nice clean-cut solution. Not something deep and mysterious. She stretched and looked over her shoulder at Hawke. He met her gaze and smiled.

A shower, her mate and sleep, in that order. He held up their bags and the room card. Standing, she followed him to the stairs and ignored the smirk from the front desk.

Chapter 30

Angus stood alone in the forest gathering his thoughts and reconnecting with the land. The trees and deep trenches in the ground bore witness to Asia and Hawke's fight against the bluebirds.

He surveyed the damage. It looked like a hurricane swept through the area and tore it apart. Uprooted trees, deep furrows in the ground, branches split apart... the Liege had a new weapon and based on the video Chacal sent, if this one was ever perfected they would have a real fight on their hands.

The animals were so fast they did not show up on scans. He chuckled. But Hawke said he knew they were coming, a serious flaw in the design. Angus glanced at his watch. Asia and her mate should return in the next hour. She had sent a message when they left the hotel a couple of hours past.

He inhaled.

The lush forest called to his beast. America was good. Silas was all he could hope for in a litter mate. But his heart... his heart was to the south, on the Continent. He had not realized how much he missed the open spaces and freedom. There were hundreds of places humans had not explored where a wolf could roam and be one with nature.

When the need arose for Asia to seek shelter, he contacted an old friend, Chacal. That first conversation led to many. When Jasmine told him to come assist Asia, his bags had been packed, his plans had been made. His pack was in trouble, unlike Chacal, he could not remain neutral. He had to help in any way possible.

Silas understood and promised his support. The next few days would set the course of action. He hoped the European Council was ready to listen, unlike the Black Clan council who shut him down before.

At least not until he devised the chameleon bracelets. Then they wanted him to turn over the device to them, to allow them to control it. Even then, he sensed something was off and refused which shocked him more than them. After hours of lecturing him on protocol and his constant refusal to explain how the device worked or how he created it, they finally agreed to allow him to work on a plan to infiltrate their new enemies, to gain information of the threat.

But they tied his hands, refused to allow him to act against the Liege. He had been the only person who knew Brix's true identity which he believed saved the young pup's life.

Someone stole a chameleon bracelet from one of his deceased operatives and gave it to the Liege. Asia recovered the device and killed the Liege Lord in the process but the fact remained that someone committed treason and betrayed the Black Clan.

Pity he could not scan Alphas or Council members for lies. It would make this next meeting so much easier. Silas didn't trust the Council and warned him to be careful. Their link had to remain open during the meeting. Silas took it a step further and required Asia to be in the meeting as well.

Everyone knew she had the best bullshit meter and would in all likelihood call the Council members on it. Silas did not care if she broke social protocol, he expected it. He wanted to see how the Council handled conflict and if those men were relevant in the quest to discover what happened to the missing black pups.

His thoughts turned toward their meeting with the European Council again. He had been surprised they agreed to meet with him and hear his concerns so quickly. The group traveled to Odessa instead of requiring him to meet them in one of the major cities in Europe. Had things deteriorated to the point they were willing to listen to a different point of view? He hoped not. Things had been bad for a long time and the Black Clan Council had done nothing.

"Angus."

Angus stilled and turned slowly to greet his former Alpha. Chacal must have allowed the man to enter the grounds and hadn't bothered to tell him. They would discuss ground rules of good hospitality later.

He nodded. "Ulric."

The man looked as if he hadn't slept in a week. His shirt stretched tight against his chest but he lacked the width Angus remembered.

Ulric's jaw ticked at the lack of proper greeting. His jet-black hair seemed to rise at the widow's peak. "I am Alpha Ulric."

Angus shook his head. "Not to me. I serve another and you know this. Why are you here? To discuss my change of Alphas?" He suspected Ulric had much to say with about his upcoming meeting and waited.

"No. It is disrespectful that you return to the Continent and do not pay your respects. I thought you were beyond our petty disagreements of the past, but I see you have not moved forward."

Angus smiled at the tall, dark complexioned man standing in front of him and the bravado he spouted. "I am here on my Alpha's behalf. Did you travel across a continent to chastise me for not coming to say hello? Come now, I know better than that. What do you want? Why are you here?"

If Ulric tightened his jaw more it would snap. Angus wondered if the man would challenge him after all these years.

"Word has come to me that you seek an audience with the European council." He paused as if Angus would or should explain. He had no intention of doing either. Instead he held Ulric's gaze and waited for him to continue.

"Is this true?" Ulric ground out.

"Why? Does it matter?"

"Yes it matters," Ulric snapped taking a step closer.

Angus changed positions and prepared to fight if attacked. "I'm not at liberty to answer you. As I said before I am here on behalf of my Alpha and cannot discuss his directives."

Ulric's eyes blazed his frustration but other than fight Angus, which his chances of winning were slim, there was little he could do.

"Things are tense everywhere. New Alphas taking over packs using underhanded tactics with no honor. The old ways ...ignored. Gadgets instead of using this," he tapped his nose, "to track prey." He sounded disappointed and disgusted by the change of time.

"Things have been tense for decades that's not new," Angus said.

"You've said so, many times." He paused and then straightened. "Is it true your Patron seeks to claim the Continent as well?"

A lifetime of hiding emotions served Angus well. He did not show his surprise at the ridiculous question. Silas had been clear in every communication with the Alphas he had no interest in expanding his territory overseas. A few Mexican packs sought to join his nation. He, Alpha Theron and the Alphas bordering Mexico were considering the possibility based on logistics more than anything else. Silas was content with the fifty state packs already beneath his crest.

"What makes you ask that?" Angus wondered who started the rumors.

"Do you deny it?"

"Yes I do. Someone is playing an interesting game among the Alphas on this part of the world."

"If he is not interested in pack lands on the continent why speak to the council? Everyone knows they have been discontent with the way things have changed for decades and would leap at a chance for fresh ideas. What does your Alpha hope to gain?" Ulric pressed.

"I will not discuss my Alpha's business with you. I have said he does not seek to claim anything on the Continent." Angus chuckled. "La Patron is Alpha to fifty tough, loyal Alphas. Each run a state with the help of their betas and protect millions of wolves across the United States. His national pack is *the* strongest and most prosperous in the world. He has an army at his command, and pups who grow up secure with the knowledge of their heritage. Billions of dollars are spent on the education and protection of the young, which guarantees a solid future for the pack."

He met Ulric's gaze. "Why would he want to start from scratch here? With this messy situation? You just said things were bad. Alphas who refuse to share information, don't honor allegiances, and do not protect the vulnerable."

Neither spoke. Angus knew he hit a hot button speaking on the young. Would Ulric speak on the problem of disappearing pups?

"I find it strange he sent you, considering your feelings about our pack."

Angus sighed. “Not strange. I am the most qualified because of those very things.” He glanced at his watch, Asia should be arriving soon. He needed to change into more appropriate attire.

“You did not approve of my position of Alpha and set about sabotaging me at every turn. You fed the council lies and sowed seeds of discord among the pack. It took a long time to recover from the damage you caused and I refuse to allow my people to go through that again. You need to leave, return to your Alpha and not return.”

Hurt burrowed into Angus’ chest at the hateful words. He had never lied or deliberately caused problems. He did ask questions and was turned away. To hear his concern for the pack twisted and maligned grieved him on a deep level.

“I did not approve of the manner in which you took the Alpha’s position –”

“He is dead! A ghost cannot lead a pack.” Ulric walked off and tipped his head to the sky. The bitter scent of his frustration reached Angus’ nostrils. “He was a great Alpha, the greatest the Black Clan ever had. But he’s dead. Gone. We needed to move forward. We were losing respect amongst the other clans; we needed to act, to come together. But you... you never supported the clan...”

“I never supported you is what you mean.”

“Right, you never accepted me as Alpha which caused problems in the ranks. And because you never challenged me for the position–”

“I have no interest in being Alpha, never have.”

“I knew that. But the pack did not.” He paused. “Your attitude caused problems. It may not have been intentional but it did and I was glad when you left.”

Angus straightened. “I was glad to leave. But I am not on the Continent. In fact, I am thousands of miles from your pack lands and you are here asking me to leave. You claim to be concerned with my Alpha taking over the Continent but La Patron has never sent anyone to Africa. All of this confuses me.” He waved his hand at Ulric. “This entire visit, your presence, your explanation, none of it makes sense to me.”

Ulric clenched and unclenched his fist. A barrage of emotions crossed his face.

Confused, Angus waited to see if the man would come clean and share what troubled him. Something had happened. Something shook Ulric so bad; he sought out the man who left his pack. Something deep and disturbing sent a flash of fear across Ulric's face.

"Ulric?" Angus said, concerned by the prolonged silence and ticking of Ulric's jaw.

"Nothing." His former Alpha said and turned away. "Just go home and stay off the Continent." Ulric ran deeper into the forest and disappeared.

Chapter 31

Asia walked into the lobby of the upscale hotel and looked around. She and Hawke arrived at Chacal's twenty minutes prior. Angus gave them just enough time to shower, change and return to their car to make this appointment with the European Council.

Remembering the last meeting with three Alphas and Greggor hijacking the floor, Asia wondered at the effectiveness of the council.

"This is a lot different than the last meeting," she murmured. Humans and full-bloods walked the hall. Two male full-bloods watched their approach and stood in front of them before they reached the lobby. Asia glanced at Hawke.

He stared down at the two wolves without expression.

"Can you follow us?"

"We can but we are not going to," Angus said crossing his arms. "First off, you need to identify yourself. I know what you are, but not who you are."

"We are here with the European Council. You have an appointment with them in five minutes. They are finishing with their current appointment and will see you next."

Asia nodded. That explained why they traveled such a great distance, they had other complaints. They followed the full-blood down the hall a bit, but opted to remain in the halls instead of going inside where she was certain they installed cameras.

She looked around the lobby, concerned. "It's too quiet."

Hawke looked down at her.

She met his gaze and recalled their lovemaking last night. It had been tender and everything around them disappeared. She floated on a cloud and they merged.

Even now she had no words to explain what had to be the most magical moments in her life. His heart beat synced with his. She had heard his thoughts, felt his joy at being with her. Nothing about him was hidden from her. And she believed. After all this time she believed this man, this wolf, her mate would always be there for her. His scent filled every nook of her being. His taste remained on her tongue and she understood why Jasmine pushed for the mating. Hawke stabilized her.

"*Quiet?*"

"*Yeah. No one is trying to kill you or me. That's unusual.*"

"*I'm okay with quiet.*"

She smiled. "*Me too, but I don't trust it.*"

A door opened and footsteps headed toward them. Alpha Verrick's gaze widened when he saw them. His pace quickened, as he and two others passed by without a greeting and left the hall.

Asia looked at Angus, who shrugged.

A few moments later the same full-blood approached them. "The council will see you now."

Asia pushed off the wall and fell into line behind Angus with Hawke bringing up the rear. They agreed she should appear the same as she had during the Alpha meeting to cut down on questions.

Three full-bloods sat on a dais at the front of the room. She heard the ticking sound. Someone else watched the proceedings. She told Hawke. His gaze sharpened and he stepped to the side leaving her right arm clear.

"Angus Black Wolf, you asked for an audience with us."

Angus nodded. "Yes. My companions Hawke and Simon." He waved toward them. Each council member nodded. A second later

Asia sensed a tingling at the front of her skull. She slapped it down.

One of the Council members stared at her and then turned toward Angus.

"What is the purpose of your request?"

"I am here as a representative of my Alpha, La Patron. He is concerned over the disappearance of so many black pups on European soil."

The room stilled. If air could stop moving it would have, that's how quiet the room became after Angus's comment.

"Disappearance of black pups? What have you been telling your Alpha? Is there any proof of your claim?" His glance flickered over each of them but remained a little longer on Hawke.

"If you do not know what is happening on your land, then this meeting is a waste of time. Thank you for seeing us." Angus turned and they took a few steps.

"How dare you?" The one who had just mocked Angus screeched. "You ask for a meeting, ask a ridiculous question and then judge us for not agreeing with your fantasy. Once again you prove to be –"

"Stop, Bendred. Just stop," the Alpha in the middle said ignoring the glare sent his way. "If we have no knowledge of his concern then he and his Alpha are right. There is no need to waste everyone's time."

"Jeddick is right." He pushed a button. The soft ticks of the camera stopped.

Asia turned and faced the three men. Maybe this wouldn't be a colossal waste of time after-all. She eyed Angus, who faced the council without fanfare. They all agreed they needed to move with haste to find answers for Silas.

"I am Connall. Before I address your concern, when does La Patron intend to keep his word and stop test wolves from attacking humans? From what I understand he said he offered to handle the matter."

"That task has been completed," Angus said.

Connall frowned. "A wolf attacked and murdered a human female last night. We have been told the deed was done by a test wolf gone mad. A request has been brought to this council to destroy all the test wolves."

Asia stared at the council in shock. They hadn't heard about another death. Chacal monitored the news like a religious zealot, and would have informed them of another victim.

"I assure you the task has been completed. Unless the wolf was captured there is no way to determine if he is a test wolf."

"He was caught and put to death immediately. The Alpha swears he was a test wolf."

"Give me the particulars and I will look into it," Angus said.

Connall nodded.

"Why is La Patron interested in the disappearance of black pups?" Jeddick asked.

"Are they are disappearing?" Angus said.

Asia watched Jeddick struggle with what to say. "If they are disappearing, why is La Patron interested," he asked instead of answering Angus outright.

"That is obvious, he is a black wolf. So am I. So is Hawke. We are all concerned." He pointed at her and Hawke.

The council members glanced at each of them. "Is that all, interest? Does he have any other plans?" Jeddick asked.

Asia narrowed her gaze at him as the implication settled.

"Does he have reason to make other plans?" Angus asked.

"We are curious," Connall said. "He never touched our shores and then sends a team to Lyrill. A member of his pack releases test wolves and he is the only one who can fix the problem. We have a right to be concerned. His name is everywhere. What exactly does he want?"

"He wants to know why black pups are disappearing," Angus said spacing out each word. "If you don't have an answer or have any knowledge we will leave."

"There are discrepancies," Connall said slowly. "Nothing conclusive. Tell your Alpha we are looking into the claims brought before this council." The look he gave Angus said let that be enough. Don't push. If Angus didn't push, Asia would have.

"Do you know why? Our concern is simple. Pups have been disappearing for decades. This is not new, although La Patron has just learned of it. How is it possible for a full-blood like Hawke," he pointed to her mate's direction, "to go missing for decades and no one rescues him? The bitch that sired him or his Alpha should have sounded an alarm. Why was nothing done?" She heard the disgust and frustration in Angus' tone.

The three men looked at Hawke. "Is this true? You were taken as a pup?" Bendred asked, his entire demeanor changed into one of surprise and sympathy.

"Yes."

They waited for him to expound but they had already agreed Angus would do most of the talking.

"You escaped I take it. What happened to you? How long were you a prisoner?"

"Lord Boris kept me for over thirty years running experiments. A lot of experiments."

Shock and excitement creased the faces of the council members. Asia wasn't sure why they were excited and waited to hear what they had to say.

"Boris Lancaster? Are you sure?"

The look Hawke gave the man would melt paint. "Yes. I am very sure."

Asia tilted her head to the side.

"What can you tell us about your experience?" Bendred asked leaning forward.

"*Don't answer. They turned the camera on again*," she told Hawke.

"*I hear it. You think someone else is watching?*"

"*I don't know or care. Notice, they have not given any information.*"

"*Yes, I noticed.*"

Angus glanced at her. She realized the room had gone silent.

"Hawke, will you answer the question please?" Connall said.

"No. I am done talking. This has been a waste of my time. You are not going to do anything. Whether you are concerned about the missing pups I cannot say. But your past actions lead me to believe you will continue to do as you always have, nothing." Hawke turned and walked out. Asia followed, leaving Angus to make up his own mind.

A few seconds later, Angus caught up with them as they headed out the door of the hotel. She felt the eyes on her back as they walked toward the parking lot, fully prepared for an ambush.

Hawke drove.

Angus sat up front and she took the rear. He waited until they pulled out and were down the road before speaking.

"What did you find out?" Angus asked.

"I thought it strange they turned off the camera while they talked but after Hawke accused Boris they turned the camera back on," she said.

"Someone else is pulling their strings?" Angus asked.

"I think so. At any rate, how can they be council and have no power?" She said. "I did not sense anything from them other than being full-bloods. Did you Hawke?"

"There was something, I tried to isolate it but could not get a fix. Based on the small display from your Alpha at the meeting the other day, and the time he called my wolf at the castle, I understand what you mean. Those men were not in the same league as your Alpha."

"What about the murder? I thought you contacted all the test wolves who met the criteria," Angus said.

"We did. I will check again. But without knowing the identity of the wolf I cannot cross reference him."

"Is there a log that gives date or time of death?" Asia asked. "If so we could do a reverse check to see who died last night. There may be some test strains we missed."

Hawke nodded. "I think so. When we get to the house, I will check the files." They pulled onto the road leading to Chacal's house.

"What's that?" Angus pointed to a large brown mound further down the road. The closer they got, the more Asia shook her head. "It looks like a pile of... shit," Angus said with disbelief. "Can you believe how high that shit is?"

Asia laughed at his play on words and the situation. Somebody went through a lot of trouble to get them to stop.

"Hawke stopped laughing long enough to speak. "I cannot drive through it. There may be something beneath the... shit. There's not much space on the side of the road to drive."

They stopped in front to the knee-high mound. Angus rolled the window down a bit. The stench hit her nose and she turned away.

"Roll that up, hurry up, it stinks."

"I'm not picking up anything or anyone nearby," Hawke said.

"Me neither," Angus said.

"That's not good, Asia said. "Can you back up, turn around?"

Hawke didn't ask questions, he shifted gears and pressed on the pedal. The car shot backward. Before they reached the intersection, a bomb exploded rocking the car as debris fell onto the roof, side and windows. Large globs of stink rained on the car when it came to a complete stop.

"Asia?" Angus called out.

"I'm good."

She sensed Hawke checking her through their link, just as she did a quick check over his vitals. They were all banged around but okay.

"*Incoming? What are they doing?*" She sensed full-bloods nearby but they were a distance from the car and not moving forward.

"*I can't get a good lock on them although their scents are familiar,*" Hawke said moving slowly and pushing the door.

"*It's the same ones who followed us the other night.*"

"Can we get out of here? I smell gas," Angus said trying to push the door open but a large tree fell across the roof and bent the door.

Hawke slammed his shoulder against the car door a few times until it popped off the hinges. He scooted out and pulled her over the front seat and out the door. Next he helped Angus. They searched the area. The wolves who had been following them the past few days remained at a distance.

"Damn that stinks," Angus said and spit on the side of the road. "Let's get out of here Chacal is going to meet us." He took off at a run and they followed.

A chorus of howls split the air. Asia looked over her shoulder and saw Alpha Radoff.

"Let's go," Angus yelled.

They dashed toward Chacal' property line. Before they reached the property line the car exploded.

Chapter 32

Disgruntled and bleeding, the three of them made their way to the Hummer as it pulled up. In the distance the dark plumes of smoke rose in salute of their day. She looked for the other wolves, hoping they had made it safely away and were not injured. After the wasted meeting with the Council, she intended to contact Alpha Radoff for answers.

Hawke touched her hand and brushed against her link. "*Are you okay? You haven't said much.*"

"*Not a lot to say. Not yet anyway. Too many unanswered questions. I get the feeling we are in the middle of a bad play with no decent ending.*" She had watched some movies with Jasmine and Rose at the compound. Most were entertaining, others were too silly. She enjoyed the thrill of pointing out the villain before the movie revealed him or her. "*There are so many players in this thing; any one of them can be involved.*"

"You don't like the council?" Chacal asked glancing at her and then Hawke.

"They didn't know much," she said.

"They never have. Their positions are symbolic now. They lost control a long time ago," Chacal said.

"So why did we waste time with them?" Hawke asked.

"Politics. Silas did not want anyone to come back later and say he did not follow protocol. That's out of the way now." He chuckled. "When you left, they were miffed but asked me to keep them informed of our investigation."

"Who left the shit in the middle of the road?" Hawke asked.

Chacal frowned. "Shit?"

Angus told him what happened.

"I've heard it all now. Why bother with that?" Chacal asked.

Hawke shrugged. "If we knew what it was from a distance, we never would've driven close."

Chacal nodded. "Radoff is nearby, he asked for permission to enter my property. He wants to talk to the two in the back. He said something happened and wanted to discuss it with you." He glanced at them in the rear-view mirror.

"Now you ask before allowing access," Angus growled.

Chacal shrugged.

"What do you think?" Hawke asked her.

"I planned to look for him anyway. This way we don't travel as far. Besides he may know something about the bomb in the middle of the road."

"Do we want to know about the bomb? We are looking into a matter and someone wants us to stop. It's simple. We don't know who is doing all of this, the cowards remain hidden," Hawke said.

"Alpha Verrick?" she asked.

"It's possible," Angus said. "He visited the council today and probably killed the wolf last night."

"Alpha Verrick is in the middle of an Alpha challenge, he suspects another Alpha set the whole situation up and is upset. That is probably why he spoke to the Council. There have been an increase of Alpha challenges lately and he barely won his last one," Chacal said.

"Why the increase in challenges? Is that normal?" Asia asked.

"No. Not at the current rate they are happening," Chacal said.

She looked at Hawke.

"Maybe that is a good place to start seeking answers," he said.

Asia nodded and stretched. She needed a shower and food first.

"What shall I tell Radoff?" Chacal asked.

"I'd like to talk with him," Asia said. "Hawke and I met him the other night. Angus, I'd like to get your opinion on him."

Angus nodded. "Will do. Have him meet us in an hour and a half. I need to wash this shit off me."

"I will modify the property shield so you can meet at the hangar," Chacal said.

<<<<>>>>

Two hours later, Radoff and five members of his pack stepped into Chacal's empty hangar. Asia and Hawke introduced Angus and invited the men to have a seat at the makeshift table. The pack members declined. Alpha Radoff sat and released a long sigh.

"An innocent wolf died last night."

None of them spoke. Asia and Hawke had checked the records earlier, all of the test wolves were alive but how did Radoff know?

"Why do you say that?" Angus asked.

"The woman died by the hands of a wolf, but not one of yours. That is another problem to be tackled on another day." He sighed and then steepled his fingers beneath his chin.

Asia hadn't noticed the lines in his forehead before. His dark brown eyes looked tired, at least that was her first impression, until his gaze met hers. An indefinable spark lit his orbs that brightened his entire being. He seemed larger than before.

"The layers of this deception run deep. Each one must be peeled carefully so that healing takes place, strengthening that layer so it can withstand being removed without breaking." Radoff stared at Asia and Hawke.

"Do you understand?" he asked when they didn't respond.

"There is a lot happening and it's deep," Asia said cutting out the extra words.

"Yes, but the most important thing you must learn is pacing, you are in a rush to expose the enemy, solve the problems, make everything better, all at once. None of this happened all at once. It took decades. My concern is that in your eagerness to complete your goal, you destroy the fabric of who we are as a people."

Asia tensed. "Destroy? Why would I do that? I have a simple job. Discover what's happening to the missing black pups and shut it down. It's not my intention to destroy your society."

"I know but hear what I am saying. The answers are not as simple as you think. There are many hands in the pie. There are some things that can never be revealed. That's not dishonest, that's good governing. No Alpha shares everything with his pack."

She nodded. "What do you want me to say? That I'll be careful? Or that we'll run things by you first? Or that we won't expose anybody?" She shook her head. "I hear what you're saying but I'm not sure what you want from me, from us." She looked at Hawke and then Angus before meeting Radoff 's gaze.

He leaned forward. "Pacing. Timing. You would not be sitting here if it were not for him." He pointed to Hawke. "And he would not be here if not for you. Do you think you are the first who tried to break into Lord Boris' castle?"

She didn't think so, but did not answer.

"You are not. Many, many have died trying through the years. Because of that, when pack members go missing, most Alphas believe they are beyond hope of retrieval. You..." he pointed at Asia. "And you." He pointed to Hawke. "Have changed all of that. When word came to the coast of Poland that Lancaster Castle had fallen, I dropped everything to come see for myself. It is a day many of our people have prayed to the Goddess to see. But it happened after many things in your life aligned for this time and purpose." He paused.

Uncertain where he was going with all of this, Asia frowned.

"Pacing and timing. Could you have accomplished your goals a year ago today?" His gaze touched her, and then Hawke and then Angus.

"No, I could not." A year ago, she was a prisoner of the Liege in worse condition than her mate because she walked freely amongst the Liege's enemies before destroying them.

"I could not either," Hawke said. "It's as you say. I needed my mate in order to step into whatever we need to do now."

"Same here," Angus said.

"You say we need to slow down and that there are many levels, I agree. But we are tasked to complete a mission in a timely manner. How do you suggest we move forward?" Asia asked to get the conversation back on track.

Radoff pointed at her. "You are from the outside with no stake in our problems. Your Alpha and his litter-mate, they are black wolfs. Your mate, he is a black wolf. On the inside our hearts weep for the loss of our pack. We mourn its fallen state, and recall glorious days of old. Not to live in the past but to learn from it."

Asia glanced at Hawke who took her hand and squeezed.

"When I ask if you are here to help, I refer to both. To open the cage is one thing; it is another to make sure the bridge to cross over to freedom is safe."

"What?" Asia frowned.

Radoff held up a finger and smiled. "I refer to stopping the problem but leaving the pack in such a state it will survive. There are layers to every problem before you reach the core. But if the layers are destroyed it makes it harder and sometimes impossible to see the heart." He stared at her.

"We understand," Hawke said. "And while my mate is from the outside, he has accomplished more for the pack in the past week than anyone has in years."

"True. As I said before, that is why I'm here. To share information and to seek help."

Angus stretched and looked at Radoff. "Our assignment is based on missing black clan pups. Our Alpha is concerned and does not wish to see that happen in his territories. This is an offensive mission until he changes it." Angus paused and then continued. "I am of the Black Wolf clan on the Continent. My heart grieves the loss of our pups and the sad state of our clan. You are right; this must be handled with both a feather and a hammer."

"*How do we do that?*" she asked Hawke.

"*I think we will know when the time comes. Our hearts will lead us. That's what all of this is about. He wants your heart involved, and not just your mind,*" Hawke said.

"*He should have said that,*" she said.

"Alpha Verrick saw the council today," Angus said to Radoff. "Do you think he is involved in all this?"

"No. He refuses to obey the Liege representatives in this area and will not be Alpha much longer. The Alphas involved in this plot are in the Liege pockets. When they have a lot of pride and emotion about their people, like Verrick, they do not work for the Liege. For one thing, it is difficult but not impossible to smell a lie from an Alpha. But if he talked a lot, like Verrick or like I'm doing now, you'll be able to weigh our words for truth."

"*That's good to know,*" Asia said.

Hawke nodded.

"Liege representatives? There are more besides Greggor?" Asia asked.

"The nephew? He only leaves the castle to dally in town with the women. He has no power or authority. No, there are men who have risen through the ranks of the organization who manage the Liege' assets."

Asia glanced at Angus. Brix, Leon's mate had infiltrated the Liege until he ran into his mate at the research lab in Pennsylvania. Angus had been the one to set Brix up for the operation. La Patron learned a lot about the structure of the organization from Brix.

"Are they involved with the pups?" she asked.

"Yes and no. I suspect they are but no one has ever been able to catch them. Which means they must have help. Help within the pack."

That did not surprise her. "I agree. There is no way they could have operated this long without someone betraying their own."

"Power is a tempting seat, but the responsibility is too heavy for many. Look at the new Alphas. They are cocky, care little for their packs, use fear to generate loyalty..." he shook his head. "That is the first layer to peel. Follow that thread." He stood and stuck his hands down his pocket while looking at her.

"I think you already know which Alphas work for the Liege," she said meeting his gaze.

"I'm old. Seen a lot, know a lot, heard a lot. You need to learn for yourself, peel the layer, follow the threads, earn the respect you'll need to get answers from the pack. They *will* talk to you if they trust you. Or trust that you won't be like everyone else, in and out at their expense."

Asia didn't know what to say. What he proposed sounded long term. This was a job. A mission to be completed efficiently with the results La Patron required. She did not get emotionally involved in her assignments.

"Do you have a list of the new Alphas in the area?" Hawke asked into the silence.

Radoff lifted his hand.

One of the men stepped forward and handed Hawke a slip of paper. He looked over it and nodded. "Interesting. Alpha Andrei is on this list. I did not realize he was new."

Radoff smiled. "He is from southern Romania. His pack is in Bucharest."

Asia looked at him. "And? Does that mean something?"

Radoff shrugged. "He has been an Alpha a year and has constant turnover in his pack. He recruits all the time."

Asia recalled Andrei made an invitation for test wolves to come to his lands at the Alpha meeting. "We told the test couples about his offer to resettle on his land."

Hawke squeezed her hand. "*They'll be fine. They have a nose for danger and probably have banded together into their own pack. Remember we saw all six of them together when we checked the files. They didn't go to Bucharest.*"

She released a breath, feeling better. "*Thanks for reminding me.*"

"Anyone else on the list we need to check out besides, Andrei?" Angus asked.

"Yeah. I'll give you a copy of this. You research some, we'll do the same so we know what we're dealing with here," Hawke said folding the paper and putting it into his pocket.

Angus nodded.

"Be careful with the Alphas. They are only top layers because they are new and easy to see. But they are dangerous. Each of them will lie, cheat and steal for what they want. They have already done that to gain their positions." He looked at Angus, Hawke and then Asia.

"When an Alpha is removed from his position, it creates a vacuum. A hole. The pack suffers. When one packs suffer, we are all at risk of discovery. I am asking that you consider carefully who you target and what you do with the information you discover. All the Alphas on that list aren't bad, just misguided. But they lead others. Someone must fill the void or the structure, pack structure, will collapse."

Hawke stood. Angus and Asia stood and walked Radoff out the entrance. Something pierced Asia's chest. Surprised she looked around, saw Hawke on the ground.

"Hawke," she screamed through their link as her knees buckled and she fell to the ground.

Chapter 33

"*Asia... dammit Asia answer me*!" The words rolled across Asia's mind but she couldn't grab hold of anything to respond. A jolt of energy sped through her, clearing bits of fog in her mind.

"*Asia... Asia. She's not answering me Silas. Have you reached Angus? I need to know what's going on. Asia... Asia*?" Another jolt cleared more gray clouds from her mind.

"*Tranquilizers...*" she moaned.

"*Silas she said tranquilizers.*" The next moment Asia sensed a rolling movement through her system. A burning sensation exploded through her veins. Her stomach clenched, rebelled and then emptied. She spewed the contents across the floor.

"*Asia?*"

"*Mistress,*" she whispered feeling a little better. The bitter taste of the tranquilizer remained on the back of her tongue. She tried to wipe her face and realized metal cuffs secured her arms to the table.

"*Sorry to be so heavy-handed, but you winked out so fast it scared me. I've been calling you for fifteen minutes. Can you talk*?"

Still fuzzy, she opened one eye and shut it from the glare of the overhead light. "*We were leaving.... And got shot with tranqs. Didn't... sense or see them.*" She exhaled and opened her eyes half-mast.

"*Do you know where Angus is? Silas can't get through to him.*"

"*We... we were all together.*" She tried to break through the hazy clouds loitering in her mind to put the parts of the puzzle together. "*I don't... know where I am.*" Something nagged at her from the corner of her awareness. A yawning silence filled her chest. It took a few seconds to figure out the problem. And then it hit her.

"*Hawke?*" Asia called and received no response. "*I can't reach Hawke. As his mate I should be able to reach him all the time, right?*" she asked Jasmine needing reassurance. At the same time she battled fears of what would happen if the Liege reprogrammed him again.

"Silas says yes. But you may need to be closer or something. You're the only one responding so we need to get you up and running to find the others first."

Warmth, like running water surged through her system and she knew La Patron assisted his mate. Grateful for the hand of experience, the last two jolts from her Mistress set her teeth jarring. The remnants of the serum dribbled down the side of her chin.

"*Hawke*," she called again and then again, unable to stop seeking that part of her. "*He is not answering.*"

"Is he in the same area?"

Clearer of mind and armed with purpose, Asia scanned the area. There were ten full-bloods in the immediate vicinity. Angus was in another area. Hawke was missing.

"*He is not here.*" She called him again and sought their link, finding it blocked. "*Hawke, you stop locking me out.*" Silence.

Pushing away her fear and anger, she pressed forward to hear a conversation on the other side of the building.

"He is on his way. Lord Roderick wants the other one and dispose of the others. Radoff got away but I have his beta," someone said. Although the voice sounded familiar, she couldn't place it.

Asia frowned in concentration. Nothing made sense except Alpha Radoff. She was glad he escaped and could send help. Maybe he saw which way these guys took them and would send reinforcements.

Who knew how long that would be or if that happened.

She couldn't wait. Hawke was in trouble, she had to find him.

The one-sided conversation continued. "No Greggor, no extra help this time. Last time in forest I lost four of my best, no sending more. I gave him another shot and then put in truck to be putty in your hands."

Greggor? Extra shot? Hawke? It took her mind a few seconds to make the connections. This person had sent those wolves before to attack Hawke in the forest when Greggor shot him. She listened more. "Lord Roderick in country? I do not know. Ask your uncle." Asia heard the contempt in the speaker's voice and wondered why he worked with Greggor if he despised him.

"Black wolf kept separate. No one can touch. I put thick gloves on his hands before lifting him." He paused. "I do not know why the gloves, just followed directions. I must go."

Asia kept her eyes closed and told Jasmine all she heard.

"I don't know why Hawke's not responding. Can you reach him through your link?"

Asia searched the link again, but it remained closed. Hawke may have picked something up and shut down their link to protect her. They needed a long discussion on acceptable mate behavior. "*No, I can't.*"

"*Can you leave wherever you are and find Angus?*"

Asia scanned the room for surveillance cameras. *"There is a camera in the corner but I don't think they're paying attention to me. Angus is the big fish. I'll loosen the cuff so I can take out the next person who comes inside the room."*

"Be careful."

Keeping her eyes closed, Asia pulled the metal cuff on her right arm inch by inch. The sound of the stretching metal echoed in the small room. She hoped they didn't have audio on the camera. Once it was loose enough to slip her hand through, she rested her arm so the torn flesh on her wrist could regenerate.

"Okay, I'm ready. Come here," she whispered, hoping the bastards would come into the room. The low hum of the camera, the tick of her watch and the vibration of the light fixture grew louder in her mind with each passing second her mate was with Greggor.

Impatient, she clenched her fist, ready to rip off the metal cuff from her left arm and break down the door. "Pacing and timing," Alpha Radoff warned. On one level she understood and agreed, but each second that passed without contact with her mate scraped her skin raw, leaving her vulnerable, exposed. Her throat tightened and she couldn't breathe.

"Asia?"

"Mistress, I need Hawke," she whispered, opening and closing her fist in desperation for her mate. A thousand ants raced across her flesh, she bucked against the restraint to dislodge them. Deep, piercing pain struck the base of her neck.

She screamed and dropped her head forward. Her chin hit her chest. "Hawke..." She screamed into the silence of their link, and heard the echo of her cry.

"Asia... Asia, calm down. Breathe. You can't help him if you lose it. Calm down... calm..." Warmth like the early morning sun spread through her allowing her to breathe, to swallow, and to think.

Think Asia, she commanded her mind. Think beyond the present. Think five steps ahead, no more short-sighted plans. She exhaled. First, escape this room. She inhaled. Second, get Angus and leave. She exhaled. Third, go to Hawke. Her breath hitched, but she continued. Four, leave the castle with Hawke. She exhaled. Five, go to Chacal's with Hawke and Angus.

"Thank you, Mistress. I will contact you when I am on my way to Angus. I will need La Patron to prepare him to move."

"Okay, he's still working on him. They gave him more of that shit than they gave you so it's taking a little longer."

"Okay."

"Asia?"

"Yes, Ma'am?"

"Remember I told you not to start shit in that country?"

Asia bit back a smile at Jasmine's tone. "Yes, Ma'am."

"Forget that shit. Do whatever you need to do to get those guys outta there alive. If you need me I've got your back."

"Yes, Ma'am. I know you do. I think someone is coming."

Eyes closed, heartbeat racing, Asia waited. "One, two, three, four," she counted off in her head bringing her heartbeat to a slower than normal rhythm. She had no idea who her captors were and what abilities they had, she focused on the sound of the footsteps.

The door opened.

"Oh shit, he messed up the floor." She saw an outline of the full-blood as he stepped closer. "Damn." He took her chin between his hands and tapped her face to wake her.

The tingling of the chameleon started in her arms and stopped when she stood in front of her old body, holding the chin in her hand. She searched his memories. Hiry, Pack Beta and her personal escort to the main room for termination. Karma was indeed a bitch.

She pulled out his cell phone and made the call. "Sir, this one's dead." She listened to her "Alpha" question her about the new corpse and wondered why they did not speak link to link like La Patron did with his Alphas. He had not been on the extraction team at Chacal's and did not know anything.

"Get up here. Lord Roderick's people are delayed but will be here within the hour. I need to make a call."

Grateful to leave the foul-smelling room, Asia stepped into the hall and sought out Angus' room. It was in the opposite direction of the area she needed to go. Damn. The clock ticked inside her mind. Hawke hadn't responded. Angus was dead weight, literally.

Each second of her separation from Hawke, a thousand needle points pierced her skin, digging and then scraping as if searching for him beneath her flesh. She took her time walking into the common area where six other full bloods sat or stood. They nodded at her but didn't say anything, which suited her fine.

"I do not know what the delay is, my men left already. If he's not there and you want him faster, go look for him. I am not your personal servant to search for your toys," the Alpha said standing in the corner with a cell phone next to his ear.

Asia noted the positions of each full-blood and the camera positions in the room. Those devices needed to be disabled, and the footage destroyed. After the destruction of the castle, the Liege would look for similarities in the incidents. They may notice the way she led with her right metal arm, her fighting style and the strength of her metal legs and guess Asia Montgomery had shut down Lord Boris' castle sending the bounty from eight million to ten. That was the last thing she wanted or needed.

The door slammed and Asia turned, getting her first real look at the Alpha Andrei. She should have known. This man looked nothing like the soft spoken Alpha at the meeting a few days back. The long flowing robe he wore to the meeting covered the colorful artwork on his arms. Today he had tied his long reddish-brown hair into a long braid that brushed against the base of his neck. His piercing green eyes radiated anger.

He pointed at her. "Go check on the bastard."

She nodded and turned. "Yes, Sir."

"I want to see more respect around here," the Alpha snarled as she left the room ignoring the glares of the other men. When she approached the room where Angus lay, another full-blood patted her down and then opened the door.

Angus lay prostrate on a table in his underwear and gloves. She estimated the temperature in the room at around forty-five degrees. Chill bumps were all over his skin.

"Mistress, I found Angus." She explained his condition while moving around the room checking to see if he was alert. She saw the pool of serum on the floor where it dripped from his mouth. Good, at least his body had a break from the full dose.

"Silas is still working on his system and needs a few more minutes before he's done."

"Okay." She started toward the door. Angus' eyes flickered and then opened. He nodded at her and then closed them again. She strode out the room and headed toward the Alpha who stood in a small room off the main area.

"He still out, Sir," she reported closing the door behind her.

Andrei stared toward the monitors and she wondered if he had seen Angus respond to her. It had been quick and if she hadn't been staring at him she would have missed it.

"Get the case, give him another shot."

"Yes, Sir," she said moving toward a small office where they kept the drugs.

"Did you say other one died from serum?" Andrei asked stopping her.

"No, Sir. I said other one dead when I went in room." She waited for him to question her further. She planned to destroy or dilute that serum before leaving this place. First thing, Hawke needed to make an antidote for his concoction.

"We wait to give him more. Stay here, watch monitors. I don't know why, but Lord Roderick excited over that one." Andrei turned and left the room. She watched him step into the room containing the serum supply. Once he entered she watched him through the monitor.

"Mistress, I am in the room monitoring the security cams. Whenever Angus is ready to make his move he can. I need Jacques to set up a virus or something to disrupt the cameras. We will fight our way out of here and I don't want anyone to see that footage."

"Got it. I'll tell Silas and Jacques."

Andrei unlocked a drawer and pulled out a vial case similar to one she had seen in an underground tunnel months ago.

Agents of the Liege had kidnapped La Patron's son, Tyrese and her for testing. The doctor administered a shot to Tyrese changing his biology. Is that what the Liege offered the local Alphas? She wouldn't be surprised. Adjusting the mounted camera, she zeroed in on the clear vials of liquid and then pulled back as Andrei injected the fluid into his veins. *"Hawke?"* she continued calling to him, aching for contact while watching the monitors. Andrei's knees buckled, and he sat on a chair with his head in his palms.

On another screen, she caught the tail end of Angus dragging the guard from in front of the room of his recent prison and placed him on the table. Angus exchanged forms with the guard and then locked the full-blood in the metal cuffs. Anyone looking in the room would see someone who looked like Angus and not sound an alarm. He tugged on the tight-fitting pants and walked out of the room. He stared into the nearby camera and nodded.

Asia rubbed her arms, to ease the persistent stinging but nothing helped. "*Hawk*e..." she called out.

"Asia." His response was the sweetest whisper she ever heard.

She closed her eyes and pushed at their link. "*Let me in.*" He remained closed off to her.

"*Not... yet.*"

She wanted to scream her frustration. *"I am not a child, Hawke. I am your mate and I need you. Now open the damn link."*

The link opened, and she fell to the ground as waves of sluggishness and pain beat at her, pushing, grinding, and knocking her back. She fought to stay conscious. How the hell did he pull out of whatever gripped him to answer her?

After getting her breathing under control, Asia closed her eyes and made their relationship her focal point. She dredged up every memory of their time together, starting in the cave. She opened herself allowing the sunlight of her affection to dismiss the darkness and burn off the listlessness. She imagined them running through the forest, fighting the bluebirds, laughing in the shower and making love.

A few moments later he added his memories, layering them with hers. Shaky, she stood. The more memories he added the clearer they became, the fog thinned. The pain downgraded to bearable.

"*Asia*," her name sounded like a prayer through their link.

"I'm coming Hawke and don't you dare tell me not to come."

"Argue later."

She gazed at the monitors and saw a reduction to three men in the main area. One of them had to be Angus. Andrei remained seated in the other room but began to stir.

"Mistress, Andrei just took a drug that reminds me of the one that altered Tyrese. He will be in the main area soon. Alert Angus. Is the virus ready to be uploaded to the system?"

"Whew! Long day. I told Silas, he'll tell Angus. Same deal as the castle computer, type in the code and a nice package will download. I'm with the kids if you need me, otherwise Silas has it covered."

"Yes, Ma'am." Asia typed in the code and downloaded the virus just as Andrei stepped out the room and looked around the area.

"Where the hell is everybody?" He growled and shifted into a large hybrid.

He stepped toward one of the full-bloods, picked him up by his shirt collar and shook him so hard, the man lost control of his bowels. Andrei laughed and threw him across the room into the brick wall, his head split like a melon.

"He has no control of his beast," Asia murmured watching him pick up the next full-blood, and the computer as it uploaded the files necessary to erase her presence.

Andrei flung the next full-blood against the wall, killing him on the spot as well. He threw his head back and roared, obviously feeling invincible. But only a fool would watch two comrades die in such a foul manner and remain for their chance to meet the Goddess.

If Andrei's thoughts were clear he would have realized the last full-blood in the main room waited for him. He would have realized this full-blood was different than the others. If Andrei had not been ramped up on drugs, he would have run to save his life. Instead, he entered the battle arena as the underdog.

Virus loaded. The cameras showed reruns of Scooby-Do. Asia stepped out of the room and watched Angus bulk to his hybrid. The look of shock on Andrei's face made her smile as she scooted around the dueling pair and made her way to the room Andrei had left.

The locked door offered little resistance after she kicked it a few times. There were two cases with tranqs on the shelves. She dumped the capsules onto the floor. The vials from the desk drawer she added to the pile, stepping on them first breaking the seals and spilling the liquid. Next, she crushed the containers holding the tranq serum. When the noxious odors from the chemicals grew too strong, she left the room wishing she had a match. She walked two steps and realized Hiry, her new body, was a smoker. After a few pats on her pockets, she found his lighter and cigarettes. She pulled out a cigarette, tossed the pack into the room, lit and then threw it in the middle of the liquid.

A loud swoosh filled the area. Smoke and heat billowed from the floor and licked the ceiling. Closing the door, she moved quickly to the area where Angus and Andrei continued their battle. She glanced at her watch. They needed to leave and get to the castle. If Roderick or his associates were on their way, they would have their own stash of the serum and she did not want to go through that cleansing again.

Angus body slammed Andrei onto the unforgiving concrete floor. Based on the screams of pain from Andrei, the fight wouldn't continue much longer. She headed toward the front of the building to search for transportation. After walking through numerous halls and getting turned around, she saw daylight. There were two full bloods walking the perimeter. In his arrogance, Andrei had not communicated with his pack. As pack beta she ordered a vehicle to be brought to the front.

The men nodded and left to do her bidding. She remained out front scanning the area. She sensed Angus before she saw him. How fitting he had taken Andrei's form. They waited in silence, her thoughts on her mate. Hawke's chip had moved from his brain and she assumed passed through his system. But that would not stop Lord Boris from reinstalling another device.

The black Land Rover pulled up front. The four of them entered the vehicle. Asia drove with a full-blood in the passenger seat. Angus sat in the back with the other full-blood. While driving she scanned them for devices. Neither had the deadly chips implanted in their brains. After thirty minutes Asia pulled to the side of the road. She and Angus got out and motioned the full-bloods out of the car.

"Go to back to the pack lands. I'll meet you there later," Angus said.

The two men frowned, and then nodded. "Yes Alpha," they said one after the other.

Angus climbed in the front seat as Asia returned behind the wheel.

She gunned the accelerator. "*Hawke, I'm coming.*"

"*No*!"

Chapter 34

Hawke inhaled and blessed the Goddess for his stubborn mate. Thanks to her, he could push through the dark clouds in his mind and think of the best way to defeat Greggor. The overhead light had been dimmed and he could see everything in the old lab.

He had not been away from the castle long but it seemed like a lifetime. So much had happened. Freedom tasted great and he refused to be a slave for Lord Boris or anyone again.

How long he had been back in his old lab strapped to the table? He had no idea but did not think it had been long. Greggor had been mumbling about delays and missing fun while he strapped his inert body to the table. From what he sensed, there was no one else in the castle other than him and his captor who acted strange.

Hawke heard Greggor on the phone. Someone called to tell him Angus had escaped and may be on his way to the castle. Greggor left the room to prepare a special surprise. Hawke had no idea what it could be, Greggor refused to talk to him, or look at him.

Asia. They knew she and Angus were coming. He had to find a way to stop Greggor.

"Asia."

"Don't tell me not to come. I am almost there. How many are in the castle?"

"Just Greggor, but something's off with him."

"Just Greggor? That's strange. I didn't get a signal on those blue-birds the other day, is it possible you're not picking up something?"

"Yes. It's possible, although I always get a read on them, one of the perks of creating things."

"Hmmm, we are going to have a long discussion about you and the things you do in the lab."

"Right now I'm strapped to a lab table."

"Let me guess. You modified it to hold a person with your strength,"

He sighed. *"Yes. I could kick myself for that."*

"Instead of that, help me figure out how to kick Greggor's ass."

"He is waiting for you. Someone called and warned him."

"Damn. I bet it was Lord Roderick; he probably arrived after we left. I wonder if he is on his way to the castle."

"I don't know him. But be prepared to get shot with a tranquilizer and held in metal cuffs like mine. Greggor is no fighter; he probably has instructions to hold Angus for Roderick."

"I want to come in under the radar, is that possible?"

"No. Every entry point is covered. That's why no one has ever been successful attacking this place. Greggor is monitoring the security cams and will see you arrive."

"You created security for that place, Hawke. Tell me how to break in and surprise Greggor. I need to get you out of there. Please... think."

He swallowed hard. Creating security had been a huge chess match for him. He made moves and countermoves three steps deep, glorying in defeating of his imaginary opponents. There had been several attempts over the years to overtake the castle. But if anyone ever came close to success he shut down that avenue. No one ever breached their defenses, except Asia. Her simple strategy of impersonating staff to gain entry would never have worked with anyone else unless they had access to the same technology.

"*What if we came in from the roof?*" Asia asked.

"*Cameras and beams.*"

"The hole in the wall?"

"It's a specific trap that tracks all and any movement. Plus, unless I open the passage you're stuck in the antechamber."

"Windows?"

"Second floor with bars, sensors and non-breakable panels."

"Doors?"

"They are probably unlocked and you can walk in. Be prepared to be shot full of tranqs."

"Garbage chutes? Sewage tunnels? Caves? Anything?" she asked and he heard her frustration. He had spent decades achieving an impenetrable fortress and to the extent of known technology he succeeded.

"*All have sensors and beams. I shut them down that night we escaped. I can assure you they are back online now.*"

"*I'm not losing you.*"

He knew how difficult it was for her to admit that. He echoed the sentiment. They would find a way to win against Lord Boris and Greggor.

"No. You're not. Give me a minute to think this through."

"Okay. We are going to run the last few miles, when does the cameras start picking up movement?"

"Not until you're in the tree line."

"Okay."

Where.... How could she slip in undetected? Below the castle on the ground where his wolf ran the length of the castle around the pillars that supported its weight. Someone tried to dig beneath the foundation twenty years ago. Lord Boris reinforced the exterior walls with solid stone creating a stair step effect. It would take heavy machinery to bore a hole through all that stone.

If she attempted to gain access from the top she would be fried. He installed so many cross beams, anything as small as an infant's foot couldn't step across without touching a laser. At the time he had been certain the next attempt would come through the roof and went into overkill mode. In retrospect he realized the roof would be the last place anyone would attempt to enter the castle. The upper floors were the equivalent of a six-story building and there were few flat surfaces.

Stumped, he lay locked to the gurney wondering how to save his mate. There was no way he knew of for her to enter the building undetected.

"Is the camera working in your lab? I remember you shut it down and locked it when we left."

He thought back to the day they broke out of the lab. "*Yes, it should be. My system is separate from the rest of the building. I was told I was the only one who could access it but I sent a virus to shut down the entire system and it's running again. I don't know if I was told the truth.*"

"*Shut down everything and isolate the sounds. Find the hum of the camera.*"

He shut out the air conditioning, then the lights, then the computer and then he searched for any other sounds. He heard nothing. Focused, he searched for more sounds and heard Greggor speaking to someone.

"I am in the security room, no matter how they try to get in, I will stop them." He paused. "Yes, Sir I'll hold both of them for your men Lord Roderick." He paused. "He is locked in the lab." He paused again. "Yes, ironic he built his own prison. He will be reprogrammed when my uncle returns."

Sweat beaded and ran down Hawke's brow at the plans they made for Asia. His mate in the hands of Lord Roderick... his wolf howled his displeasure. He pulled on the metal cuffs, nothing. A scream curdled in his throat, but did not escape. He swallowed hard.

Frustrated, he clenched and unclenched his fists, he had to do something. He couldn't lay there and not do anything.

"*I don't hear a camera.*"

"Thank the Goddess," Asia whispered.

He didn't understand, he couldn't move from the table, couldn't help her. "*What?*"

"Nothing we have an idea, it's a long shot but we're running out of time. I think Lord Roderick or his men are on the way."

"You are right."

"Good I would love to greet him and rid the earth of another Liege Lord, but we need to free you first." The cavalier way she said free him made him think it might happen even though he couldn't see how.

"*Great.*" He thought he should say something and stared at the ceiling.

Asia chuckled at the pout in her mate's voice and looked at Angus, marveling how well he blended with the tree next to her. She told him what Hawke said.

"It's the best shot we have before there are reinforcements. I will open that door for you as soon as I gain access."

Asia swallowed hard. "Okay." She watched the tree slide into the trees closer to the castle. She touched the tree, merged and followed Angus at a slower pace. It took longer to reach the portion of the forest in front of the hidden entrance she had used to re-enter the castle the last time. Angus had entered the same vent she and Hawke used to escape.

Minutes passed. She swallowed her fear of failing Hawke. "This has to work. It has to work," she murmured over and over while listening for the sound of approaching vehicles. The door clicked open.

She stared in disbelief and then elation as she raced to the entry. Closing the door behind her, she morphed into Hawke and took the stairs two at a time. When she reached the exit, she eased it open slowly and peeked out. Across the floor, Angus sat in the communications room working his magic. So far their plan worked. She waved at him and took the stairs down to Hawke's lab and listened to the voices coming from inside.

"How did you do that?" Greggor demanded. The sound of flesh connecting to flesh pissed her off. "Answer me or I'll kill you."

Asia smelled Greggor's anger and knew he was on edge. They calculated he would be disoriented and possibly violent. That's why each moment outside wrecked her nerves. She strolled to the lab, placed her palm on the security panel and stared down at Greggor. His altered appearance stunned her and she forgot her punch line.

Gone was the thin, dorky man who panted behind Hawke. His uncle had turned him into a human bluebird. The pale blue speckles on his skin were not good. His shaggy hair hung in thinned, lank clumps in a weird patchwork on his oversized skull. Thick legs and arms that hung lower than normal made him stoop forward.

He stared at her and then blinked, wiped his face with his huge palm and blinked again. "What is going on?" Greggor yelled and stormed toward her.

"What the fuck?" she said hoping Angus unlocked Hawke's restraints from the computer.

Greggor's skin turned a darker shade of blue. Red streaks multiplied in the white of his eyes as they bulged. He jumped up and down like a toddler having a tantrum. He ran back to the table clenched his fist and punched Hawke in the stomach over and over again.

Horrified at the sight, she hadn't realized she moved until she saw Greggor slide across the floor and land into the glass wall. Pieces of glass rained all over him. A week ago, he would curl into a ball and send her dirty looks. Now he shook it off in a King Kong imitation and charged. She waited until he was close and leapt over his head. He hit the wall behind her but did not stay down. He sprung up and ran toward her. She had little room to maneuver and dropped to the floor in a split and punched him between his legs. He bent over and ran into the table. Pushing away, he punched Hawke again in the stomach and between his legs.

Hawke's growl of pain pierced her. She grabbed Greggor and punched him in the face. He spun and clipped her on the jaw. She flew backward and landed on the floor.

Shaking her head to clear it, Greggor lifted her from the ground and threw her across the room. She hit the wall so hard, dark spots flew in front of her eyes. Gasping for air, she stood slowly. Greggor had grabbed Hawke's balls and held them tight in his hands. The look of sheer maniacal delight in his gaze meant Hawke was in unspeakable pain.

She tried to open their link to help but he refused. She ran, jumped and kicked Greggor in the chest. He stumbled back and fell on a metal chest. His loud scream of pain filled the room. She ignored him and went to Hawke.

"How do I unlock you?" she asked walking on the other side of the table toward the computer.

"Push the button on the table," he hissed his face a mask of pain. His scrotum reddish blue and bruised with claw marks. "Son of a bitch," she swore. Greggor tried to rip off Hawke's balls. She pushed every button. The cuffs unlocked and Hawke rolled onto the floor holding his side, spitting up blood.

Enraged, Asia jumped up on the exam table and then in front of Greggor.

Brow furrowed, he looked at her and then down at Hawke and then back at her.

"You visited any hookers lately? Beat them with your belt? Have they lied and said I love you?" She asked drawing his attention.

Greggor's face crumpled and then he screamed, arms outstretched he ran toward her. She sidestepped him. He followed, caught a part of her shirt, whirled her around and punched her in the face. She spun and hit the wall.

He pulled her from behind and slammed her into the wall again smearing blood from her face against the glass.

Asia's vision dimmed. She shut down her links and centered into her quiet place. One, two, three, she counted in her mind to crystallize her focus. She spun and caught Greggor's chin with the heel of her boot. He flew backward and crashed into some equipment.

She glanced at Hawke, he stood slow and watched. Zeroing in on Greggor she targeted her next hits. When he stood, he looked at her and moved forward in slow degrees, no doubt weighing his next move.

Like lightning he swung at her. She ducked feeling the breeze from the missed blow. She jumped and kicked him in the back knocking him headfirst into the concrete floor. The equipment moved from the force of his fall. Under normal conditions, hitting the ground as hard as he had would have split his skull open. Instead, Greggor leaned up on one arm and kicked back hitting her in the leg.

"*Either you finish him or I will. Angus is going to need us.*"

She glared at her mate who leaned against the exam table with his arms crossed. Greggor stood slower this time. His steps wobbled a bit before he straightened.

Asia tested her right arm, and her legs. Hawke was right, she needed to finish this. "Greggor, you got a thing for me? You want some Hawke? I know you do. Come get your Hawke," she taunted. With each sentence his face turned bluer. She knew the moment he snapped. His eyes turned pitch black and his snarl ended on a hiss.

With clenched fists he stomped toward her and swung. She ducked and sidestepped him. He swung again, missed but continued moving. She jumped and kicked him in the chest. He flew back into the stone wall and this time she heard the crack of his skull.

Eyes wild, he stood, roared and charged. Blood ran down the side of his face and back. She sidestepped and hit him beneath his chin with her right arm. His head snapped back and he slammed into the wall again. Another cracking sound resonated in the room.

She waited.

He raised his arm toward Hawke, opened his mouth and then slumped forward.

Chapter 35

Asia and Hawke left the lab heading for the communication center. Angus waved them in. "It worked? He was more confused?" Angus had entered the castle through the vents by merging with the materials and then dropped to the floor in the mechanical room. He changed his appearance to resemble Hawke. When he opened the door and headed upstairs, Greggor saw him on the monitors and thought Hawke escaped. He left the communications room to check on Hawke in the lab.

They were prepared to take Greggor down if he went after Angus or she would take him out in the lab. Greggor chose the lab.

"Yes, he's down. Can we leave? Roderick is on his way." Asia asked looking at the monitors. Two blue monsters, a couple of hybrids and a Hummer parked a distance from the castle.

"Okay it doesn't look like it," she said swallowing a groan. She had burned a lot of energy on Greggor; her body throbbed with the need to rest.

"I locked everything down but Boris keeps overriding my commands," Angus said pressing keys.

"Where's the serum? Let's tranq them," Asia said looking at the beasts.

"Those darts won't penetrate the metal on the bluebirds. It will take out the hybrids." Hawke grabbed a piece of paper and wrote. *"Boris is listening. He cannot see but sound is always on."*

Asia nodded and morphed into her male form. "Here's a tranq gun, I'll target them now and take them out." She picked up the gun and left the room.

"*Did he move them?"* She asked Hawke through their link.

"Not yet... yes. The hybrids are moving toward the Hummer and the bluebirds are walking up the steps. Hold onto the gun in case they send the hybrids after the bluebirds enter."

"Okay." Asia headed back to communications when she noticed Angus left with Hawke. The hybrids remained near the truck, she watched all the screens. One blanked.

"*Hawke, one monitor blinked and returned on line. I don't sense anything extra but you may have more incoming. Boris is running the cams from wherever he is."*

"Got it. We do this old school." She heard the tearing of metal.

"What are you doing?"

"Taking a few seconds to pull the right cables and stop Boris' remote control. It should buy a little time. Wherever he is operating he has to be connected to this building in some way. I am shutting one way down."

"Okay. You have incoming. Front door."

The front door opened and then shut. The growl of the blue bird ended on a screech. The sound filled the hall. The cameras went off line and then rebooted. She rescanned the area. Two hybrids had entered from the same door she had and were moving up the staircase.

Tranq gun in hand she strode out the communications room, flattened against the wall and waited. Seconds ticked.

Hawke and Angus looked at each other and morphed to their hybrids. Hawke would wait to see how many bluebirds showed up before he morphed into his largest hybrid. His body had taken a pummeling from Greggor; he had morphed to his wolf for a short period while Asia fought. But once she hit the wall and he saw blood, he returned to human, prepared to rip Greggor apart.

But Asia did her own ripping apart, and Greggor lay dead. One bluebird growled and flew toward him. He ducked. It hit the wall. To the side Angus and the other beast fought.

"Watch out for their claws, they are tipped in serum to weaken you," he yelled to Angus and jumped out of the way of a claw swipe. The beast screamed its frustration as it skidded across the floor before stopping.

Out the corner of his eye he watched a hybrid fall to the ground and knew his mate watched from a distance. The bluebird came at him again. This time he waited until the last moment, jumped and kicked it in the chin.

The beast stumbled backward. Hawke lengthened his claws and swiped it across the face, tearing through skin and flesh. Unaffected the beast jumped up and punched him in the gut and then his chin. Hawke flew backward and hit the wall. Paintings and wall sconces fell to the floor, shattering. Before he could catch his breath, the beast was on him. Hawke avoided being clawed by squeezing its hand, crushing the bone and rendering it useless. Next, he broke the beast's other arm leaving it dangling.

He looked around the room for something to cut off the head and saw nothing.

The beast ran toward him and swung. Hawke leaned back and the limbs swayed loosely. This inherent defect was another reason the bluebird was not ready for release. To put it out of its misery, Hawke punched in the neck and pulled out the spinal cord.

He turned and two blue birds ran into the room. Angus had defeated the blue bird but lay on the ground bleeding. Hawke bulked to his largest size, grabbed the first beast and slammed it into the other. The loud sound of flesh hitting flesh resounded in the open area.

He picked up one and then the other and slammed them together like a pair of cymbals. He sensed Asia's distress. Something was wrong.

"Asia?"

He dropped the beasts. They jumped up and flew at him. He ducked and caught one, piercing its metal shield with his claws and hit it against the wall in rapid succession. The other beast went after Angus who tried to stand and fight. The beast Hawke held was a bloody pulp missing multiple body parts. Hawke ran in front of the other beast, deflecting it from attacking Angus and knocked it back. He threw the remains of the bluebird in his claws at the remaining beast. It ducked and flew toward him. Didn't matter how fast they were, Hawke always heard them coming. He avoided the outstretched claws and kicked the beast in the stomach sending him flying in the opposite direction. Hawke ran to the downed bluebird and ripped out its spinal cord.

He turned, looked at Angus as he returned to human. "Are you okay?"

"Tired. Sick. Nauseous. All of the above. Silas is working on it, go find Asia. We had more company than we see."

Hawke nodded and didn't bother with an explanation. He ran up the stairs in time to overhear a part of her conversation.

Chapter 36

Blow after blow, the fight with the blue birds continued. Asia listened and watched. The staircase door cracked open. She aimed the gun. The moment the first hybrid cleared the door she shot into the mass directly behind it and then shot the hybrid running across the floor. Both dropped to the ground.

After checking to make sure they were out of it, she pulled the one in the staircase into the hall so she could see him. Next, she shot them again before heading back to the communications room to see who else breached Angus' security. Three full-bloods were on the roof. She recalled the security codes from before and entered a few key strokes. A light flashed on screen and then stabilized as the security system on the roof rebooted. Laser beams incinerated the full-bloods before they could escape.

The Hummer moved closer to the castle. She checked all the monitors. One blanked and went dark. She had a blind spot. Where was it? She checked the gun and then scanned the building for intruders. Two hybrids had entered through Hawke's lab and were making their way up the stairs. Boris must have opened the door. She grabbed the gun, and ran to a vantage point so she could see downstairs.

The first hybrid walked out and ran across the floor. She shot him before he reached the fighters. The other hybrid ran behind the first. She aimed and fired, dropping him before he got far. The lift was moving. She ducked behind the wall, scanned for heartbeats and waited.

The door opened and she heard footsteps. Tranq raised she aimed and shot the hybrid. A bullet hit her in the chest and she jerked backward, dropping the gun.

"You were a disrespectful baggage," Connall, from the Council, said pointing his gun on her. "You refused to answer the simplest questions and then leave." He shot her in the leg.

"*Asia*," Hawke yelled through their link.

"*He shot me in the chest, and in the leg. The bullets are working their way out. It's the guy from the Council. Strange, I thought it'd be Chacal.*"

"*One second, let me finish this and I'll be there.*"

"Get that system back online so we can finish here," Connall said over his shoulder. A full-blood walked into the communications system and sat down.

"*They are trying to reboot the remote system.*"

"*They can't.*"

Connall, looked at the full-blood and then at her. "What is going on?"

"Cables are missing."

"Which means?"

"There's no way to reconnect."

"Damn." He pulled out his cell and tapped a few buttons. "The cables are gone, what next?"

Asia closed her eyes and listened. Blood continued to leak from her chest and leg at a normal wolf pace.

"There are four blue birds down there, the fight is almost over. I will take both men to Roderick's lab. I want to know about the chips, why they stopped working." He paused and looked at her.

"Will do."

"*Are you fighting two blue-birds? He's counting on your losing.*"

"*Down to one. Angus is hurt.*"

Shit. La Patron was going to be pissed.

Connall stooped in front of her. "How did Angus do it? I just left Andrei, or what's left of him. We were able to salvage some footage from the camera and he switched from man to man, killing them as he went along. He murdered an Alpha, his pack members and then burned down a legitimate business. As lead council member I assure you I completed a thorough investigation." He smiled and she smelled his fear.

What was he afraid of? Did he think she was Angus? Hmm.

"If I touch you, will you take me over? Learn my secrets? How would you handle the darkness growing inside me every day?" He stared into her eyes and she sensed he wanted her to do as he described.

"I made a mistake," he whispered. "A big one. I wish I could change it but I cannot. It is too late. Maybe you can unravel it?"

"*He's talking crazy.*"

"*I know, I hear him.*" She realized Hawke stood in the hall and had taken out the full-blood.

"Angus?"

"His Alpha is working on him. He's out of it right now, he got swiped with a claw."

Connall touched her hand. Nothing happened. Frowning, he touched her again, squeezing her hand this time. He looked at her puzzled.

Hawke removed the gun from his hand and assisted the man to his feet. Then he extended his hand to Asia.

"He said you had magical powers that you could take away all of my problems," Connall said searching her face.

"I'm not Angus," she said into the silence.

"No? Where is he?"

"Downstairs. He fought the bluebirds."

Connall's eyes widened. "He took over a bluebird? They don't think much."

"No. He fought the blue-birds."

"Why would he do that?" The council member asked. She wondered if he were on some type of drug.

"So we could leave," she said, watching him.

Connall laughed. It was a dry mocking sound. "We are not leaving here."

Asia stilled. "Why do you say that?" She glanced at Hawke who walked to the monitor in the communication room.

"We are destroying this building. It's my last assignment as a Council member. To rid the Liege of Angus and Hawke if the beasts failed. Both are too dangerous outside of our control. If you would have listened to me the other day all of this could have been avoided."

Pissed, Asia stepped closer to him and snarled. "How? How could this have been avoided?"

"If you would have left town, left things alone as I suggested to Angus."

She snorted. "They never would have allowed Angus or Hawke to leave town."

He did not deny her claim.

"We have other problems," Hawke said tapping keys. "Boris has locked most of the system down. When I pulled the cable he was in the middle of something, it's not aborted but it's not completed. If I reconnect enough cables we might be able to get a door open to leave, but he could complete his plans. Right now, we are stuck. Everything is frozen."

Chapter 37

Hawke stared at the configurations on each monitor following a series of steps Boris initiated. He noticed a common thread running through the base of the building, the newer section added to the castle. Green lights blinked at four of eight points.

He searched his memory and did not recall the construction of the additional base with extra elements. Boris must have contracted someone on the side and snuck them into the building. That did not make sense. Hawke had access to the entire castle and installed cameras everywhere.

"*How does it look*?" Asia asked.

"*Not good.*"

"*Wrong answer. Why? What's going on?*" She stood behind him and kept an eye on Connall who sat on the floor with his eyes closed.

"*Flashing lights in the base exterior wall, the new section. I don't know what they are, had no idea they were there.*" He glanced at her. "*Go check on Angus while I make sense of this.*"

She nodded. "*Should I take him?*" she tipped her chin toward the Council member.

"*Yes, he may want to unburden his conscience and say something to help discover the problem with the pups.*"

"*Good forward thinking.*" She touched his shoulder, and walked to the door. "Come Connall."

The older man glared at her and didn't respond. Hawke did not blame his mate for not addressing the traitor by his title.

"Where?"

Asia bulked and lifted the full-blood by his collar and dragged him out the room. Connall shifted and Asia backhanded his wolf sending him sliding across the floor. She waited until he returned to human before morphing into her male persona.

"Why didn't you take steroids or whatever that was Andrei took?"

Connall stood slowly and wiped the blood from his mouth. "I did. It's poison and over time it robs you of everything." He shook his head. "Everything starts off bright and shiny. I believed the offer of help would be that, help for our people. But it is not. Just as humans are enslaved by drugs there are drugs to enslave our wolf. Count yourself lucky if you have not been exposed. If your Patron is able to keep it from his shores he is a better leader than any of us have ever been."

"I have seen the drug. It does not affect everyone the same," Asia said. Hawke sensed her discomfort speaking on that part of her life.

"They discovered much later the vaunted black wolf is immune. It took decades and hundreds of tests to come to that conclusion," Connall said with a touch of bitterness.

"You took the serum when they first started testing?" Asia asked.

He nodded.

"How long has that been?"

"A day is too long."

"Are you sick? You look healthy."

Hawke half listened while running diagnostics on castle operations. Since he created most of the programs he overturned Boris commands but the perimeter wall was not in the system. He re-routed commands to get one door open so they could leave.

A warning popped up.

He cursed. Boris had indeed been busy making it impossible for them to leave the castle alive. Hawke entered another string of code to over-ride Boris' command.

Another warning displayed.

He frowned. Boris should not be able to layer his files like this. Something was off. He entered information for the next exit. A warning sign did not pop up; three of the remaining four lights lit up and flashed leaving one light. A caricature of Lord Boris laughing flashed across the screen and then a large chess board.

Hawke sat back staring at the monitor. He hadn't considered Boris as a challenge and had just been out maneuvered. His cockiness may get his mate killed. That was unacceptable.

"Go check on Angus, I need to focus on this." He stood. *"I am going to the lab below."* He needed to use his system to plug holes and shut this one down.

"Okay." He heard their voices but paid no attention to their words as he left. When he entered his former lab, he glanced at Greggor and veered to his storage area. He pulled out his blade, unsheathed it and separated head and body.

Moving quickly, he found the hybrids lying in the hall and did the same. He took the lift to the main floor where Angus sat in a chair in front of Asia and Connall. He nodded at Angus, glad to see him feeling better.

"Heads?" Asia asked.

He nodded and made quick work of separating heads and bodies of the bluebirds. When he returned to the lab he had removed the threat of regeneration from all hybrids and bluebirds. He sat at the console and booted up the system. Nothing happened. He smiled at Boris' attempt to trick him. But Hawke had all but built this operation and knew it like the back of his hand. He laced his fingers, cracked his knuckles, typed in strings of code and the cursor blinked. He continued entering data, rebuilding, and pulling information to link information. It took a little time but eventually he had a picture of what Boris had done.

"This is not good."

"Connall said that already. What's going on?"

"Boris is blowing this place up and decided it will be our graves. If any exit opens the last light will activate the bomb. It's in the pillars of the castle. Some of them. My lab has separate explosives with a different trigger. I'm trying to figure that out now." He continued running sequences and patterns to locate a flaw in Boris' plans. Chances are Boris ran these same formulas and based on the results, plugged the holes.

He had to think. Was there anything Boris had not accessed? Or seen? All of his files were open to Boris and anyone he designated.

The scan pinged. There were no holes in the plan.

His fist hit the desk. There had to be a way. He just needed to think. He could not bear allowing that arrogant bastard to win.

He walked to the door that entered the antechamber which eventually led to outside. The door did not respond to his command. His passcodes had been wiped; it would take time to reinstate them. Time they did not have. What would be a trigger?

He looked around the room, nothing stood out, except Greggor on the floor. He pulled the body into one of the rooms and tossed his head in behind him.

Asia mentioned Angus came in through the vents by merging with the material. They were running out of time. "*You and Angus should leave through the vents. Head toward the forest, get as far as you can. When the castle explodes, it's going to send shockwaves for miles.*"

"*No.*"

He closed his eyes. She couldn't have heard him right or understood. The clock on the bomb could go off at any time. He did not know what would trigger the final link.

"*I cannot fix this. He used my own diagnostics to beat me. The bomb is ticking and will go off no matter what I do. Please... please leave. I cannot have your death on my conscience.*"

"*Then find another way to stop him. Someone said you were a genius, smart. Beat him. Win this or we both meet the Goddess.*"

He slumped against the wall. "What does she think I have been doing all this time?" His wolf growled at the thought of their mate being in danger. "I know... what can I do? I don't know what to do."

Find another way to stop him... her words rang in his ear. He moved to the keyboard and sat. Time to visit the clouds. He searched through his unfinished work files. Often he had ideas, and started them but did not find solutions right away. Lord Boris wanted him to toss them in archives so he and his cronies didn't think something was safe and it was not.

He kept these in his personal cloud, something his computer chip could not access. Once he had an idea to interrupt triggers with sound waves. The research had been interesting but he had become sidetracked and put the work aside. He pulled down the file, and read.

Asia watched Angus struggle to remain upright. He had been healing in wolf form when she and Connall entered the area. When Hawke came upstairs to decapitate the beasts, Angus morphed to his human form and remained. He had been given lethal doses of the serum. The scratch from the bluebird had been too much after the huge amounts he had been infected with earlier. La Patron had been working non-stop to keep

Angus alive, given the great distance that was the most he could do.

Connall sat near Angus asking questions, most went unanswered.

Her heart bled for Hawke, but he was their only hope. Angus wouldn't make it very far in his condition. She would never leave either of them behind, they were in this together. Turning to the Council member she saw the longing in his eyes as he watched Angus.

"Why don't you share with Angus what you shared with me? It might help him understand why you want him to relieve you of this burden." She knew Angus would never morph into a stranger who asked him to do so. There could be all sorts of mental traps involved. She had done a quick rifling through Connall's mind when he took her hand. He carried a load of guilt and the stain of blood. She wanted no part of him or his memories. The blemish of those types of memories resided with her mind already.

He seemed eager to re-tell the early days when he accepted assistance from a group of men who claimed to offer assistance to full-bloods. Things had been brutal and it seemed they were dying out as a clan. He later discovered the opposite was true, as a whole full-blood's thrived. But in the small area where he lived, he was easily deceived.

"Who approached you? In the beginning?" Angus asked.

"Lord Griffith. He claimed there were drugs that assisted in fertility and overall good health for our wolf. It worked in the beginning. My mate had many litters but they were frail, unhealthy and we lost most of them. Over time the opposite happened. But by then it was too late."

"It's never too late to do right," Angus said, sounding stronger.

Connall smiled. "For me the last option is death. I cannot undo all that I have done and I will not shed light on others. We were all masterfully played and damaged our people. It is unforgivable and the penalty should be a thousand deaths. Unfortunately, a man only dies once."

"What about your mate? Does she know what you are doing?" Asia asked, thinking of Hawke.

He sighed. "She suspects it but I do not think she is concerned."

He shook his head. "I will only speak of my sins, no one else's."

"What happened to the black pups? Why are they disappearing?"

"I told you. The Black wolf is the only shifter who can withstand the surgeries, absorb the chemicals and process the chips while remaining their duality. They do not turn into monsters. They have a level of control no other clan has."

"Someone is selling the pups? Giving them away? What? How are they disappearing?" She asked.

He shrugged. "I never got involved with that. The Black Clan watches their pups close. To take one requires help from the inside. I have not been a trusted ally of that clan for decades."

"You think someone on the inside is involved?" she asked glancing at Angus who sat still without looking in their direction.

"Yes. I do."

She nodded. "What about Alpha Radoff? Could he be involved?"

Connall nodded. "Yes, he could. He and Verrick."

Asia stood, turned and punched him in the face. His head snapped back and blood ran down his nose.

Angus grinned.

"You son of a bitch, stop lying. I smell the stench of your lies."

Connall jumped up, snarled and shifted to attack. She bulked to hybrid, unsurprised when he did the same. Instead of coming after her he attacked Angus.

Angus ducked and shifted mid air, slamming his elbow into Connall's back, sending him to the floor. Growling, Connall leapt at her. She backhanded him sending him spinning toward Angus who gut punched him.

"*Wait, don't kill him,*" Hawke said through their link. "*He's the final trigger.*"

She held her hand up to stop Angus. "*What do you mean?*" "*I ran a separate set of probability tests. Greggor was the first trigger. It was set in his neck piece, something he wore on the outside. Connall is the trigger, he controls the detonation. I don't know if it's inside him or in his clothes. I don't see a neck piece like Greggor's."*

No of course not, that would have been too easy. She nodded and watched the older man rise slowly. His eyes gleamed with curiosity as he faced the three of them. He waited for one of them to speak.

They remained silent.

"What? Nothing to say? No words of condemnation for what I've done? I betrayed my people, sold them out, I am the lowest of the low... you cannot say anything I have not heard before." He pointed at Hawke.

"You betrayed our people but you get a pass. You get forgiveness. Yet I am evil." He spit on the floor and stared at them. "What is wrong? You cannot figure out how to save your friends? Boris laughed when he thought of this game. That is all it is to him, a chess match, a game. He admits you are a genius but you will never win against him. You do not think outside the box. Things must have rationale explanations. Like why am I here spouting drivel when I want to gut you like a fish?"

Asia filtered out all the sounds in the room, isolating them one by one. The familiar tick of the computer chip reached her first. Connall was under Liege control. She searched closer for a detonation device. Would he hold the switch? Or had they placed the explosive inside him. She had seen and heard of the damage from suicide bombers.

This time she hoped he had a switch to flip.

"I hear the computer chip but nothing else. If he has a trigger, it is not ticking or humming."

"Good to know. But he is the trigger, we need to find out how," Hawke said sounding confident. Asia did not know what happened in the lab to generate this level of assurance but she appreciated it.

"I am curious why you lied?" Asia said.

"All of it was not a lie. Some parts are true." Connall grinned and wiped the blood from his chin.

"Are you mated?" Hawke asked.

Connall nodded. "That part was true. We lost most of our litters."

Angus returned to human and sat in the chair.

Connall morphed to human and Asia followed. The older man slid down the wall and sat on the ground. "Did you have to hit me so hard?" he asked holding the side of his face.

"Yeah, I did. Lying stinks like hell, makes me antsy," she said drawing attention from Angus to herself.

"I did not lie. I exaggerated."

Her brow rose and she crossed her arms staring at him. "Why are you here? What's your assignment this time? Who's watching? Who's listening?" she asked.

He stared at her and then laughed. "I am here to make sure Hawke and Angus die. I hope your lie detectors are on so you know I am telling the truth. We needed a little time to get things lined up and that should be done by now."

"*First part is true, but they don't have the second part in place. I ripped the cables out and they would need to be reconnected from the inside. Even if they slipped in a team, they would need to connect to communications.*"

"*Not if they are installing a perimeter bomb, on the outside,*" she said.

"*I've been monitoring the cameras and there has been no movement out there.*"

"*Which is strange, don't you think?*"

"*Think outside the box...*"

Hawke met her gaze and shook his head slowly. Before she could blink, he ran forward and smashed Connall into the wall, robbing him of his next breath. Then he grabbed the older man's head and twisted causing it to rest a weird angle. Hawke tossed Connall aside to the ground. Bulking to hybrid, he picked up Angus and strode to the front door.

Asia grabbed the tranq gun and ran behind him.

It took two kicks against the steel panels before it popped open. She did not sense anyone nearby, but did not relax her guard.

"*Let's go.*" Hawke took off in a blur. She raced behind them without looking back.

The first vehicle, the Black Hummer, sat empty but she did not trust it and ran past the car. Next, they saw the black land rover. All four tires were flat, they continued running to put as much distance between them and the castle as possible.

They had run several miles from the castle when it blew. Asia stumbled forward and stopped to watch the collapse of centuries of abuse. Like a drunk refusing to fall, it took time for the towers and peaks of the castle to join the base of the building on the ground. She imagined the graceful demolition of the landmark could be seen for miles around.

"*We need to go, I want to find a place so Angus can rest and regain his strength,*" Hawke said.

She nodded and glanced at him. He stared into the distance at the building and then met her gaze. "*That's the past; let's walk through our present into our future. First thing, we need food and rest.*"

"*Yes.*" She took off behind him at a slower pace but every now and then she turned to look at the fallen castle.

Chapter 38

Hawke ran until they reached the main road and set Angus down. The man had morphed to his base form at some point during their escape and now stood on all fours as a wolf to complete his healing.

"Head back to town, stay at the hotel for the night?" Hawke asked Asia.

"Sounds like a plan. There is a short cut through the forest."

"Good, we are too far from Chacal and I don't know how far Angus can run in his condition." He glanced at the wolf and then back at her.

"*Okay.*" Asia took off running. Hawke adjusted his speed to match Angus and jogged behind her. Thirty minutes later they stopped. Angus shifted and sat on an overturned log breathing heavily.

"Are you okay?" Asia asked concerned.

Angus nodded. "Yeah. What the hell is in that fucking serum? It knocked me on my ass." His words were spaced apart like he had a difficult time breathing.

Hawke's face warmed. "A complex chemical compound created specifically for that purpose, to knock a wolf on his ass."

Angus growled but the sound lacked menace. "Silas will love you. Patten and Matt will probably sit at your feet for hours. No doubt you will be a hit in the lab back home."

Hawke looked at his mate and then back at Angus. "I thought you were staying here for a while." She shrugged and stiffened.

"Shit," Angus said as Hawke pushed him to the side and stepped in front.

Ulric, Angus' former Alpha stepped into the clearing along with two other full bloods. Asia moved to Hawke's side prepared to fight and Angus stepped to his other side.

Ulric held up his hands. "No fighting. There has been enough of that. I came to talk. To discuss important issues."

"What issues?" Hawke asked crossing his arms. He remembered Ulric from somewhere, but could not place him. Maybe he should ask Asia to check his memories again.

"Pups from my pack are missing." He looked at Angus. "When you first mentioned the inconsistency to me years ago, I dismissed your concerns. I thought the questions regarding missing pups was your way of undermining my leadership."

"No, I was not," Angus protested. "The pack accepted you as Alpha and that settled the matter. I never tried to harm you or the pack."

Ulric nodded and stepped closer to Angus. Hawke moved to intercept. Angus took a step forward, as well.

"I know that now," Ulric said after glancing at Hawke. "But things were different then and the pack had a lot of challenges to overcome."

"Something has happened? What?" Angus asked sounding more alert than Hawke had heard him before.

Ulric released a long stream. "My pups were taken."

Shock raced through Hawke. "From where?"

"How did someone have access to an Alpha's den?" Asia asked and Hawke sensed her concern.

Ulric glanced at Asia and then turned to Angus. "I don't know." The tortured look on his face told its own story and touched Hawke. "One moment we were running through the forest during a training and the next they were gone. We searched every inch of the area and there was no trace of them or anyone else."

"Are you saying there was no scent of an intruder?" Hawke asked, wondering if someone else utilized a device similar to his mate.

"Yes. I mean no. Yes that is what I am saying," Ulric said watching Hawke.

"And you came to the southern Ukraine? Why?" Angus asked.

"I heard Lord Boris collected black pups."

"What?" Asia said before Hawke could speak or show his surprise.

Ulric nodded. "That is an old rumor, but once my pups were missing I came north to check into it. So far I have not found anything to connect Boris to the pups or this Lobo place."

Hawke's mind latched onto the lack of scent problem. That thread needed unraveling.

"Lobo?" Angus asked, his brows furrowing. Ulric nodded. "Yes. That is the name I was told."

"What have you done so far?" Angus asked.

"Chased down every lead, searched too many places to count and saw more than we needed to see. We spoke with the European council before they arrived here. They told me that your presence threatened the lives of the pups because of what happened with the test wolves. That was a red flag. No wolf would be angry over the release of enslaved full bloods. But if there was a chance they spoke the truth I wanted you to stop and go home. Later I discovered they work for the Liege."

"Are you still linked to Angus? Is that how you found us?" Asia asked.

"Yes. It is also why I'm asking for your help. The three of you have been inside the castle; did you ever see any black pups?" He looked at Hawke.

"No. I have never seen any pups at the castle. But the castle is one of many places the Liege uses. Each place is outfitted for a specific purpose," Hawke said thinking it through.

Ulric's gaze dropped.

"Connall said that the Black Wolf Clan was immune to the negative aspects of the drug he and Andrei used to magnify their abilities. It is possible they take the pups to use in experiments," Asia said watching Hawke and then facing Ulric.

Ulric nodded. "That is my fear." He looked at Angus. "We need help to find out if Lobo is real, and free the pups. I do not say this for just my pups, but for all black pups, including La Patron's. None of our pups are safe as long as the Liege uses them for experiments."

Hawke heard the frustration in the Alpha's voice and agreed. He glanced at his mate and wondered if they would have pups. The Liege would love a pup from Asia. He shuddered to think of his pup in the hands of his enemies. Asia brushed against his link with a cool calming breeze. She understood his fear and concern, any pups they bore would be targeted by the Liege. Before they started a den, the enemy needed to be destroyed.

"I will talk with my Alpha and we will discuss a plan," Angus said. "You are correct, this problem must be corrected and the Liege must be stopped. No pups, or black clan wolves will be test wolves for the Liege."

Ulric nodded. "Agreed. Come I have secured a house, we can rest and talk."

Hawke wondered if Angus would return to Chacal's.

"Thank you but we have a place to rest and will return there shortly. I wanted to speak with you first. Tomorrow we will talk," Angus said walking toward his former Alpha.

"Agreed," Ulric said and left the clearing.

Hawke watched Angus turn and walk in the opposite direction. "What do you think?" He asked Asia who stood next to him staring at the path Ulric had taken.

"No pups should be taken from their den and made slaves to the Liege. Lobo needs to be shut down." She paused and met his gaze with a concerned look. "Two of the pups they have are yours."

"What?" Hawke had no idea what she was talking about, he had no pups.

She exhaled and he knew whatever she said next would hit hard. "When I worked in the lab, Chuck or Henry said only two of your pups lived. They said you had pups. The Liege were using you as breeding stock. That was the purpose of the bitches we brought to your lab that night. Didn't you know that?"

Stunned, Hawke traced his memories and hit a wall. Pain speared his skull and for a few seconds he couldn't move. "I was never told about any pups. They always provided bitches for sex, and within the past ten years the bitches were always in heat. Hearing you say it now, I can see it, but no... I never knew." He gazed at his mate and spoke from his heart through their link. "*My main concern was the Liege attacking any den you and I would have.*"

Her eyes widened and she took a step back. He took a step forward. *"One day, I want a den... with you. It will happen but first we must make certain our pups will be safe."*

Her mouth opened and closed. Hawke bit back a grin. It was not often she looked uncertain.

"A den? I do not think I can do that," she whispered.

He pulled her into his arms and held her tight. *"Don't worry, I will help. You won't be alone."*

Her arms tightened around his waist.

Content with her agreement, his beast howled. He placed his finger beneath her chin, stared into her eyes and saw his future. *"Thank you."*

She frowned and he wished she could morph into her base form, but it was too risky.

"Why?"

"Because I have a future. I never had one before. A mate, pups, a den... none of those things ever seemed possible before. You have brought the sun into my world. For the first time in my life I am seeing things clear." Unable to fully explain the jumble of emotions rolling through him, he released the love he felt for her through their link. Her grip tightened around his waist. He held her close as tremors shot through her frame. She grabbed his face, pulled him down and kissed him with so much heat it scorched.

"Hawke..."

The hoarseness of her voice, coupled with her need for him made his blood sizzle. He deepened the kiss, needing more and more. He would never have enough. Her arms wrapped around his neck and he lifted her easily loving the feel of her legs around his waist.

The kiss deepened. And then she released a barrage of emotions through their link. He staggered and then firmed his hold on her ass. Fear of being hurt or deceived, her desire to know who she was, her family, how she wanted to love but was afraid, and those conflicting thoughts ran through the link on a loop.

Until finally her need for him, her pride in his work, her excitement at building a future with him and not being alone rolled through their link, bathing him with hope and affection. She called him her do-over. He wondered at the meaning but did not ask, not now, perhaps later.

Hawke gasped and sucked in air. She rested her forehead on his shoulder. They remained in that position while their emotions touched and merged through their link.

"Our ride is here," Angus yelled.

Hawke placed a kiss on the tip of her nose and let her down. No words were necessary. He took her hand and they followed Angus' trail to the road where Chacal sat behind the driver's seat with Angus in the passenger's side.

Before they reached the car, Alpha Radoff waved from the opposite side of the street and approached them. He looked well considering the last time Hawke had seen the man they had all been under attack.

"It is good to see you are safe and well. I have spoken briefly with Angus, he will bring you current. We will talk more after you are rested. I do not need to tell you the hornet's nest is truly stirred now, so be careful." He nodded and returned to the other side of the road where members of his pack waited.

Hawke opened the door for Asia and slid in after her. He met Chacal's glance in the rear-view mirror and pulled Asia close.

Chacal nodded and looked ahead.

"We can talk about all of this later. I must rest and so do you two. A lot of things will be decided in the next few days. But tonight, we savor our victory, Lancaster castle has fallen," Angus said sounding more like himself.

Asia squeezed his hand and leaned into him. Hawke placed a kiss on her head and looked ahead. She knew better than most how vast the Liege holding were. There were many heads, like a hydra, and she hoped three new ones would not sprout to replace the castle. At any rate, her mate was free; Greggor was dead and somewhere in Hawke's mind information regarding all the Liege experiments was locked away. Eventually they would defeat the Liege. Pacing. Layers.

Tomorrow Alpha Radoff said.

Asia glanced at the darkening skies as she snuggled closer to Hawke. Tomorrow was a future concern. Tonight, she would spend in the arms of her mate.

Chapter 39

Lord Boris sat in the chair staring at the blank monitor as the camera from Councilman Connall flickered and died.

Connall was dead.

Four bluebirds, the last of their stock, destroyed. Alpha Andrei, dead. Even Greggor, the worthless mutt, died in service to the Liege. After a century of service Lancaster Castle was no more.

The moment Connall's heart stopped the explosives in his body activated. That explosion triggered another, deadlier one in the base of the building. Boris did not need to watch the news channels to see the destruction of his castle; he sensed the end of an era in his bones.

Seconds turned into minutes and then hours as he waited for the circulation to return to his limbs and mind.

Impossible.

How did Hawke know? What made him suspect Connall as the answer to the riddle? The Councilman should have bought them more time to set things in place. Instead, the castle fell before Boris' team arrived. The taste of failure was indeed bitter and one he had little acquaintance with.

He stiffened at the sound of footsteps moving toward the room and turned on the computer.

"Boris." Roderick's deep voice scratched against Boris' tattered nerves. Rather than allow his comrades to sense the depth of his desolation, his brow rose in greeting.

"Roderick." Boris' fingers flew across the keyboard, re-running sequences and re-closing files, anything to appear too busy to answer questions or admit the failure of Lancaster Castle.

"Connall is dead."

"Yes. I know," Boris said without turning or looking in Roderick's direction. "I received notice of his termination earlier."

Roderick moved further into the room and sat across from him. "My men arrived to find Alpha Andrei missing and later dead. Angus and Hawke are still missing." He paused. "We have lost much these past few days. A high-ranking council member, a loyal alpha, a facility we have used for a century and our bluebirds, all gone." With each reminder, Boris nodded, ashamed.

Roderick slammed his palm against the table.

Boris' head snapped up and then he looked away from the anger and derision in Roderick's gaze.

"Are you trying to ruin our organization?"

"No... no of course not. I made a few bad decisions, but I am working to make things right."

Roderick snorted.

Boris did not blame him, that comment sounded ridiculous.

"How comrade? How will you make this right?"

Boris cleared his throat. "Hawke had help. There was someone else involved, a player we have not identified yet." He glanced at Roderick and then returned to the keyboard.

"True. Why is this person of interest?"

"Hawke is analytical and would still be running probabilities and sequences if left to him. Someone changed that dynamic. Can that happen with other test subjects? How do we maintain a high level of quality for our customers if anyone can change basic components in our product?"

Roderick stared at him for a few seconds and then started clapping. "Bravo. Bullshit but your delivery was excellent." He pointed at Boris with a cruel twist of lips. "Do you know why I am here? Alone? The others are angry. Your thoughtless actions have set us back for months and before a vote of credibility is taken, the others want you to step down from Lobo. They no longer feel you should be trusted with such a serious project."

Boris mouth dropped open and then snapped shut. "What? A credibility vote? Over this? That is absurd." He refused to believe anyone with half a brain questioned his loyalty to the group. Until recently his exemplary record shined brighter than anyone else, Roderick included. The Lobo project was his creation. How dare they expect him to relinquish control when his team was on the brink of a major breakthrough?

Roderick sat back in the chair and laced his fingers on his lap. "Absurd? If memory serves me correctly, and I am sure it does, you petitioned this type of vote for far less infractions from the other Lords, including myself."

Boris mouth went dry. He tried to defend his previous actions. "No, that is not true. Well it may be true but at the time the situation was critical."

"The others believe the current situation is critical. You removed creatures with major deficiencies to fight a battle for you before they were ready. Now we must start from the beginning with that project without Hawke. According to the lab his files are riddled with errors. That sounds critical to me, comrade."

"Yes, but at the time we all agreed the bluebirds were the best weapon to capture Angus and return Hawke to the lab. I did not make that decision alone and refuse to shoulder the full responsibility."

"Perhaps. But, our warehouses are almost empty. We have lost capable researchers. For now, we must fill the orders to replenish our coffers. The others feel and I agree, you must take a break from seeking vengeance."

"Vengeance? When?" Boris stalled, unable to believe anyone saw through his motives. He had covered his tracks well.

Roderick waved a hand. "Tell me you are not plotting revenge on Hawke and this person who helped him? You are a creature of habit, mean, nasty and vindictive. It makes you a great Liege Lord. You were too focused on your personal battles and lost sight of the broader vision which serves and impacts us all."

"Hawke is a key, just as Asia is a key. Hawke unlocked many mysteries of the Black wolf. To merge beast and man without a meltdown, the study must continue or we have lost the battle."

"That has never been the battle for the Liege. It has always been your crusade and as long as profits flowed, we agreed. Now, the reins must be pulled back so that we can regroup and prioritize."

Boris listened in horrified silence as years of personal sacrifice were whitewashed with the equivalent of a gold watch retirement speech. Roderick couldn't be serious. Pull the reins? On his research? He was the reason these men lived long lives and now they wanted him to stop? He could not. More to the point, he would not.

"I trust we can agree that the needs of the group rank higher than the individual." Roderick repeated a phrase Boris always used to justify disciplinary actions amongst them.

"Do you believe continued research of the Black wolf is in opposition to future success of this organization?" Boris asked while staring at Roderick. The man had no idea what lengths Boris would tread to reach the brass ring. For him, that ring meant the merger of man and beast at will. He refused to allow anyone to interfere.

"No, I agree we need to continue research. The merger can happen and when we perfect the transition, the world will be ours. Imagine mass production of our shining star, Asia, at will. Or Hawke."

Boris frowned and glanced at the computer screen again. "Asia... have we located her?"

"No? Why?" Roderick sat forward.

"What if?" Boris pulled up clips from the previous fights with the bluebirds, and Greggor and stared. Could it be?

"What?" Roderick demanded.

"What if Asia is on the continent?" He glanced at Roderick and enjoyed the look of shock on his face.

"What?"

"What if she met Hawke and helped him escape?"

Slack-jawed Roderick slumped in his chair. "How? How would she have done that?"

Pleased to have Roderick's attention diverted, Boris keyed in Asia's file and ran a probability study. The odds were not in her favor but he could not let go of the idea she was somehow involved in this recent setback.

"Angus Black Wolf wears a bracelet..."

"Yes a chameleon. I am not certain all that it does but he alters his appearance."

Boris deflated. The odds were Angus helped Hawke. But why? They were not from the same clan. According to his spies, Angus arrived after Hawke left the castle. None of this made sense.

"What are you thinking?" Roderick asked.

Boris explained the twists and turns of events.

"Makes more sense that Angus helped Hawke. But how does that explain the chip? Alpha Andrei said Hawke's mate could stop the chip from functioning."

The two men looked at each other.

Roderick smiled. "Hawke and Angus? Mates?"

Boris' heart sped as he ran another probability study using Angus' information. He grinned. "Yes, there is a high probability on that match. That explains why Angus is here; he came to rescue his mate. The bond is strong." Boris congratulated himself for revealing an important piece of information.

"I want that bracelet," Roderick said looking at Boris with a calculating smile. "Imagine being anyone in the world. We could run governments and raise an army for our bidding."

Boris nodded with understanding. Now he wondered if he had been played by a masterful hand. Had the others sent Roderick? Or had the cunning man seen his current failures as an opportunity to barter a deal?

"If the bracelet delivers as you believe then it would indeed be worth whatever is involved to retrieve such a prize." Boris waited for Roderick to make an offer.

"It does indeed." Roderick frowned. "There is a problem with how it works but I am sure we can work around that." His eyes narrowed while looking at Boris.

"If we take Angus or Hawke, one will bring the other. This time go and oversee the operation yourself. No more Alphas or hybrids. You need to be on the continent working this coup."

Boris didn't want to leave in the middle of his research but the lure of outwitting Hawke proved too strong. The bonus of seeing Hawke fall apart over the loss of his mate would be icing on the cake.

"I see that gleam in your eyes. Alive, not dead. A dead Angus is of no value."

Boris smiled. Accidents always happened. "Hawke is mine."

Roderick nodded. "True. That black wolf always belonged to you."

Boris stood to prepare for the trip. Several possibilities to trap Hawke filtered through his mind. Chess had always been Hawke's strong point. Boris filed that information to beat Hawke at his own game.

Next installment in the La Patron Sword series:

Sword of Mercy

In their quest to discover more information on Project Lobo and the missing black pups, Asia and Hawke slam into Hawke's past. Asia must keep Hawke from destroying the family who sold him into slavery while maintaining their focus on their current task and to survive numerous assassination attempts from the Liege.

Another Liege Lord decides he will rise to the forefront of power by single handedly bringing in both Asia and Hawke. His greed and ambition keeps the newly mated pair on their toes. More black pups disappear and Silas is more concerned than ever, he sends Brix and Leon as backup for Asia and Hawke.

Asia and Hawke learn how difficult it is to extend Mercy when they see the emotional scars each mate bears, but realize the importance of forgiveness for the future of their relationship.

Here's a peek:

Chapter 1

The plane landed in a small private landing field, 50 miles from Bucharest in Romania. Boris Lancaster gazed out the window at the dreary landscape and felt a connection to the old country. Animals grazed nearby and barely glanced in the direction of the plane as they taxied. There were no overt signs of prosperity. If crops had been planted in the fields opposite the small landing strip, nothing showed above ground. From his vantage point inside, everything appeared frozen in time.

Had it been a century ago, he had bartered his soul for a position of power with Lord Konstantin? Or longer? His father had been certain the stately older man had the answers to all life's problems and all but worshipped Konstantin. Those had been the days, the government sat back and allowed men to rule men without interference. He sighed and shifted in his seat waiting for the plane to come to a complete stop, and longed for the comfort of his Colorado condo. The weather was cold, crisp and perfect this time of year.

Roderick, the leader of the Liege, sent him to oversee Hawke's downfall and to capture his mate, Angus. Time confused Roderick, made him forget critical elements of the Black Wolf 's nature. Once a black wolf tasted freedom, they would die rather than return to captivity. The chances of Roderick "unwrapping" Angus were slim to none. But since Roderick had allowed him to bring the crown prince of project LOBO, Damian, he kept those facts quiet. Especially with the last insult, they had asked for his resignation as lead on LOBO, Boris was not inclined to remind any of the ingrates of many things, like the covenant, or the limitations of their products or that Damian lacked a proper tracking computer chip. Next time they won't be so hasty to undermine him.

Damian, seed of Hawke, his prize protégé, had been born and raised within the Liege compounds and was one hundred percent loyal to them. He had no idea of pack, or family or memories that needed altering. The pup had been refitted with metal arms and legs when he reached his teens. Damian passed every test they had, and scored higher than everyone, except Asia and Hawke, while maintaining control of his beast. He and Roderick agreed field testing for the young Alpha would help prepare the wolf for future jobs. Several countries requested services similar to the ones Asia had performed and they wanted to send Damian after testing. Gordon, another Liege, requested they spend additional funds on surgeries for the pup and insisted they invest the same money and time on Damian as they had on his sire, Hawke, or at the very least, Asia. Dealing with Gordon would tax his patience, but he would complete his version of this assignment and return to LOBO by the end of next week, or sooner.

The door to the plane opened and Councilman Jeddick stood at the bottom of the stairs. Damian walked out first, scenting the air as he buttoned his sports coat and scanned the area. He took a few steps looking around and then looked over his shoulder and nodded. Boris stepped onto the ladder, holding his satchel filled with documents that needed work. Hawke made a mess of the files and some would never be recovered, which set them back on the projects he'd been working on. The tranquilizer formula for one thing had been erased and a team of scientists had been trying to recreate it in the lab but hadn't gotten it exact. Which put a dent in their financial and marketing plan since they had to cancel pending and incoming orders.

"Welcome home, Lord Lancaster," Councilman Jeddick said bowing low. Boris walked past him without acknowledging the greeting. Instead, he headed to the car and slid into the back seat while Damian rode up front with the driver leaving Jeddick on the tarmac.

There had been too many losses and he needed to rectify that as quickly as possible. Jeddick would be eager to get on his good side and would make a decent sacrifice to the cause. Pity they'd lost Councilman Connall, he had been a quick thinker and kept the Liege current on things they needed to know. Jeddick made it known to them that he welcomed a closer alliance with the Liege, but refused the surgical implant, which would allow them to monitor his movements and see through his eyes. The kill chip had been the deal breaker in the end stopping negotiations.

Boris opened his bag and pulled out two pictures. Hawke and then his mate, Angus Black Wolf. Of all the rotten luck, Hawke and Angus, those two would be difficult to destroy, but that was his mission and he refused to fail again. His phone beeped with an incoming message. He shook his head.

"I knew you'd be pissed," he murmured reading the message from Lord Gordon. Boris glanced at his watch and then shoved his phone into his pocket as they turned onto the main highway leading to Odessa. Gordon would be a problem. The man thought of Damian as a son of sorts and objected to him being on the continent without a full vote of the board. With Lord Phinneas' recent filling of Griffith's spot, and Roderick approving Damian's trip, Gordon would have been out-voted but that wouldn't stop the hard-headed man. Even though the man had not mentioned his arrival, Boris expected Gordon to arrive within days.

When the car pulled in front of the luxury hotel, Damian got out, checked the area and then opened the door. Boris walked into the lobby without looking right or left, expecting the hotel manager to meet him and escort them to the floor he'd reserved for his use. The manager, a short, stout Midwestern man stood in the middle of the lobby and personally ushered them to their space.

Once alone, Boris placed a laptop on the table and motioned to Damian, who stood near the kitchen area, to boot it up. Boris pulled out a sheaf of papers and made plans to bring Hawke to his knees. After all the surgeries Hawke endured, killing him would be near impossible. Plus, who knew what a mated Hawke could do at this point. The only way to get to Hawke would be through his mate. Angus's age, over three hundred, and his connection to La Patron, made taking him down hard and risky. The challenge of defeating these two powerful Alphas caused his heartbeat to race with excitement.

He glanced at Damian. The young wolf favored his sire, but lacked the mental sharpness and strong will of Hawke. Boris couldn't think of a more fitting end, Hawke destroyed by his son's hand.

He pulled out a private cell phone and placed the call. "I'm here. Pick up the package so we can finish this. No failure, no excuses, no second chances."

Hello,

Thank you for taking the time to read the first book in the La Patron's Sword series. I love paranormal books and characters in general and shifter stories in particular. Throw in the romantic element, strong Alpha characters who bend beneath the power of love and I'm over the moon. Sighs...

In her quest to learn her past, Asia bumps into her future. The Liege is stealing black wolf pups for research. Silas Knight, La Patron, has four black pups in his den and is determined to stop the Liege before they attempt to take his pups. Asia and Hawke are chosen to discover the Liege's plans and shut it down. First Asia must learn to trust someone other than Jasmine. Next she must merge with Hawke as a cohesive unit to infiltrate and take down the Lancaster Castle which belongs to the Liege. The Liege refuses to go down without a fight. They have been operating for centuries and have no intention of stopping, even if two of their most prized products are the ones gunning for them.

You're invited to journey with me through all the books in this series. If you like fast paced action, suspense and great love connections like me, you won't be disappointed. Feel free to drop me a line, SydneyAddae@msn.com or join my Facebook group, La Patron's Den, where discussions regarding Silas and the Wolf nation abound. Also, you can find me at my website, SydneyAddae.com.

Knight Chronicles is a newsletter for my Readers Group from the characters of the series to keep you informed of what's going on in the Wolf Nation. Each issue has a personal message from Silas Knight, La Patron, or his mate, Jasmine. Character profiles with indepth interviews and thoughts you won't find anywhere else. Also works in progress, new releases and special give-aways in every issue.

If you would like to receive Knight Chronicles click this sign up[1]link! Thank you. (http://eepurl.com/bb3csz)

---

1. http://eepurl.com/bb3csz

La Patron, the Alpha's Alpha is my first paranormal series and I'd like to ask a favor. When you finish reading, please leave a review, whatever your opinion, I assure you I appreciate it.

The following books are in the La Patron Series, enjoy!

Thanks again

Sydney

BirthRight
BirthControl
BirthMark
BirthStone
BirthDate
BirthSign
Sword of Inquest
Sword of Mercy
Sword of Justice
La Patron's Christmas
La Patron's 2nd Christmas
La Patron's New Year – Leigh West, Catherine Marsh
KnightForce 1
KnightForce Deuces
KnightForce Tres'
KnightForce Damian
KnightForce Ethan
Angus

Booksets
La Patron Series Books 1-6
La Patron Series Books 4-6
Sword Series Books 1-3

Bear With Me – Bear Mountain Patrol
Jewel's Bear – Bear Mountain Patrol

Last in Line- Vampire Story

Jackie's Journey – La Patron's Den – Book 1
Awakening the Alpha, Adam – La Patron's Den – Book 2

www.SydneyAddae.com